THE VICTIM HAS NO LEGS!

The living room of the trailer was unairconditioned and smelled of stale cigarettes, whiskey, and death.

When Detective Willette entered, he noticed the grotesque body of Grady Stiles, Jr., slumped over in a large armchair. His head and face were covered in fresh blood. His massive upper torso supported him from falling and hid his arms from view. Willette put his age at between fifty-five and sixty-five. All the dead carny wore was a pair of plain briefs.

"The victim has no legs," the investigator noted in his report.

Finishing up his examination of the murder scene, Willette signaled the coroner to remove the body. As the body was loaded onto the stretcher and taken outside to be driven to the medical examiner's office, he noted something else. Not only were the man's legs stunted with pointed extremities in place of feet, but his hands appeared claw-like, with what might have been fingers deformed into two large digits apiece.

He'd awed thousands of people by sporting his grotesque deformity at sideshows across the nation as Lobster Boy— Half Man, Half Monster.

Now, he was just dead.

LOBSTER BOY

FRED ROSEN

PINNACLE BOOKS
KENSINGTON PUBLISHING CORP.

PINNACLE BOOKS are published by
Kensington Publishing Corp.
850 Third Avenue
New York, NY 10022

The P logo Reg. U.S. Pat. & TM Off. Pinnacle is a trademark of Kensington Publishing Corp.

First Printing: May, 1995

Printed in the United States of America

FOR THE COOLER KING

ACKNOWLEDGMENTS

Paul Dinas is easily the most unique editor I've ever worked with. It is Paul who saw the possibility of this book way before I did, and who provided unparalleled support in its research and writing. He has more journalistic integrity than most journalists I know.

Thanks, too, to my family and friends for their support, especially my wife, Leah, and my mother and stepfather. My researchers Billy Koskotos and Michael Shapiro also deserve credit.

And my special thanks to Michael Willette, Ron Hanes, Brian Donerly, Sandra Spoto, Mike Mahan, and Rob Sumner in Tampa; Merrill McCubbin in Norfolk; and Tony DeCello and Commander Ron Freeman of the Allegheny County Homicide Division in Pittsburgh, for their openness and candor.

A WORD ABOUT SOURCES

This book is based upon an extensive amount of interviewing, including all the members of the Stiles family in Tampa, all the attorneys involved and investigating officers. Two people I wanted to talk to, however, I did not.

Chris Wyant was never released on bond and was not available to be interviewed. Neither was Barbara Stiles. Despite efforts by the police and the Florida state attorney's office to locate her, she remains a phantom.

Merrill McCubbin filled in a lot of gaps on the last summer of Grady's life. Commander Ron Freeman of the Pittsburgh Homicide Squad went out of his way to give me special access to the police records of the Layne homicide in 1978.

Official court and police documents provided invaluable information. So did other background research materials, including newspaper and magazine articles.

Dialogue has been reconstructed on the basis of the memories of those interviewed and the official documents. As with any homicide case, there are sometimes different memories of the same event. In those cases, I have evaluated the competing claims and presented an account based on my considered judgment of what happened.

The worst abusers are the abused.
— Don Banks

Part One

The Murder

One

Gibsonton, Florida.

The four-lane blacktop that is Federal Highway 41 rises gently into a bridge that spans the Alafia River.

The Alafia is a lazy body of water filled with recreational boaters and fishermen. But it was the Cargill Fertilizer Plant on the river's western banks that really dominated the scenery.

Smoke spewed from long stacks that climbed toward the sky. Set off by its ominous-looking, gunmetal-gray machinery encroaching on the water's edge, the fertilizer factory gave the river an ugly, grayish pall.

On the other side of the Alafia, a sign at the bottom of the bridge reads GIBSONTON.

The first building on the right is the "Giant's Camp." It literally is that, a place where a giant camped.

At eight feet six inches, Al Tomaini was a giant of a man. During the 1930s, he was exhibited in the "World's Fair Freak Show."

It was there that he met and wed his wife, Jeanie Tomaini, "The World's Only Living Half Girl." Jeanie was born with the lower half of her body missing.

Al and Jeanie had heard from their friend "The Crocodile Man" that the place to go during the off-season was Gibsonton, a town on the Gulf of Mexico, twenty miles south of Tampa.

"In those days," Jeanie recalls, "there wasn't much here, just swampland and not much else."

But the carnies came nevertheless, to winter away from their public. After a while, the town had a thriving population of dwarfs, bearded ladies, human blockheads, magicians, fire-eaters, sword swallowers, clowns, strippers, and the real backbone of the carnival, the roustabouts.

When Jeanie and Al decided to quit touring for good, they opened the Giant's Camp, a combination restaurant/bait and tackle shop/trailer court. On any given morning, you can still see Jeanie behind the counter, "The Bearded Lady" in the corner, "The Human Blockhead" shoving unimaginable things up his nose, and out back, a fire-eater working on a new trick.

Decorated like somebody's kitchen, you can get a complete meal of home-cooked food for $4.

The men and women in the small restaurant, which formed the main room of the Giant's Camp, shared a hard-bitten look that they wore like the uniform of their trade. The carnies came by their money the hard way. They work at least seven months out of every year on the road, traveling throughout the United States, wherever a carnival could be set up with its tents and rides and midway.

Be it a deserted field in Holcomb, Kansas, or the parking lot of the Nassau Coliseum in Uniondale, New York, sooner or later the carny would play your local town.

Beginning with films like *Nightmare Alley,* in which Tyrone Power became a geek—a sideshow performer who bites the heads off live chickens—carnivals and carnival folk have become the focus of derisive portrayals in all facets of the media.

Yet with all the bad publicity, they never told the real truth, carny people asserted. Carny people are kind and caring. For instance, you never see a crippled child on the midway without a toy given them by carnival people.

Most nights, Gibsonton residents gather for a drink in the famous Showtown USA on Highway 41. A mid-sized local pub with a well-stocked bar and a small stage area for live local bands, it affords the locals a place to blow off steam and swap stories.

Many of the carny folk live in trailers cemented to a foundation. They build on room additions as money permits, but most of them look unfinished. Number 11117 Inglewood Drive, on the east side of town, was no exception.

Number 11117 was a long, wide, dark brown, aluminum trailer set on a concrete slab, with a room addition on the east side of the structure that opened on the street.

On the night of November 29, 1992, the side door of the trailer was open, spilling light on the ground. Standing in the doorway was a haggard-looking woman. Her name was Mary Teresa Stiles.

"Come on, Glenn, you wanna come with me?" she said to her teen-aged son in the trailer.

"Sure, Mom," he called from one of the back bedrooms.

"See ya in a few minutes," Teresa yelled back to her husband, Grady.

In the shadows, their neighbor Chris Wyant, 17, watched them go. He waited a few moments before going inside. He wore a black leather jacket with a Raiders hat turned around backward, black Nike Cavericis tennis shoes, a black-and-white IOU T-shirt and blue jeans.

Having been to the house many times before to play chess with Glenn, Chris knew the layout. He sneaked along the passsage, passing the kitchen and stepping into the living room.

"What the fuck are you doing here?" Grady barked at the boy.

"You son of a bitch, get the fuck out of my house!"

Wyant said nothing.

"I said get the fuck out of my house! And don't ever come around here again."

The boy mumbled something and waited. *Grady had seen him.*

To Marco Eno, it sounded like four gunshots in rapid succession.

In the third trailer, which sat on the northwest side of the property, Marco Eno was lounging with the gorilla. It was actually a gorilla suit, used in a carnival illusion done with mirrors and light that purported to show a woman changing into a gorilla.

Marco had been working as a roustabout for years. In his mid-thirties, his body was all edges—slim and sharp, arms tattooed. On his upper left arm the inscription read "Carnie Power." He had lank black hair, and a jet-black handlebar mustache.

Marco was watching TV about eleven o'clock when he heard shouting coming from the brown trailer out front, then the shots.

Eno ran outside to see what had happened. A moment later, a young man in a dark jacket whom Marco did not recognize sauntered out the side door of the brown trailer like nothing had happened and disappeared into the night.

Eno strained his ears. The yard gate creaked. And then . . . silence. What the hell was going on?

When Glenn heard the shots, he ran out of his half-sister Cathy's trailer in back of the property. He immediately recognized Chris Wyant fleeing from the back door of the brown trailer. Then he saw Marco Eno running toward him from the other side of the yard.

"Did you hear those shots?" Marco asked breathlessly.

"Oh no, it might be Grady," Teresa said with anxiety in her voice. She had joined her son along with her daughter, Cathy, and son-in-law, Tyrill.

"I'll go, Ma," Glenn said quickly. "You all stay here."

"Come on," said Marco.

They tramped across the grass to the side door.

"I'll go in first," said Marco.

He threw the screen door open and stepped into the trailer. The TV was on.

"Grady?"

No reply.

He walked into the living room.

Grady was sitting in his favorite armchair. Dressed in undershorts and nothing else, he was slumped over, his face almost in his lap. And there was blood. Lots of it.

Beginning to go into shock, Marco plodded forward unsteadily. It was like a dream, or some horror movie. There was Grady all right, but he wasn't alive like he had been a few hours before when Marco saw him. He looked stone-cold dead.

The blood came from bullet wounds on top of his bald head. It dripped down his face in rivulets, and some of it had coagulated in a dark reddish pool on the floor, under his chair.

"Hey, Marco, what's happening?" Glenn called in.

"Glenn, call 911," he yelled. It sounded like it was someone else.

"Why?"

"Your father's been shot!"

Two

Northeast of Tampa in one of the city's bedroom suburbs, Det. Michael Willette was asleep in bed. His wife, Melanie, was curled up beside him. When the phone rang, he woke up quickly. In his line of work, he was used to being woken up late at night.

He listened for a few minutes, mumbled a few things, wrote down the address, and climbed out of bed. He dressed quickly. Melanie awoke briefly, then turned over. She'd been through this before.

Outside in the dark, he fit his stocky five-foot-ten, 220-pound frame behind the wheel of his 1988 Ford LTD, an old police car painted white for unmarked duty.

Traveling south on Interstate 75, the super highway that paralleled Federal Highway 41, Willette made Gibsonton in forty-five minutes. While he'd been to Gibsonton before, he had never been to Inglewood Drive and had to consult the book of maps he always carried with him.

Willette arrived at the crime scene at 12:25

A.M. Opening the LTD's trunk, Willette rum-
maged through a pile of rumpled clothes before finding a simple tissue-sized cardboard
box and extracted a couple of pairs of surgical rubber gloves. Thrusting them into the
pockets of his jacket, he slammed shut the
trunk.

There were already a lot of squad cars in
front of the brown trailer.

"What's going on?" Willette asked the uni-
formed deputies, who were milling out front.

"Some carnival guy got shot," said one.

"Where's Chuck Phillips?"

"Over there," the deputy pointed.

Willette made his way through the crowd
of cops and medical personnel.

"Hey, Chuck. What have we got?"

"A carny was murdered."

Phillips consulted his notebook.

"We took a statement from a guy named
Marco Eno, who lives in a trailer out back.
Says he heard the victim arguing with somebody and then shots fired. Says he saw a
young guy leaving the trailer right after the
shots were fired. Then he went in and found
the body. The vic's stepson called it in."

"What's the vic's name?"

"Grady Stiles, Jr."

Willette nodded, writing down the name
in his notebook. He pulled his jacket tighter
around him.

Like a doctor entering surgery, Willette

donned his surgical gloves and entered the crime scene via the front door. It was unlocked, and Willette immediately noted no signs of forced entry.

Willette made special note that "The head area of the victim had visible trauma, possibly caused by bullets."

Continuing his examination, Willette noticed that the kitchen area was on the south side of the room, separated from the TV/family room by kitchen cabinets that backed up to the chair the victim sat in. On top of the kitchen cabinet directly behind the victim, Willette spied blood that had splattered across the top and down the sides of a carton of Pall Mall cigarettes. On the counter itself was more blood, mixed in with what appeared to be human body tissue. There were also a single pack of cigarettes with one cigarette sticking out invitingly, and a notebook filled with paper.

The carton, the single pack, and the notebook were damaged. Willette had the impression that a bullet or bullets had passed through them. Looking further, Willette saw an indentation in the countertop surface. He figured that a bullet had struck the counter surface first, traveling from south to north, toward the victim's head.

Willette noticed he was standing in an enclosed porch filled with dusty knickknacks. He walked up two steps into the living room, passing through an aluminum door. Again, the door lock showed no visible signs of forced entry.

The living room smelled from stale cigarette smoke and whiskey. The furnishings were plain, cheap but understated. High on the walls above what appeared to be a hamster cage was a selection of photographs. The room was dominated by the body in the armchair near the Tiffany lamp.

The man was slumped over in the heavy armchair. Blood was visible on his head and face. From his cursory examination, Willette figured the victim to be between fifty-five and sixty-five years old, with a balding head. All he wore was a pair of briefs.

"The subject has no legs," Willette wrote in his report.

Willette concluded that the killer was approximately eight to ten feet south of the victim facing north, probably standing when he shot in a downward angle, the bullets striking the victim in the back of the head.

Willette found "one projectile" in the north bedroom area lying on the floor underneath the north window, implying that the victim was shot at from the kitchen hallway area, near the back door. Willette took out a small, white pillbox and placed the bullet inside.

He found a "second projectile" in the ceiling area of the living room, approximately five feet north of the body. The trajectory of this bullet was not readily identifiable. It was gently placed in another white pillbox.

Looking around the room, Willette noticed the victim's pants on the couch facing directly across from where Grady now sat in the frozen tableau of death.

The detective searched the dead man's pants and found his wallet, which contained identification, and a large amount of money.

Who kills a man during a robbery and doesn't take his wallet? Willette wondered.

Going from room to room, looking for clues and finding none, Willette finished his search of the trailer. Dr. Robert Pfalzgraf, associate medical examiner in the Hillsborough County Medical Examiner's Office, arrived to make the official pronouncement of death. Tall, blond, in his mid-thirties, Pfalzgraf looked ten years younger.

"Three gunshot wounds to the head with what appeared to be one exit wound," he said.

Therefore, the two "projectiles" Willette had recovered had probably passed through Grady first, before coming to rest on the outside. The third was probably still inside the body.

Willette examined the recovered bullets again. They were .32 caliber with copper tips. That meant that a small-caliber gun had been used to commit the crime.

"Finished with him?" Pfalzgraf asked.

Willette nodded.

"Okay, guys," said Pfalzgraf to his assistants.

As the body of Grady Stiles, Jr., was loaded onto a stretcher and taken outside to be driven to the medical examiner's office, Willette noticed something else. Not only were the man's legs stunted with pointed extremities in place of feet, but his hands appeared to be claw-like, with what might have been fingers deformed into two large digits.

Later, Willette would discover that Grady Stiles, Jr., was known on the carny circuit as Lobster Boy.

Three

Grady Stiles III is a barrel-chested teenager who favors dark T-shirts, jeans, and sci-fi paperbacks. His thick, straight, brown hair falls over a low forehead. Scattered bloodred blemishes mar an otherwise innocent-looking face. His eyes are a soft, bright blue.

Willette and Stiles were in the rear of the trailer in the boy's bedroom, furnished simply with a bed and dresser. Apparently, he'd been sleeping and the bedclothes were turned around a little bit.

"You're Grady Stiles, Jr.'s, natural son?" Willette asked.

Little Grady, as he was known to his family, nodded. He felt uncomfortable talking to police. In the carny world, cops usually meant trouble.

"When was the last time you saw your father alive?" Willette asked.

"I was watching this video with my parents. When it ended, I went to bed."

"At about what time was that?"

"What time what?"

"What time did you finish watching TV and go to bed?"

"About ten-fifty-five."

"Alone?"

"Yeah."

"Which bedroom?"

"This one."

Grady brushed hair from across his eyes with his claw. He was born with the same affliction as his father had been.

"Hear anything?"

"I heard at least three bang noises while I was sleeping."

"Then what? Did you go out to see what the noises were?"

Little Grady shook his head. "Went back to sleep. I didn't know anyone'd been shot until Mom woke me later."

"Got any idea who did it?"

"I don't know who killed my father. I didn't see or hear anything else."

Despite the fact that his father had been shot in cold blood, Grady III didn't sound too upset about it, Willette thought.

While only fifty-four years old, Mary Teresa Stiles looked much older. She had mousy brown hair and brown eyes. Most people described the middle-aged woman as looking like someone's grandmother.

Detective Willette interviewed her in the

hallway of the trailer by the washing machine near the back door.

She began by describing the day as brisk. By night, the air had cooled into the mid-forties, positively chilly by Florida standards. Inside 11117 Inglewood Drive, Grady, Little Grady and Teresa were watching television, specifically one of the tapes Teresa had rented that afternoon. The film was *Ruby*, starring Danny Aiello as Lee Harvey Oswald's murderer.

Grady Stiles, Jr., sat in his underwear. Teresa said he was "half in the bag," drinking whiskey like there was no tomorrow and never seeming to get any drunker than he already was, while chain-smoking Pall Mall cigarettes.

After a while, Little Grady tired of the program and went to his room.

At eleven o'clock, Teresa said, "Grady, I think I'm gonna go on back and see how Misty's doing." Misty had been ill that afternoon.

Grady and Teresa's daughter Cathy had married Tyrill Berry and had one daughter, Misty. They all lived out back in another trailer on the same property.

"Guess I'll take Glenn along, too," Teresa said. Grady just grunted, absorbed by the new video he was watching.

Glenn Newman, Teresa's son by her third husband, was out back in his bedroom. He rarely came out, preferring his solitary pursuits. But that evening he decided to join his mother.

Together they left by the southwest door, the one next to the kitchen, leaving it open. They walked on back to Cathy's trailer and went on inside.

"Well," Teresa continued, "I was inside my daughter's trailer sitting on the couch for about five minutes. Then a neighbor, Marco Eno— he lives in another trailer out back— he came over to my daughter's. He asked if we'd heard the shouting and the shooting coming from here. I told him I hadn't. Then me and my son Glenn, along with Mark Eno, we went into the trailer and found my husband dead."

"Mrs. Stiles, I know this is a difficult time for you, but do you know who would possibly want your husband dead?"

"No, sir, I don't," Teresa stated.

"Does anything, any property appear to be missing?" Willette wondered.

She looked around. "No, sir."

Once more, Willette had eliminated robbery as a motive. Still, you never know what might turn up during the investigation of a murder scene.

"Mrs. Stiles, we'd like to search the trailer. Maybe we could find something that would help catch your husband's killer."

"That would be fine, sir."

"All we need, then, is for you to sign a

'Consent to Search' form that would give us the right to search the trailer legally. It's common procedure in homicide cases."

Teresa readily agreed and signed the form that Willette produced.

Unlike his father, Glenn Newman, Sr., who was a dwarf and went by the carnival names of "Midget Man" and "The World's Smallest Man," Harry Glenn Newman, Jr., was anything but.

He packed 250 pounds on his five-foot-eight frame, with brown hair and brown eyes and had a temper that could flare up when provoked. In the carnival, he worked as "The Human Blockhead." He would pound nails and other implements up his nose with nary a nosebleed.

Once, while with the carnival in the Bronx, New York, he had been attacked by a gang of youths, who beat him up. Undaunted, Glenn had returned to the carnival, armed himself with a hammer, and set out through the mean streets of the South Bronx, searching for his assailants. He never did find them.

"So, tell me what happened."

"Well, I was in my bedroom watching TV at about eleven o'clock. My mom went outside to check on my niece and I went along."

"How come you decided to accompany your mom?" Willette wondered.

"Yesterday, there'd been some reckless shooting in the neighborhood and I was afraid something might happen again. So, anyway, while I was inside my sister Cathy's trailer, I heard a gunshot. I went outside the trailer and met up with Marco Eno, who said he'd heard shouting and then shooting, and he saw someone leaving the trailer."

"And you? Did you see or hear anyone?"

"No."

He then recounted how he and Eno had gone to see what had happened, how Eno had entered the trailer first, how he had gone in afterward with his mother to find his stepfather murdered, and how he'd called 911.

"Any idea who'd want to kill your stepfather?" Willette asked.

"No, none at all," Glenn answered emphatically.

Willette was moving quickly from interview to interview, none taking longer than ten minutes because as far as he was concerned, nothing was being said. "If we get a lot of relevant information, I'll sit down and take time with them. If I'm not getting any more out of it, then I'm not gonna dig up shit that's not relevant," Willette explains.

Still, the lack of relevant information bothered him.

Most homicides are solved within the first twenty-four hours after the crime is committed. The further away you get in time from the act, the more difficult it is to pick up the trail of the murderer, and the more difficult it is to get a conviction. Detective Michael Willette knew this, and so he pressed forward with his interviews, late into the night.

Cathy Berry was up next.

Cathy Berry said that she was Grady Stiles's natural daughter. Willette didn't have to be told this: She, too, suffered from the "lobster claw syndrome." Claws for hands, no legs below the knee.

"I was inside my trailer with my mom, Teresa Stiles, and my brother Glenn Newman, as well as my husband Tyrill and my child. Anyway, it was at about eleven o'clock. I was brushing my teeth when our neighbor, Marco Eno, came over telling of the shouting and the shooting going on in my parents' house."

"But you didn't go over immediately?"

"No, I didn't go in until after Glenn told me my father had been shot."

"Do you know anyone who'd want your father harmed?"

"Well, no, but there's a person by the name of Howard Gallick. He's a former carnival worker who had an argument with my father."

"Where's he live?" Willette asked.

"Around here," Cathy replied. "In Gibsonton."

After the interviews, Willette processed the crime scene with the crime-scene technicians, taking a more detailed look, "getting my bullets lined up," so he was clear about the trajectory. He also collected any more physical evidence that might be present.

Crime-scene technician Sharon Sullivan took color photographs of the dead man and the crime scene. Measurements of the interior of the trailer were also taken for a crime-scene sketch.

Aside from his professional abilities, of all the detectives in Hillsborough County who could have been assigned to the Stiles murder case, Michael Willette was probably best equipped emotionally to handle it.

"I've got a brother who's a quadriplegic and over the years I've become very understanding of people with abnormalities and disabilities," he admitted.

While Willette processed the crime scene, helicopters hovered over Gibsonton, their spotlights cutting through the dark night, trying to spot any suspicious people from the air. Squad cars began prowling the side streets. One of those squad cars drove up to the trailer.

A patrolman got out of the car, spoke to Willette briefly, then went back to usher out his two passengers, seventeen-year-old Dennis Berger and his stepfather Rick Ardry. They'd been walking near the Stiles trailer at the time of the shooting and Willette needed to interview them.

"What were you doing out so late?" Willette inquired.

"Well, me and my stepfather were out walking," Berger said.

"You're his stepfather?" Willette turned to Ardry.

"Yes," Ardry replied dutifully. He'd been a soldier in Special Forces during the Persian Gulf War and he knew how to respond to authority. And also how not to be intimidated by it.

"Look, we were out walking. When we were near Symmes Road—" Berger continued.

"Where is that? What part of town?"

"Just east of 41, Officer," Ardry replied.

"Anyway," Berger said, "we heard one gunshot."

"You're sure of that?"

Both men nodded.

"We didn't see or hear anything else. Then the copters started flying around and that police car stopped us. This is even the first time I been on Inglewood Drive," said Berger.

"Did you know Grady Stiles or any members of his family?"

"No. Never met any of them."

"What are those spots on your jeans?" Willette asked. It was because of those spots that the patrolmen had picked them up.

Dennis Berger looked down at his pants, stained a dark red. "Oh, those. I got those from a cut elbow that I got from skateboarding."

Ardry corroborated everything his stepson told Detective Willette.

"The first time I was on Inglewood Drive was when the sheriff's deputies brought me to the scene tonight. I'm telling you, my stepson just wanted to talk about personal problems and that was the reason we were out walking."

Willette asked the teenager to submit the pants for serological (blood) analysis. Berger readily agreed.

At 5:45 A.M., with the sun peering over the horizon, Det. Michael Willette secured the crime scene. There was nothing more the brown trailer could tell him. It was up to the coroner now.

* * *

Dr. Robert Pfalzgraf had performed dozens of autopsies, but this was the first one of a man with lobster claws. As a doctor Pfalzgraf was fascinated by the deformity, even more so since Grady had passed it on to his kids.

Pfalzgraf wore a perpetually bemused expression. Maybe that was a defense against his job, because Dr. Pfalzgraf's patients were the dead, most of whom had died violently.

The sooner the autopsy was done, the sooner the police would have the most accurate information possible from which to build their case once the bad guy or guys were arrested. If they were arrested.

Pfalzgraf began by having the body photographed. He wanted a complete photographic record of the body in the condition it was brought in. This would be important later on as evidence for the prosecution.

Pfalzgraf's X rays found that two bullets were still in his head. That meant that one of the deadly pellets had exited.

There was no powder residue around the wounds. That meant that the victim had not been shot at close range. Using surgical saws, drills, and scalpels, Pfalzgraf was able to enter the brain and recover the bullets.

Examining the inside of the brain, it became clear that at least one of two shots had been fatal and that Grady had slumped forward after the bullets had entered. The third shot, though, was different. His head was already slumped down when it exploded through his cranium. And that bullet came from a different angle. It was almost as if the killer, not content to have shot twice, wanted to be sure the job was finished.

Pfalzgraf turned to a further examination of the body. The skin was already mottled, which meant lividity had set in.

He noticed that Stiles had tattooed a bunch of names on his arms. The left had the names *Barbara, Tamara,* and *Grady* in blue lettering. The name *Grady* was contained in a box that curved upward into what looked like a pictorial representation of his lobster claw. The right arm had names tattooed on it as well: *Teresa, Donna, Cathy,* and *Grady* in descending order. Once again, the last name was in a box that curved up into a lobster claw.

Pfalzgraf made an incision down the length of the body, removing and examining the organs and taking samples of bodily fluids, particularly the stomach contents, which would help pinpoint time of death. Though it was obvious how the victim had died, it was also remotely possible that the victim had ingested some sort of substance, like poison, that had hastened his demise. The blood tests would show the presence of any unusual substances, including drugs and alcohol.

Eventually, when he was finished, Pfalzgraf would make out his report, which would be forwarded to the investigating officer, Mike Willette.

Four

Willette was up bright and early, and drove over to headquarters in Ybor City, where he linked up with his partner, Det. Rick "Fig" Figueredo, who'd been poking around the crime scene late the previous night. They got together with their supervisors, Al Luis and Cpl. Lee "Pops" Baker, to talk about the case.

"I think it's a little too convenient that the mother and the stepson just happened to leave the trailer five minutes before the guy is shot," said Willette.

All agreed suspicion was focusing on the two family members.

"Oh, listen," advised Pops Baker. "Make sure when you're down in Gibsonton you look up Chuck Osak."

"Who's Osak?" Willette asked.

"He owns Showtown USA out on 41. Everyone in Gibtown comes in to drink at that place."

"Including Lobster Boy?" Fig voiced.

"Maybe. But if anyone has his pulse on the community and would know what was happening with the Stiles family, it'd be Osak."

As Willette and Fig rode along in their un-marked police car, they could see that there was a depressed look to Gibtown, as it's known to its residents, like modern progress had passed it by. No McDonald's or Pizza Hut, no fast-food chain restaurants of any kind. The local flea market was actually a few rows of clothing and trinkets attached to the side of a weather-beaten trailer. The clothing, sec-ondhand and lifeless, sat forlornly on hang-ers, flapping in the dry afternoon wind.

The one shopping center, Twin Oaks Plaza, has a bar, a video store, a restaurant, and a supermarket. The U-Save Supermarket stocks twenty-five different types of chewing tobacco, nine different types of snuff, and cigarette and cigar brands too numerous to count. The liquor section offered an equally wide selection as well.

The Gibsonton Post Office, in the same mall, has hundreds of post office boxes, re-flecting the nomadic existence of the town's inhabitants.

Despite its poor condition, the town is a modern rarity. Gibsonton's zoning regula-tions allow for the billeting of animals on residents' properties. "Residential show busi-ness" is the way the local zoning classification defines it. What that means in nonbureaucratic language is that Gibtown residents are allowed to bring their acts and equipment home with them every winter.

If you catch them at the right time, on some lawns you can see circus animals grazing, everything from dwarf ponies to five-legged cows to chimps.

But Willette and Fig weren't interested in the local sights. They knew the history of Gibsonton. They knew who lived there. They were there to solve a murder.

They found Marco Eno at his off-season job at Ruth's Steakhouse off Federal Highway 301 outside of town. He worked there as a cook.

While Eno had already given his statement to the police at the scene, maybe he would have something to add after having thought things over. Many witnesses to homicides remember important details the day after the crime has occurred.

It turned out that Eno had known Grady for five or six years. "I worked for Grady at a lot of carnivals," he began.

"How long you been living on the Stiles property?" Willette wondered.

"I moved into that small trailer in the back about a week ago," Eno interrupted. "It's actually a travel trailer. We store the gorilla illusion in it."

"Gorilla illusion?" Fig asked.

"Yeah, you know, where a girl turns into a gorilla."

The cops exchanged looks.

"What else can you tell us about Mr. Stiles?" Willette continued.

Eno thought for a moment.

"Grady has a temper when he drinks and gets verbally abusive."

"Have you ever heard any fights between Grady and his wife and kids?"

"Well, Glenn . . . he occasionally gets cocky and mouthy with Grady. They've had fights but nothing physical."

He then related how he'd heard the argument in the trailer on the previous night, the gunshots, the young man he saw leaving by the back door, how he raced over to the Berrys' trailer and how he'd entered the crime scene.

"Do you know Howard Gallick?" Willette asked.

Eno did.

"Was he the guy you saw running from the trailer?"

"No, he wasn't."

In fact, Eno couldn't say who the guy fleeing was.

"Something's not right here," Willette said to his partner after the interview with Eno was over.

"Like?"

"Nobody's showing any emotion. Guy gets killed in his house and his family doesn't seem to bat an eyelash."

"Coupled with the wife and stepson leaving right before the guy gets shot—"

"It sucks."

Willette put the car into gear.

Sometimes, a feeling that something's not right is all an investigator has to act on. A feeling here, a glance there. Whatever it was, it wasn't important to identify it, just to go with it and see where things led.

So Det. Michael Willette and his partner Fig Figueredo went back to Inglewood Drive to talk to Teresa Stiles.

"The first night, we'd just been looking for preliminary stuff," Willette relates. "I wanted to go back and see if I could dig up some more dirt."

The first thing Willette asked Teresa was why she and Glenn had gone out back at eleven P.M.

"Well, sir," Teresa said politely. "I had been walking over to my daughter's trailer on a regular basis because my grandbaby was sick. Glenn was concerned, too, and decided to come along."

"Did you leave the door open?" Willette prodded.

"The doors to the trailer are left unlocked and open a lot because Grady has high blood pressure and he overheats himself.

"He likes to sit in his underwear and sit in the chair where you found him. The chair's position allows a cool draft if the door is open."

Willette had noticed the fan in the living room the previous night. Despite the Florida heat and humidity, the Stiles residence had no air-conditioning.

"When I walked outside last night to check on the grandbaby, Grady said that he was going to use the rest room, and for me to hurry back so he could watch the remainder of the videotape we was watching. It's called *Ruby.*"

"Did your husband drink?"

"Oh my, yes."

"Was he drunk last night? Your husband."

"Yes, sir, he had two double shots of Seagram's 7 whiskey. You know about his arrest in Pennsylvania?"

Willette and Fig looked at each other.

"What arrest?" Fig asked.

"My daughter's boyfriend was shot and killed by Grady in Pittsburgh in 1978. He's currently on probation for that."

Not anymore, Willette thought. But that made things interesting. A murder victim who was himself a murderer. And he shot a guy in Pittsburgh. How? He didn't have hands.

"I wasn't married to Grady at the time of the murder," Teresa added. "We were married the first time for fifteen years and then divorced in 1974. We remarried again in 1988."

"Did your husband have a life-insurance policy?"

She nodded. "But I don't know the amount." If they wanted that information, they could call the agent, Walter Neff. She gave them his phone number.

"Think she killed her husband for the money?" Fig wondered aloud when they were alone.

"Maybe. But she'd have to hate him awful bad."

"Or love him," said Fig and added, "Maybe the son-in-law can tell us something."

The detectives went on back to the travel trailer to interview Tyrill Ray Berry, Cathy's husband.

Tyrill hails from Kansas. In the Stiles family, he takes a lot of ribbing for coming from the "Land of Oz." He's been down South so long that his flat, Kansas twang has been enhanced by a slow, Southern drawl.

A tall, heavyset man with sad eyes and an

inquisitive face, Tyrill remembered that on the evening of the murder, at about 10:45 P.M., he was out on the street in front of the brown trailer.

"I was picking up flea-market stuff that I had on display, when I saw a pickup truck with no headlights on, just parking lights, cruise on down the street very slowly."

Light blue or silver in color, the pickup truck drove by and went to the mobile-home park at the end of the street. Then the pickup made a U-turn and traveled back down the street, passing the brown trailer again.

"See who was inside?"

"No."

"How about the license plate?"

"It was too dark."

After the suspicious pickup faded from view, Tyrill went on back to be with his wife and daughter, Misty.

Willette wondered what kind of relationship Tyrill had with his father-in-law.

"I worked with Grady on the carnival circuit," Tyrill volunteered. "I run an oddity museum of rare animal species."

Tyrill said he and Grady got along well, but they'd had verbal arguments in the past. "Nothing that would cause me to want to kill him," Tyrill added.

"Would you know of anyone who would?"

"I know of no one who would want to kill him."

Investigators know that some communities are more open than others about offering information. In some wealthy communities, the residents are forthcoming because they are less afraid of the consequences of involvement with the police. In poorer communities, people can tend to be less forthcoming because they fear any contact with law enforcement officials.

Gibsonton falls into a different category. It's a carny town and carny folk keep to themselves. Partly because they know how difficult it is for the non-carny world to understand their peculiar lives. Partly because their world is so deeply rooted in presenting illusions as "real life" that they can often lose sight of simple facts in favor of something more interesting.

Always vigilant for the hard truth, Willette and Figueredo knew they had to be particularly careful about the information they gathered during their interviews in Gibsonton.

Every community has its good ole boy who made good, a guy who made it but never forgot his roots. The residents of Gibsonton looked to Chuck Osak to fill that role.

Osak's parents were in the carnival; he was raised on the road. He remembers his parents being so desperate for money that when he was a child they once sold his toy boat for gas money. Today, Chuck gets carny people license tags for their show vehicles. He estimates that he has 105 accounts.

Osak works out of a trailer off Highway 41. The trailer is actually an office, with a bank of desks and phones stretching its considerable length. It also doubles as a Western Union office, where residents can come and wire or have wired to them money from anyplace in the country.

Osak is a prosperous man. Adjacent to his office/trailer was another property that he owned: Showtown USA.

Chuck Osak told Willette and Fig that he'd been a booking agent for Grady Stiles, booking him into various carnivals throughout the country. He also got license tags for the vehicles Grady took with him on the road. The latter were necessary because of the numerous states that the carnival troupe would travel in.

"What was Grady Stiles like?" Willette asked.

"Grady Stiles was a very rude individual. He was rude to his wife and to his employees," Osak answered.

That afternoon the serological tests on Dennis Berger's pants came back negative. The blood did not match Grady Stiles's. The boy had been telling the truth when he said he'd cut his elbow skateboarding. Berger, though, was never really a suspect. He had no motive and had an alibi in Ardry for the time of the slaying. No, the answer, the detectives were now convinced, lay closer to home.

Why was it that out of all the people in the Berry trailer at the time of the murder— Teresa, Cathy, Tyrill, and Glenn— Glenn was the only one who stated that he'd heard at least one gunshot? Yet, in fact, there were a total of four.

And the reason he went with his mother to check on his niece's well-being was because there'd been a shooting in the neighborhood the previous night? And he just happened to leave with his mother moments before the shooter burst in and killed Grady?

Clearly, it was time to talk to Glenn Newman again.

Willette and Fig drove back to the brown trailer.

"Glenn, you know, we're having some problems with some of the things you said."

Glenn looked at them anxiously.

"Yeah," Fig continued casually, "but we think we can get a lot of answers if you'd come with us to police headquarters at the Buchman Plaza building in Ybor City to take a lie-detector test."

Most citizens are not Constitutional scholars. They are not aware that unless they are formally taken into custody, they do not have to accompany the police. Glenn Newman readily agreed to accompany them "downtown."

Soon after arrival at Buchman Plaza, headquarters of the Hillsborough County Sheriff's Office, Glenn was taken to an innocent-looking room, where a polygraph machine sat on a table. Glenn was introduced to the polygraph operator, Herb Metzger, a former detective who is an expert in the administration of polygraph tests.

Glenn was told that the questions were going to be brief, that he was to answer simply "yes" or "no." Glenn nodded and Metzger strapped him in. The examination began.

"Is your name Harry Glenn Newman, Jr.?" Metzger queried.

"Yes," Glenn replied.

"Do you live at 11117 Inglewood Drive in Gibsonton?"

"Yes."

"Are you nineteen years old?"

"No."

"Do you go to high school?"

"Yes."

"Is your mother Mary Teresa Stiles?"

"Yes."

Alone with Metzger in the room, he was strapped into the machine, staring straight ahead, concentrating on the questions. Metzger, meanwhile, was concentrating on the needles that played out over a graph. Sharp rises and falls of the needles would indicate a "blip," that the person was being disingenuous, or at worst, lying.

"Glenn, did you know Grady Stiles?"

"Yes."

"Was he your stepfather?"

"Yes."

"Did you kill him?"

"No."

"Did you have anything to do with killing him?"

"No."

"Do you know who killed him?"

"Definitely not."

"Yes or no."

"No."

After the test was over, Metzger unstrapped Glenn. He tore the graph paper with its myriad of lines out of the machine and went out to talk to Willette and Fig.

"How'd he do?" Willette asked.

Metzger was studying the graph paper. He looked up.

"I feel this man is being deceptive," Metzger responded. "Especially on the questions where I asked him directly if he had anything to do with the murder or he knew who had killed his stepfather."

"Thanks, Herb."

Willette and Fig walked into the room.

"How'd I do?" Glenn asked eagerly.

"You blew up the machine," Willette answered.

Glenn looked puzzled.

"You lied when asked certain questions," Willette translated.

"About who was responsible for killing Grady," Fig added.

Glenn's head sagged and his whole body followed. They ushered him to a green, washed-out interrogation room, furnished with a desk and some cheap chairs. They sat down to talk, Glenn on one side of the table, the two detectives on the other.

"Glenn, we have a big problem we think you might be able to help us out with," Willette said in a gentle voice.

"Look, Glenn," Fig continued, "why don't you tell us what really happened and get it off your chest. You'll feel better."

"A lot better," Willette added.

"We know you didn't mean to kill anybody."

"I didn't kill anybody!"

"Then why don't you tell us who did."

"Why should you take the fall for them?" said Fig.

Glenn began to cry. After a long time, he looked up.

"Okay," he said.

Glenn signed a "Consent to Interview" form, in which he agreed to be interviewed by the detectives without an attorney being present.

It was Figueredo's turn to take the lead. With Willette present, he would be the principal officer during questioning.

A tape recorder was set up.

"Today's date is November thirtieth, 1992. Present for this interview is Detective Mike Willette, Detective Rick Figueredo, and Harry Newman, age eighteen. Harry, do you understand that this interview is being recorded?"

"Yes," Harry Glenn Newman replied.

"Do you have any problem with us recording this interview?"

"No."

"Okay," Fig continued, "I'm going to read you something and please listen closely and ask any questions if you have any. Okay, you understand we're investigating a murder?"

"Yes."

"Okay, you understand the following: I hereby consent to be interviewed by the below listed Hillsborough County Sheriff's Office Law Enforcement officials concerning the above listed incident and I further understand that I have the right to remain silent and can invoke this right at any time during questioning?"

"Yes."

"Do you understand that?"

"Yes."

Fig wasn't taking any chances that a judge

would throw out what he hoped would be a confession on some technicality like the suspect was not properly advised of his rights.

"Do you have any questions about what I've read so far?"

"No."

"If you make a statement it can and will be used against you in a court of law. Do you understand that?"

"Yes."

"Okay, do you have any questions?"

"No."

"I have the right to the presence of an attorney during questioning. Do you understand that?"

"Yes."

"Do you have any questions about that?"

"No."

"If you can't afford an attorney, one will be appointed to you without charge and before any questioning if that's your desire. Do you understand that?"

"Yes."

"If I wish to make a statement I may invoke my right to an attorney or remain silent at any time during the questioning. Do you understand that?"

"Yes."

"Do you have any questions about that?"

"No."

"I understand these rights and no one has threatened me, coerced me, or tricked me, or promised me anything in order to induce me to make a statement. I presently wish to make a statement and answer questions without an attorney being present."

"Yes," answered Glenn.

"Okay," said Fig. "I ask you to initial this box here and sign your name right there."

Glenn did as instructed.

"Okay, we've spoken for the last hour or so . . ."

"Yes."

". . . Another detective, Herb Metzger . . . here on the death of your stepfather . . . what's his name?"

"Grady Stiles."

"Where does Grady Stiles live?"

"11117 Inglewood Drive."

"What part of town is that?"

". . . Right off Symmes . . . about the same . . . down in Gibsonton."

"Do you have a phone number there?"

"Yes."

"What is that number?"

He stated the number.

"What I'd like for you to do at this time is to go back as early as you can remember the plot, for a lack of better words . . . Tell us how this all came about."

"Well, this happened about a week ago. I talked to this one kid Chris that my father's been abusing my mom, beating her up. He had threatened to kill her. Things like that.

He'll lay in bed at night when he's drunk, says 'I should just kill you to get it over with.' He's turned around and threatened to kill my sister. Beat her up already, he has, made her jaw swell up."

"When you refer to your family member, could you be more specific and mention which sister, first and last name?" Fig asked for clarification.

"Cathy Berry is the one that got beat up at one time. He punched her in the jaw, made her jaw swell up. And Mary Teresa Stiles is my mother. That's the one that he used to get drunk and lay in bed and say 'I should just kill you. Get it over with.' He knocked her down. Choked her, beat her in her head, hit her mouth with his forehead. He killed a man in 1978."

Part Two

The Family

Five

In 1937, Edna and Grady Stiles already had two children. On a carny's salary, it was hard to make ends meet.

Grady Stiles worked in the carnival, where he exhibited himself as one of life's human oddities. Grady was born with a birth deformity that gave him fused hands in the shape of lobster claws.

"Hurry, hurry, hurry, and see the Lobster Man," the bally man would shout to the throng assembled on the midway. "Hurry, hurry, hurry."

They would pay their nickel and step inside a tent. On a raised platform sat Grady Stiles.

"Ladies and gentlemen, I am Grady Stiles, the Lobster Man," he said, holding his claws up proudly. "I am a product of a genetic condition, which has run in the Stiles family since 1840. In scientific circles it is known as ectrodactyly.

"Ectrodactyly is a genetic condition. Affecting one in ninety thousand at birth, a baby is born with the absence of the third digit and the fusing together of the remaining fingers and toes into claws. Sometimes it affects all four limbs, sometimes two. In my case, as you can see, I have normal legs.

"Once the gene has latched onto a family, every child born has a fifty-fifty chance of getting the condition, which is also known as 'lobster claw syndrome.' "

He never bothered to add that the only way to get rid of the offending gene was not to have children, a choice the Stiles family had rejected.

Since Zachary Taylor was president, the Stileses bore children. Their attitude was "Hell, if a child was born a freak, it was the child's problem, the child's and God's. Besides, fifty-fifty weren't bad odds."

Grady and Edna Stiles had had three children. Big sister Margaret was born normal, but her life came to a tragic end. One day while selling tickets at the carnival, she keeled over and died of a cerebral brain hemorrhage, only weeks before she was to be married.

Their middle child Sarah was born with the "lobster claw syndrome," in her case, with a lobster claw for one hand, and one stunted foot with lobster claw for toes. She later had the foot amputated and an artificial leg made. A marriage to an alcoholic ended in divorce, but the products of the union, one boy and two girls, grew up to marry and have normal lives.

Then came Edna's third pregnancy. Grady, Jr., who came into the world on July 18, 1937, was born with ectrodactyly. The condition was so bad that not only did he have claws for appendages, he had legs whose growth was stunted and ended at the knees.

On the north side of the Ohio River, which cuts the city of Pittsburgh in two, is a series of slums. It is the place where those without money and those without hope settle. Every city has a place like that and in Pittsburgh it's called, not coincidentally, the North Side.

Edna and Grady, Sr., rented an apartment on the North Side. As a toddler, Grady, Jr. crawled on his back and on his stomach on the apartment's bare, wooden floors. Without legs, he could not stand; without hands, he would gradually have to learn a special type of manual dexterity.

In the eyes of the residents of the tough North Side, he was a freak, constantly pointed at whenever he appeared on the street, constantly made fun of and demeaned by children and adults alike. Grady, Sr., was always on the road with the carnival, traveling throughout the forty-eight states, so Grady, Jr., had no father to teach him what it meant to be a man, to teach him how to weather life's adversities, of which there were many for a child who was called "freak" to his face.

Parents held their children tight and pointed with mixed awe and revulsion at the freak with lobster claws. Silent prayers of "There but for the grace of God go I," superstitious women spitting to ward off the evil eye, and taunts from schoolmates of "Hey, freak" accompanied him wherever he went. The world did not accept him. And then, fate gave young Grady a reprieve.

The Stileses had already discovered the Gibsonton area. It was the place to winter when the carnival shut down for the cold weather. Real estate was cheap in Florida in those days and from his carnival wages, Grady, Sr., was able to buy a house on Marconi Street in the Palmetto Beach area, across the bay from Gibsonton proper. In 1944, Grady, Sr., settled his family for good in their new Florida home. But young Grady, then seven years old, had little time to enjoy his new locale.

The Stiles family was still struggling along from day to day. Everyone had to do their share, including Grady, Jr. It was time for the child to go out and make a living like everyone else. His father decided he would join the family business. Young Grady would become a carny.

Grady, Sr., forced his son to quit school and join the carnival. From small town to small town, across the northern plains and the southern panhandle, into the cool New England forests and the muggy northeastern states in the summers, young Grady climbed up onto the platform with his father.

"Hurry, hurry, hurry," the bally man shouted. "Step right up, pay your money and see 'The Lobster Family!'"

People would pay money, get a ticket, and enter a small, canvas tent. Upon entering, they would see a raised, wooden platform, on which Grady Stiles, Sr., and his son sat in chairs. As they gazed at this exotic form of human oddity, Grady, Sr., began his routine. As he had throughout his carnival life, Grady would entertain the folks by relating the story of his family's disability, pointing to his smiling son, Lobster Boy, as the next generation who had to grin and bear it.

In those days, the carnival was indeed a family. There were none of the "forty-milers" you have now, those that join the carnival briefly and move on. In those days, people joined up for the duration; they stayed with the same carnival through thick and thin, through mud and rain or locusts or whatever. They were there for each other, The Fat Man, The Bearded Lady, the roustabouts, the strippers, the workers in the "grab trucks," who sold the equivalent of junk food.

The living conditions in the back of drafty trailers and tents were abysmal, but young Grady, Jr., enjoyed being a showman, exhibiting himself on the platform, earning a salary like his father.

The Stileses signed on with the Lorow Brothers and were put in a "10 in 1" show that featured ten "freak" acts under one tent for the same price. The Lobster Family became the star attraction.

During the winter months, Grady traveled with his father back to Gibsonton and lived there with his mother and sisters. Unlike his experience in Pittsburgh, he was not ridiculed for his appearance. After all, the odd was usual in Gibsonton. It was a show town, filled with carnival and circus oddities.

Young Grady fit in with the local kids. He could play baseball like they did and he loved to wrestle. It was fun getting his strong arms around his opponent and squeezing until they had no choice but to submit and cry uncle or be further crushed in Grady's python-like arms. As for locomotion, he was as fast on his hands as most people were on their feet. Even faster.

Yet despite his adaptation to his handicap and the acceptance he received in Gibsonton, Grady grew up bitter at the world at large for not accepting him. Determined to prove to the world he was just as good as they were, he got stronger than anyone else.

All Grady had was his arms. Years of crawling around on them, of supporting his entire body weight on those appendages, made them strong. His claws had bone and muscle and sinew in them, too. He gradually learned how to use his claws, to do nearly everything anyone else could, from simple tasks like washing to more complex ones like writing, and later, much later, firing a revolver . . . accurately. And they became powerful enough to crush anything he grasped with them, powerful enough to inflict pain. His strength allowed him to indulge a sadistic side that had built up in him over the years. He enjoyed inflicting pain, especially when he was drunk.

If anyone bothered him, Grady's claw shot out and slapped the malefactor alongside the head. Those who were hit by his claw said it felt like being hit with a board. Before his victim could stand, Grady would scuttle over and head butt him in the stomach. An explosion of air and his opponent went down again. Then Grady would place his powerful arms around the target's throat and began squeezing.

As for his parents, not much is known about Grady's relationship with them. In later years, he talked rarely to his wife Teresa about his childhood and adolescence. If his parents abused him in any way, he did not tell. He did, however, acquire a taste for liquor, and drank with Grady, Sr., and Edna as he grew older. Grady favored Seagram's 7.

Years later, all that bitterness he'd stored up as a child and adolescent would come raging out of control when he drank too much, which was, his family would say, every night. God forbid if you were a family member who got in Grady's path when he got drunk.

His carnival career pretty much precluded Grady from having a formal education. The schooling he got was life's experience. He could read print in a book, but as for cursive writing, it was unintelligible gibberish. He couldn't write except for his name, which was done in an elementary school-type of scrawl.

Grady was an extremely intelligent man, smart enough to eventually run his own sideshow. What he lacked in formal education he more than made up for in street smarts. He was also charming and effusive to those he liked. In those early years, he dressed well, and when he was flush, he ate in the finest restaurants.

Of course, getting around was still a problem. In public, he used a wheelchair for locomotion. In private, he just crawled on his

hands and delighted in showing anyone who
was interested how he could walk just as
quickly on those hands as the so-called "normal" people on their God-given feet.

By the 1950s, Grady, Sr., and his son had
tired of working for someone else and went
out on their own. In 1954, at the age of seventeen, Grady married Deborah Brady in
Tampa, Florida. But the marriage didn't
work out; they were separated after a year
and eventually divorced. They had no children. And so Grady continued, up on the
platform with the carnival, but eyeing the
girls, looking for another one to make his
own.

Mary Teresa Herzog was born April 23,
1938, in a small town in Vermont, where a
cold winter's day could find the temperature
plunging to ten below zero. What she remembered most from her childhood was the
cold, mostly the frost in her home.

Her mother Jean and father Harvey did
not get along and when she was six, they
divorced. Her mother married Frank Tyler.
Until Grady, he was the most important man
in her life.

In those days, incest was not talked about.
It was even more taboo than now. And so,
having no choice, having no power, young
Teresa submitted to her stepfather's frequent

sexual abuse for years. However, one of the things that made her life bearable was the circuit carnival that stopped at her town several times a year.

"The carnival fascinated me. I guess it fascinated most young people. I thought the lights and the excitement were just great," Teresa recalls.

Teresa wanted to get closer to the carny, so whenever the carnival came to town, she helped sell tickets—until one day in 1956. When she was eighteen years old, she shook off that small-town New England routine for good and joined the carnival.

Three years later, she had grown into an attractive young woman with a pretty face and a good figure.

She fell in love with a carnival roustabout named Jerry Plummer. A good-looking young man, Jerry operated one of the bulldozers that moved the carnival paraphernalia during setups and takedowns from one dusty, backwater town to another.

Teresa and Plummer got married. It was not a happy marriage.

The girl abused in childhood had married a man who abused her as an adult. Within months of their marriage, Jerry beat Teresa. He threw punch after punch in anger, breaking most of her teeth. One night, in a fit of rage over some unnamed slight, he threw hot coffee at her and scalded her skin.

But that was just the beginning of her humiliation.

On another occasion, Jerry thrust the sharp point of his switchblade against the small of Teresa's back and forced her to walk in front of hundreds of people on the midway.

When Teresa got pregnant with his child, he knocked her down the stairs, getting pleasure out of her pain. Jerry, though, grew tired of the sport. "He left me," Teresa recalls. The game just wasn't fun anymore.

Unlike many abused women, who feel helpless, alone, and depressed when their abuser is out of the picture, Mary Teresa took responsibility for her own life. Still legally married to Jerry, she engaged an attorney and got a divorce. Now she had to support herself and her new daughter, Debra.

On a warm May day in Trenton, New Jersey, in 1959, the charming Lobster Boy and the incest victim from New England met and fell in love.

Grady had already seen her selling tickets and secretly admired her. But within the hierarchy of the carnival, he was on the top as a performer and she was on the bottom as a worker. Grady and his father, while still a team, were now billed as "The Lobster Family— 4th and 5th Generation" of freaks. They worked for Stan Wright and Jimmy

Steinmetz in the World of Mirth carnival that toured the forty-eight states.

Fate intervened when the bosses, sensing her potential, offered her a job as a bally girl working the sideshow. Grady knew that if she were closer to the show, he would be able to date her more easily.

For Teresa, it meant more money and a chance to escape the monotony of the ticket booth. Teresa readily accepted. She became a full-fledged carny. Soon, she had graduated from bally girl into part of an act, as the "Blade Box Girl." Her role was to enter a box and seemingly be stabbed by swords thrust into it from every angle.

Teresa became a carnival jack-of-all-trades. She was so good as The Blade Box Girl, she also became "The Electrified Girl."

Teresa would sit in a throne-like chair similar to one used to execute prisoners. When her assistant threw the switch, an electrical glow formed around her, and lightning bolts leaped from hand to hand. She seemed in a semistupor, yet she remained unharmed. When the current was finally turned off, she stood and gazed down at her adoring crowd, as they applauded the illusion.

To Grady, it made no difference whether she was in an electric chair or a blade box. It was all just making a living, and who cared what you did? What he really cared about was that once he set eyes on her, he wanted to have her.

Grady courted her with attention and presents. Never had Teresa been so loved and so wanted by anybody as she was by Grady Stiles. He wined and dined her, made her feel like part of his family.

"Grady was such a charming man," Teresa recalls, her voice filled with love and nostalgia. "Everyone enjoyed being in his company."

Here was a man, a real man, despite his deformity, who wanted to take care of her. Finally, they began living together.

They made a decent living in the carnival. During the off-season, Teresa took a job in a shrimp factory in Tampa to help make ends meet. She and Grady lived together for nine years before he officially married her.

Grady was a good provider. However, when he was drinking, Grady started beating Teresa early in their relationship, taking care to keep his blows to the body. It wouldn't do for her to be seen on the midway with a battered face.

The first child born to Grady and Teresa was named Margaret. Margaret died after twenty-six days. Teresa says the cause of death was pneumonia.

The second child born to Grady and Teresa was named David. David died after twenty-eight days. Once again, Teresa says the cause of death was pneumonia. Apparently, the constant travel and the drafty living conditions on the road caused both infant deaths.

The family problems continued.

"Grady's father became ill and couldn't really do the work," Teresa recalls. By 1961, in failing health, Grady Stiles, Sr., quit show business for good.

"His father wasn't making it here in Florida, and the cost of living was too much for him, so he moved back to Pittsburgh. Grady was still living in Florida [with me] and he'd go to Pittsburgh when his father got ill. He got an apartment to be close by. We almost lost him a couple of times."

While Grady was in Pittsburgh, Teresa recalls that he "drank with his parents. They drank a lot. They drank beer while Grady drank whiskey."

To make ends meet, Grady and Teresa went into Tampa and opened up a single low— carnival slang for a show just featuring one act which, of course, was Grady on the platform. And during the season, they would travel.

In 1963, their third child, Donna Marie, was born. This time, the Stileses were blessed. Not only was Donna a healthy child, she was born without her father's deformity.

She would not have to go through life a
freak. It was something he should have been
thankful for. Instead, it embittered Grady
even more.

Right after Donna's birth, Grady started
drinking heavily. He would stay out late at
night drinking liquor and playing cards with
his carnival buddies. Sometimes, he'd go on
drinking binges and be away from home for
days at a time. When he did come home, he
would generally make it to the living room
and pass out on the floor. Sometimes, he'd
throw up first and then sleep in his own
vomit.

In the morning, Debra and Donna would
get up, get washed, and change into their
school clothes. They would have to step over
Grady to get out of the trailer.

None of this was lost on Grady. He might
not have had formal schooling, but he was
still a smart man. Part of him warred with
himself to become more of a father, someone his kids could look up to, at least figu-
ratively. He made a strong effort to change.
He stopped drinking as much and started to
come home more often.

During this brief period of semisobriety,
when Teresa heard him come home, she
would make the children go to their room.

"I want you to be very quiet," she told
them, "and not disturb your father."

What she did not tell them was that it was

in their own best interests because when he was drunk, Grady liked to beat his kids. There is no indication that Teresa ever tried to stop him. Perhaps she was too busy protecting herself. Sometimes, Teresa says, the beatings she suffered were so severe that she could barely get out of bed in the morning.

Their fourth child, Catherine, who would become known as Cathy, was born in 1969. She was born with the same deformity as her father. She would have to grow up with lobster claws and stunted legs that ended just below the knees.

Six

Strolling by the trailer in Gibsonton, the Stiles place looked like any other, slightly run-down, but not seedy. Just hard-working carny people trying to make a go of it.

Inside, Donna Stiles, a sad-eyed, tow-headed child, would see the same thing every day. And it seemed normal, just like other families. When you're five or seven, everything seems normal, just like other families.

Donna was born April 29, 1963, in Syosset, a middle-class suburb in Long Island, New York. Grady and Teresa had been on the road playing Long Island when her water broke. Teresa was rushed to the hospital. The child she gave birth to was completely normal.

Donna was raised in Gibsonton, and most of her early childhood years remain a blur. Her earliest memories come from about the age of seven. "There was nothing really good I can recall," she says now. "He [her father] always drank. Continually drank. I really started noticing it at about seven because he would yell at us if he was drinking at home."

Her father would get up around eleven or twelve o'clock every day. He'd have a "glass of tea" in his bedroom and then he would come out of the bedroom and sit on a chair for a couple of hours. A few more glasses of tea and then he'd wheel himself out the door.

In those days, he had a car with handheld controls. He would drive, or get someone to push him in his wheelchair down to Harry's Bar, the local watering hole that was a quarter of a mile from the house.

Donna and her half sister, Debra, and later her sister, Cathy, went to school every day. If Grady was there when they came home at night, invariably, he'd be drunk. And he would yell, heaping abuse on his children in a drunken rage.

Sober, though, Grady was subdued, rarely raising his voice. "I never seen him much when he wasn't drinking. If he didn't have a drink in his hand, he was sleeping," Donna recalls.

That didn't leave much in between. Once April rolled around, the respite of school didn't help, either.

At the start of the carnival season, Grady needed all the help he could get. While he was insistent that his children get a good education, he routinely pulled them out of school three months before the end of the term.

Together, The Lobster Family would hit the road, traveling from town to town, the children working side by side with the adults during setups and takedowns of the tent, under which Grady plied his trade. The kids would also work with their mother selling tickets, counting money, whatever their father required of them. He was the complete and absolute boss in his home.

Teresa, fully aware that the kids were getting cheated out of a proper education, would make sure to take books along. Maybe there was nothing she could do about them being on the road, but if they had to be out there, she would make certain they continued their reading.

Day after day, Grady would get drunk. He'd scream at the kids. Then he would give them beatings or spankings. Sometimes, it would happen if one of his kids talked back to him.

"Who the fuck you think you're talking to like that?" Grady would shout, and the claw would shoot out like lightning and smack his child across the mouth.

Sometimes, he'd beat his kids without provocation, just to keep them in line.

All the children suffered the same punishment, including his stepdaughter, Debra. Still, Donna was probably disciplined the worst.

She noticed that within the context of his rage, the other kids didn't get as many beatings. Maybe that was because Donna had been born the only normal child, and she had to suffer for it.

Teresa stood by while Grady beat her kids. But Teresa wanted to protect her children; when Grady beat her, she tried to keep the violence confined to the bedroom, behind closed doors. Frequently, she wasn't successful.

"Go get me a drink," Grady would shout at his wife.

Teresa would obediently comply. As she took the drink to him, Grady would grab her butt or her leg and punch her hard. Hidden under the long-sleeved shirts and pants she wore year-round, were bruises where Grady's claws had done their dirty work.

Year after year they all took it. Even when the kids were old enough to do something about it, they took it. To them, abuse was normal.

Donna remembers one night in particular during the latter part of 1972. They were home in the trailer in Gibtown. "He was arguing, he was really drunk, real bad. And he was fighting, arguing with Mom."

While World War III raged in the living

room, all the kids went to bed. They were in a separate part of the trailer. Lying in bed in the dark, staring up at the ceiling, they could hear their parents arguing and fighting.

"Then I heard a big bang," Donna says, "a very *loud* bang."

They got up and came running out of the bedroom, into the living-room light.

"He had my mom in the middle of the living-room floor, and he was punching her in the sides, and the legs, and in the arms and face."

"Stop it, stop it," Debbie screamed in tears.

"Daddy, please, stop . . . ," Donna sobbed.

Teresa collapsed in Grady's arms. Her eyes rolled back in her head. Her breathing became shallow.

Debbie raced across the room and put her thin arms around his neck, pulling him back. Trying to help, Donna took hold of his arm, too.

Looking down at the limp rag of a woman in his arms, Grady's rage subsided. He let her go and she collapsed to the floor in a heap.

"I ought to finish you," he snarled. "I ought to finish you off right here. I don't need you. You're nothing but a dirty bitch!"

He turned and looked at Donna.

"You're too much like your mother," he

muttered coldly, staring at the petrified child. "Too much."

Taking in deep gulps of air with every breath, Grady put his claws down on the floor and scooted across the room to his armchair. He turned on the TV and finished drinking his Seagram's 7 and Coke like nothing had happened.

As the television's light flickered across the room, the children knelt down around their mom and tried to wake her up. Struggling mightily, they half carried and half dragged her out. Eventually, Teresa regained consciousness.

"Mom, I'll call the cops," Debbie said.

"No, no," Teresa answered anxiously. "Don't worry about it. He's just drunk."

The night her parents separated remains indelibly etched in Donna's mind.

"I don't remember where it was, or the exact month, or the town, but we were on the road, and he was drinking all day. He drank all the time when he was working."

Many times, when the marks would come into the tent to see Grady on top of the platform, reciting his speech about how long the "lobster claw syndrome" had been in his family, his words would be slurred from all the booze he'd been drinking.

"That night, after closing, he called Mom out in the show. They were arguing. She came back into the trailer, crying. And then he came back to the trailer, pulled the door open, let it slam real hard, and he took twenty dollars and he threw it at her."

"Take your fucking kids and get out of my face," Grady screamed.

"She did," Donna continues. "She told all five of us to go get packed. She was scared and crying real hard. She packed a couple of suitcases herself and she took us with her across the street to a motel. There was no way she'd leave us alone with him when he was drinking."

After Teresa and the kids checked in, she called Midget Man to come to her rescue.

Harry Glenn Newman, aka Midget Man, was actually a welder by trade. Unlike normal-sized welders, at a little over three feet, Glenn was lower down to the material he was work-ing on and consequently inhaled some of the fine metal filings he shaved with his blow torch. Respiratory problems followed. Rather than keep risking his health, he joined the carnival.

As Midget Man or The World's Smallest Man, he toured the carnival circuit, eventu-ally hooking up with Grady Stiles, who be-came one of his friends, and later, his employer. To see Lobster Boy and Midget Man together was indeed a strange sight for the casual bystander.

Over the years of their friendship, Glenn came to know and admire Teresa Stiles. A truly compassionate person, he had a friendly shoulder she could lean on. Glenn was always there to help out.

"When my mom called Glenn the night she was thrown out, Glenn quit work. He had a little camper. He came over to the motel and tried to calm Mom down. He says, 'Don't worry, if he throws you out, I'll help you get straightened around.' "

The entire family traveled to Ohio and moved in with Glenn's mother.

Things were quiet then. Glenn would come around every day. Frequently, he played with Cathy. One day, he brought her a puppy as a present. For the first time in their lives, the Stiles family, minus Grady, lived a normal life. There was no fighting. Teresa was more relaxed.

"When we got up for breakfast every morning, it was quiet. Glenn would come over for dinner, and it was nice. He would joke around. We were able to go shopping," Donna recalled.

With Glenn footing some of the bills, the Stiles family was able to make a go of it. Then, one day, four months into the honeymoon, "Mom took us someplace to this courthouse. I think it was in Pennsylvania. I remember the day because Cathy had just lost her first front tooth that day.

"We were sitting in a room, and Dad and Mom was in another room. I don't know what happened. We went downstairs to a cafeteria, and then she took us off to the side and said we had to go with him, had to go with my dad. Cathy was crying, and I ran to Glenn's pickup and locked myself in it. I think it was Mom that eventually talked me out of there."

Without Teresa's knowledge, Grady had filed for divorce. Since Teresa never knew about the proceedings and didn't participate in any of them, the court awarded Grady an uncontested divorce and custody of the kids.

"We left the courthouse, but I don't know where he was living at the time. But we ended up in Florida, back on Trenton Street in Tampa. He still had the house."

Not for long, though. They were only there long enough for Grady to sell the house and all the furniture in it. "He gave all of Mom's whatnots, lamps and all of her stuff to his sister. He would not let her come back to the house to get her clothes, which included a fur coat and some evening dresses. He gave away all of her clothes. Jewelry, and everything else, he gave to Barbara."

By that time, Grady was living with Barbara Browning Lucille. With his divorce final, they married.

"Barbara had a sunken face and stringy,

light brown hair. She was very, very skinny. She wanted to put herself in my mom's place. She wanted to be our mother. She tried to force herself onto us."

Donna hated her. But the idea wasn't to be a nurturer, the way Teresa was. It was "a role [she was playing] to try to get closer to my dad, and to try to get us away from my mom. I think she had a drinking problem like my dad did, because they would go out drinking together a lot," unlike Teresa, who so hated drinking she would only do it if Grady forced her.

Barbara had one child from a previous marriage, a daughter named Susan. Along with Susan, who everyone called Susie, the reconstituted Stiles family consisted of Grady, Cathy, Donna, and Barbara. Debra, who was older, went out on her own.

Being the oldest, Donna was forced to adopt adult-sized responsibility. Though she wasn't close to her stepsister Susie growing up, she helped raise her.

"My dad had me take care of [all] the kids," Donna continued. Sometimes, the responsibility overwhelmed her and she cut school. When Grady found out, he beat her with his belt. "I'm gonna send you to juvenile," he threatened, as the belt bit into her skin.

Grady beat his new wife, too, but unlike Teresa, whom he preferred to beat around the body so the bruises did not show, he wasn't as careful with Barbara; when she appeared in public, it was not uncommon to see her face bruised, her eyes blackened, her lips puffy.

Donna still had her own survival to consider.

By 1974, Grady had relocated the family again, this time back to his hometown of Pittsburgh. He was hoping to organize a sideshow with him as the star attraction. They settled in his old stomping grounds on the city's North Side, in a tenement, which had a fine view of other tenements. Then, in 1976, Barbara became pregnant.

"My dad knocked Barbara down and continued to punch her in the stomach when she was pregnant with [Little] Grady," Donna recalls.

Grady Stiles III was born on July 26, 1976. He had the family trait of lobster claws and truncated legs.

Teresa continued to live with Harry Glenn Newman. He was a good husband and made a living from a tire business he had established.

On June 8, 1974, Teresa gave birth to Harry Glenn Newman, Jr. He would become known as Glennie to the family.

The joy of having her sixth child, a

healthy baby boy, should have lasted, but Teresa's heart ached. She missed her kids terribly. "He [Grady] wouldn't allow me to have contact with the kids," she remembers.

In May 1975, Grady had a friend drive him to the mobile home in Smock, Pennsylvania, where Teresa and Glenn now resided. Teresa happened to be watching from the window inside.

She saw a car pull to the curb. Grady jumped out. Walking on his hands, he ran toward the door.

"You fuckin' whore," he shouted. "You bitch, you good for nothin' cunt! Open the fucking door!"

Grady pulled the screen door wide open, breaking his watch in the process. He continued to shout obscenities and pound on the door. Finally, seeing it was doing him no good, he left.

Teresa went down to the Highway Patrol and put a warrant out on him, but the authorities never caught him and the warrant was never served.

By 1976, Grady still had custody, and Christmas was approaching.

Against Glenn's best advice, Teresa called Grady anyway.

"Grady, I was wondering if I could see the children so I can take them home with me to Vermont to see my mother for Christmas."

"That would be okay," said Grady.

"Okay, so I'll come by your place—"

"No, why don't we meet at Harry's Bar? You remember where that is, right?"

"Yeah, but—"

"Okay, so we'll meet at Harry's, have a couple of drinks, and then go back to my house to pick up the kids."

"I don't trust him," Glenn warned, after Teresa hung up. "You never know what Grady might do."

"Look, Glenn, I miss those kids. I really want to be with them."

Midget Man knew better than to argue with his wife when she had her mind set on something, especially seeing the kids. He knew how much they meant to her. Still, he felt uneasy about the trip. But they went anyway, along with baby Glennie.

They met at Harry's, where Grady tossed back double shots of Seagram's and 7-UP on the rocks.

"The girls are at my apartment," Grady said, slugging the drinks down. "You gotta go in to take them."

Glenn didn't want to. He smelled something wrong, and told her that. But Teresa was heartsick. She needed her babies.

After he finished his fifth double shot,

Grady took them all to his apartment. The kids were nowhere to be found.

"Go fix yourself a cup of coffee," Grady said casually.

Teresa didn't know what was happening. She decided to play along. When she came out of the kitchen, Grady leaned back on the couch. Deftly, he reached underneath the cushions and pulled out a revolver. He pointed it at his guests, who stood paralyzed in fear.

"Ever see a gun like this?" he asked menacingly.

"Yes, I've seen a few," Teresa replied.

Grady put his free claw in his mouth and whistled.

The back door opened. They heard a lumbering sound getting closer and closer. He plodded into the living room, all six hundred pounds of him.

His name was Paul Fishbaugh, a carnival "Fat Man" whom Grady employed. To Teresa and Glenn, he was distinguished not so much by his impressive bulk but by the even more impressive shotgun cradled in his fleshy arms.

Fishbaugh sat down on a chair by the kitchen door. It was surprising the chair would support his weight.

"Cover them, Paul," Grady said.

Fishbaugh pointed the shotgun at Teresa, Midget Man, and their baby boy. It is doubtful that Midget Man could have taken The

Fat Man under any circumstances. Still, Lobster Boy was taking no chances.

"Come over here to the couch, Teresa," said Grady.

Teresa did as she was told.

He hit her with the claw that was hard as a board.

The baby screamed.

"For God's sake, Grady, let them leave! I'll stay," Teresa shouted.

Grady ignored her pleas and continued to beat her. Teresa's mind drifted. It seemed like forever.

When he finally finished, Grady told Teresa, "Don't bother me anymore or next time, I'm going to kill you, Glenn, *and* your son."

Then he let them go.

Seven

On April 29, 1978, Donna turned fifteen. Escape from Grady was paramount in her mind. But what kind of escape could a fifteen-year-old hope for?

Her hope for freedom resided with Jack E. Layne, Jr. A strapping eighteen-year-old, six feet three inches, and a solid 210 pounds, he had black hair and a handsome face.

They were introduced by Donna's cousin, who had previously gone out with him. Jack and Donna, who was then attending Allegheny Junior High School, hit it off almost immediately.

In early September of that same year, Donna ran away from home. She met Jack in a public park, which was about four blocks from the apartment she shared with her family. Jack took her to his sister Jenny Layne's house, in the Brighten Heights section of Pittsburgh. A few days later, Donna called Grady.

"Where the fuck are you?"

"Dad, listen—"

"No, you listen," he screamed into the receiver. "You get right back here now, or else!"

Donna said no.

"All right, all right," Grady acquiesced. "I'll let you go with your mom. You come home, I'll call your mom, and you can go with your mom."

"You're lying." Donna spit the words out. "You won't even let us talk to her and you expect me to believe you'd let me go and live with her?"

"Listen, you fucking—"

And Donna hung up the phone. Three or four days later, she called again.

"I got detectives looking for you," Grady said menacingly. "They'll find you and when I find that boy that's with you, I'm going to kill him and—"

Donna hung up.

Pit Loan was a pawnshop on the North Side. Philip Archer was behind the counter on September 11 when he saw a strange sight: a legless man in a wheelchair with lobster claws for hands. He wheeled himself up to the counter.

"I want to buy a gun," he said.

Archer filled out the state-mandated "Application for Purchase of Firearms," and noted the following information:

APPLICATION FOR PURCHASE
OF A FIREARM

Name: Grady F. Stiles, Jr.
Date of application: 9-11-78
Date and place of Naturalization: 7-18-37
Male, 41 years of age, white, 4 feet 3 inches, 185 pounds, black hair, blue eyes.
Make: H&R
Model: 732 .32 caliber
Length of Barrel: 2.5 inches

In a scratchy script, Grady signed the document. As the seller, Archer countersigned.

Another few days passed. Donna made another phone call.

"The cops are looking for you this time," Grady said evenly. "With my detectives. I'm gonna send you to juvenile," he added.

This time, Donna was scared. Something about this threat made her sit up and take notice.

She hung up. She needed to do something before the door burst in and they came to get her and sent her back.

She picked up the phone and dialed.

"Dad."

"Yeah, Donna."

"Dad, listen. Jack and I want to get married. I— I'm pregnant."

Nothing could have been further from the truth. Donna was playing on Grady's paranoia. In fact, not only wasn't she pregnant, she was still a virgin. The most they'd ever done was neck a little bit.

Grady got very quiet on the phone. He didn't say anything for a while. Finally, he said, "Since you've already been with him, I'll sign the papers."

Being that she was underage, she needed her father, as her legal guardian, to sign the papers allowing her to get married.

Before returning home, she went with Jack to inform his father Jack, Sr., what they were going to do.

It was not surprising that he was at home; Jack, Sr., lived on disability. His mother, Geraldine, had died years before.

After that chore was finished, it was back to the house to face Grady.

"I went home," Donna recalls. "Dad and I, we talked for two days about what was happening, really."

September 28 was set as the wedding date. During the week, Grady made one last effort to dissuade her. When Donna remained true to her dream of escape, Grady relented and told her that he would keep his promise and let them get married.

As promised, Grady signed a form agreeing to the marriage.

Letter in hand, Donna and Jack went to the county clerk's office where, on September 20, they applied for a marriage license.

September 27, 1978, dawned with a chill in the air, but by midmorning, the temperature was climbing into the sixties and the sun came out.

Donna walked through the sunshine, and got to Jack's house at approximately eleven A.M. Together, they went to Dr. Rob Slotkin's office, where blood was drawn from both of them, as required by the state for couples marrying. Then they walked over to the barber's school on East Ohio Street, where Jack got a haircut. Jack then walked Donna to her father's house where she was to clean the house, getting ready for the planned wedding reception. When they got there, Grady was already gone.

A few blocks away at Harry's Bar, Grady was perched on a barroom stool, doing what Harry loved: being one of his best customers.

By seven o'clock, Grady had consumed twelve whiskey doubles. It was a wonder he could still crawl without tipping over, let alone talk. Because of his years of alcohol abuse, his alcohol tolerance was so high that to the average bystander, he appeared barely inebriated.

Grady left the bar in his wheelchair and headed home. He got there just as Jack, Donna, Barbara, and Grady III were leaving to buy food for the wedding reception.

They were planning on buying a lot of potato chips to feed the guests. While the others left, Donna stayed behind at Grady's behest.

"Look, I really don't think you should marry him."

"Daddy, we've been over this—"

"You know, I love you so much I paid an investigator one hundred dollars up front to find you?"

"Daddy—"

"And then I owed him another two hundred dollars, so I went over to Dover [Ohio] and worked in the sideshow to pay the guy off."

"Look, Daddy, I'm going to marry Jack!"

"He's not good enough for you!"

Grady reached for his jug of whiskey. Grady usually had a gallon jug of whiskey around. He would drink almost a whole one of those by the time he went to bed.

By 7:30, the group was back with the chips. Donna has a vivid recollection of what happened next.

"We went out, Jack, Barbara, me, and Little Grady, and I think Susie was with us.

Cathy was behind the house in the alley, playing with one of her friends.

"We went to the mall. My father gave me some money. I was supposed to pick out a dress to get married in. We selected a dress at Zaire's Department Store and put it on layaway to be picked up tomorrow morning. We had an appointment with the judge to be married on the morning of the twenty-eighth.

"A few hours later, we came back. Susie ran out back to play."

The first thing they noticed when they got back was that Grady's wheelchair was missing. Usually, Grady's wheelchair was kept right outside the house for easy access. Donna, Barbara, Jack, and Little Grady went inside.

"What happened to the wheelchair?" Barbara asked.

"It was sitting here," Grady replied. He sat calmly in his briefs. "Pittsburgh, in the streets, people steal things."

"Okay, we'll go out and look for it," said Donna, and she, Barbara, and Jack trooped to the door.

"No, you, why don't you stay, Jack? Close the door and sit down."

Jack stayed.

"So, Barbara and I went around into the metered parking lot out back, looking for the wheelchair," Donna continued. "Still not finding it, we searched in the bushes.

"We were just about halfway around, and I heard a bang. And I looked at Barbara and said, 'What do you think that was?' "

"Don't worry about it, it's not your father," Barbara replied.

"Then I heard a bang again immediately after and I said, 'Yes, it is something,' and I ran back toward the house. When I got there, Jack comes stumbling out of the house. He was holding his chest in the middle."

"He shot me." Jack coughed out the words, and fell straight down to the ground in front of Donna.

"It didn't seem real. It seemed like a joke. And I shook Jack. He didn't move. And he was coughing. There was blood coming out of his mouth. And I looked up, and Dad was standing on his knees looking out the window, smiling at me. It really surprised me that he was doing that. I said, 'Why did you do this?' "

"Because I told you I would," Grady smirked.

"You'll die for this, you son of a bitch!"

"Don't give me that shit!" Grady shouted back.

"I'll see you in your grave!"

From off in the distance, Donna could hear sirens. And then she heard the crying and screaming from inside the house. Little Grady.

Panicking, her heart beating wildly in her chest, she ran to her grandmother's house twelve blocks away.

It was a cool night for late September. Officers Jake Carlson and Jay Fazio were cruising in Unit 95 when they received the call from headquarters.

"Shooting at 511 Foreland Street. See the woman."

"Roger."

When Car 95 arrived on the scene, Carlson and Fazio found Jack Layne lying on his stomach. Bending over him was Barbara Stiles.

"What's the victim's name?" Carlson questioned.

"Jack Layne," Barbara replied.

"Was Mr. Layne shot?"

"Yes," and she pointed up at the house.

They went inside and found Grady seated in a stuffed chair at the far end of the living room. Near him on the nightstand was a .32 caliber H&R, six-shot revolver. It was the same one he'd purchased at the pawnshop exactly sixteen days before.

"Take me. I'm ready. Take me," Grady said calmly.

After getting Grady's name, Carlson informed him of his rights, then confiscated and emptied the gun of the remaining shells. With Grady in tow, they walked outside.

On the porch, Carlson and Fazio happened to look down. Carlson picked up a spent bullet and put it with the gun.

Once Grady was inside their squad car, they called homicide.

At 8:45 P.M., detectives Joe Stottlemyre and Ray Condemi of the Homicide Squad received a call from central dispatch. "Proceed to 511 Foreland Street. There's been a shooting and the victim is in critical condition. He's presently being attended to at the scene by Medic Four."

They raced downstairs into their unmarked car. On went the siren, around went the bubble top as they sped to the scene.

Donna didn't know what to do. She was so confused. She doubled back, in time to see the cops and ambulance attendants crowded around Jack on the sidewalk. They were talking to him.

"I waited until I seen them cut Jack's shirt off to see if the bullet went through. I seen them turn Jack over, and then I ran. I was really scared, so I ran out again."

* * *

By the time detectives Stottlemyre and Condemi got to the scene at 8:52 P.M., the medics already had Jack on a stretcher.

"This guy's in very, very serious condition," said Sam Switzer, the attending medic.

"How bad?" asked Stottlemyre, pulling out his notebook and taking notes.

"Gunshot wound to the left chest just above the nipple, exiting the right upper shoulder."

Still breathing, Jack was rushed to Allegheny General Hospital for emergency treatment. It wasn't a homicide yet, they realized, and with luck, it wouldn't be. Unlike most major eastern cities, Pittsburgh had very few homicides per capita. It was a safe, clean place to live.

The detectives met with Carlson and Fazio, who told them what they had already learned. They handed over the revolver and spent bullet. "There were two empty casings in the revolver," Carlson said, implying that the gun had been fired twice.

After interviewing the officers further, the detectives examined the scene of the crime.

They noted that the sidewalk was divided into four sections, that Jack's head was in the northeast section of the sidewalk and his feet in the southwest section. He had been lying on his stomach. There was debris from the medics left in the area where Jack collapsed, and a little spot of blood in the southeast section of the sidewalk near the steps leading up into the tenement.

511 Foreland was a two-story building of brick composition. To get inside, you climbed three steps to the front entrance. The front entrance then opened into the living room which measured fourteen by twelve feet. On the south wall, west of the opening of the dining room, was a gold, stuffed chair.

"Grady was sitting in that chair when he shot Jack," Barbara told the detectives.

"Was the front door open or closed?" Condemi questioned.

Barbara couldn't recall.

The detectives looked around and their keen eyes spotted a bullet hole in the wood of the front door. It appeared that the bullet had gone through the door on an upward angle and struck the roof of the porch. It then fell to the porch floor where Carlson had recovered it. Based on the condition of the bullet which Carlson had handed them, they figured it wasn't the one that had traveled through the victim.

Putting a pencil through the bullet hole in the door and aligning the trajectory with the mark in the porch roof indicated to the investigators that the front door was open approximately ten inches when this shot entered the door. The detectives then surmised that Jack Layne was shot trying to leave the residence.

In other words, as soon as Jack Layne opened the door, Grady started blasting away. That made it a cold and premeditated murder.

Still, there were unanswered questions. Carlson had said there were two empty shells left in the revolver. However, only one bullet was recovered. The detectives, while not certain if the bullet recovered was the one that traveled through Jack's body, were nevertheless inclined to believe that it wasn't. That left them one bullet shy.

They conducted a preliminary search in front of the tenement but it was too dark to do a thorough job. That would have to wait for morning.

Meanwhile, the lab-tech boys arrived. The gun was taken by the crime-unit officers to be fingerprinted and then sent to the lab for further analysis.

In addition to the gun and the spent bullet, a small piece of wood had been knocked from the door as the bullet passed through it. This piece of wood was recovered on the porch floor and was also submitted to the crime lab to determine if any lead wiping was present. Lead wiping would be any residue of lead left by the bullet.

"Mrs. Stiles, I know this is a difficult time,

but I'd like to ask you some more questions," said Detective Condemi.

Barbara nodded. After a few preliminary questions, she related her version of the events.

"Jack was to marry my stepdaughter Donna tomorrow. Donna's fifteen and she's known Jack for about a month. And she ran away with him and stayed with him for about five days.

"When she returned home, we told her that we would let her get married. In fact, they got their blood-test papers today. Anyway, today, myself, Donna, my two-year-old baby, and Jack went to the mall so Donna could get a dress and shoes for the wedding."

"How'd you get there?" asked Stottlemyre.

"We used my car. It's a 1973 Chevy, green wagon. Parked out front."

"Go on."

"We got home from the shopping spree at about 8:30 P.M. When we got into the house, I didn't see Grady's wheelchair and I asked him where it was."

"Where was your husband seated?" asked Condemi.

"In the stuffed chair in the corner opposite the front door. Anyway, he says he didn't know where his chair was. While Jack goes out the front door, Donna follows him. Then I was the last one to go out. I was going to look for his wheelchair because I thought my two younger daughters had it and they had been playing with it. Donna was with me when we got outside. As we were leaving, Grady called to Jack and said he wanted to talk with him. And Jack went inside the house.

"I then heard two shots and I turned around and seen Jack on the sidewalk and Donna ran to him and grabbed him and he fell to the pavement. Donna got hysterical and was running around and she came back and called her dad a son of a bitch.

"I went to Jack and he was groaning. When I went into the house, I asked Grady 'Why?' He said, 'Better him than her and that's the only thing I could do. I couldn't let her do it,' and then he told me to call the police. And I called the police and told them that a man was shot on the sidewalk at 511 Foreland Street."

The detectives got Barbara to sign a document giving them the right to search the premises. It wasn't necessary, though. Barbara readily turned over the box that the revolver had come in, as well as a box of .32-caliber shells. The crime lab was subsequently given this evidence to analyze.

After leaving the scene, Condemi and Stottlemyre drove to Allegheny General. They got there too late; Jack was dead on arrival. It was now, officially, a homicide.

At eleven P.M. Stottlemyre and Condemi interviewed Donna in the hospital's emergency room. While the pandemonium of a big-city hospital room reigned around them, it took Donna no longer than fifteen minutes to give her statement. By then, the detectives were anxious to question Grady. They were close to clearing the case. With a little luck, they could actually do it before midnight.

The public safety building in downtown Pittsburgh was the home of the Pittsburgh Department of Public Safety. At 11:23 P.M., Condemi and Stottlemyre removed Grady from the bull pen holding cells on the second floor and took him to the homicide office, and sat him down on a chair in the interrogation room. Condemi read from a prepared form.

"At this time, it is my duty to inform you of the rights that you possess while in custody. Under law, you cannot be compelled to answer and you have the right to refuse to answer any questions. While you are in custody, if you do answer such questions, the answers given by you will be used against you in a trial in a court of law at some later date. Do you understand?"

"I understand," Grady replied soberly.

"The answers are to be recorded in the suspect's own words. You are also entitled to talk to a lawyer and have him present before you decide whether or not to answer questions or while you are answering questions. If you do not have the money to hire a lawyer, you are entitled to have a lawyer present before you decide whether or not you will answer questions and while you are answering questions. Do you understand?"

"I understand."

"You can decide at any time before or during to exercise these rights by not answering any further questions or making any further statements. Do you understand?"

"I understand."

"Knowing these rights, are you willing to answer questions without the presence of a lawyer?"

"Some of them," Grady replied.

The detectives signed the form as witnesses and Grady gave his statement.

"I suffer from emphysema, cirrhosis, and various other ailments," he complained. "Two of my five children have the 'lobster [claw] syndrome' and my income at the present time is derived from social security."

"I use the wheelchair when I'm out of the house, otherwise I have to crawl around. I have the equivalent of an eighth grade education. I'm so concerned about my kids. What's going to happen to them?"

The detectives noted in their subsequent report Grady's ". . . sincere concern for the welfare of his children. He appears to be sober at this time."

"Mr. Stiles, why don't you tell us how all this happened?"

"Well, about three weeks ago, Donna, she's fifteen, she ran away from home with Jack Layne. I went to the city police and the state police to do something about Layne running away with my underage daughter, but I received no help. No help."

"What did you do next?"

"Well, I-I contacted a private investigator to help me find her."

"You know the PI's name?"

"No, I don't recall. I do remember that his fee was like eighty to a hundred dollars a day plus expenses. I gave him one hundred dollars to start with. Then a little while later, I got a call from Donna. Donna told me that she did not want to come home."

"Did she say why?"

"Yes, she said she was in love with Jack and wanted to marry him."

"How did that make you feel?"

"Oh, I was so upset. This is hard to talk about."

"Take your time, Mr. Stiles."

"Well, Donna, she, uh, she was a virgin

and a good girl until Jack Layne came along."

"What did you do?"

"What could I do? I finally gave in and told her I'd sign the necessary papers for her to marry him. She came home the next day. By that time, she'd been gone six days, and I owed the investigator two hundred dollars."

Neither detective bothered to tell him that his math didn't add up. They just let him keep talking.

"So, last week," Grady continued evenly, "I went to Dover, Ohio, and worked in the sideshow for the Dine Amusement Company. I worked from Wednesday to Friday, earning a little over three hundred dollars. And then I paid off the investigator.

"When I got back, I heard some street talk that Jack Layne was bragging about Donna living with him. This really upset me but I didn't say anything to Layne or Donna, but I did try to talk Donna out of the marriage. With no success, I might add."

And then he related what happened that day.

"I woke up about ten-thirty and went down the street to Harry's Bar. I was there until seven P.M., when I came back home to watch the news."

"How much booze did you drink?"

"About twelve doubleheaders of whiskey."

"That's a lot."

"I'm good at holding my booze."

"Go on."

"Well, Donna and Barbara, she's my wife, and my son, Grady, and Layne, they went to Allegheny Center to buy a wedding dress. They came back about nine and that's when I called Layne into the living room."

"The others went outside?"

"Right. To look for my wheelchair."

"What'd you say to Jack?"

"He was sitting on the sofa. I told him, 'You have her. Don't laugh and make a mockery of this.' "

"What did Jack do?"

"He smirked, and said, 'I told you I'd get her.' "

"And that's when you shot him?"

"I pulled my gun from the side of the cushion of the chair I was sitting in and shot two times at Layne. Layne got up from the sofa and walked outside. I had taken all I could at the time. The guy gave me no choice."

"How about the gun?"

"What about it?"

"When and where did you buy it?"

"I bought it about three weeks ago from a loan company down on East Ohio Street."

"Know how to use a gun?" Condemi asked, looking dubiously at Grady's claws.

"I've owned several in my time."

"Well, why'd you buy this one?"

"In the evening, when I'm alone downstairs, I watch TV. I like to keep the gun with me to ward off any intruders, who may be thinking about breaking into my home."

"Have you ever been robbed or broken into?" Stottlemyre asked.

"No."

"Where do you keep the gun?"

"In a drawer in my upstairs bedroom."

"So, since you haven't been robbed or broken into, you really wouldn't have any reason to bring the weapon downstairs?"

"Right."

"Then why'd you bring the gun downstairs today?"

Grady thought for a second.

"Now that's a good question," Grady smiled. He wouldn't answer any more questions. The interview ended.

At approximately 11:55 P.M., the detectives notified the coroner's office that they had the accused in custody and they wanted him arraigned as soon as possible. Could a deputy coroner come to their office for the arraignment because the accused was in a wheelchair?

At approximately 1:10 A.M. on September 28, 1978, Deputy Coroner Phillips came to the homicide office and began the arraignment at 1:18 A.M. Grady Stiles, Jr., was officially charged with the murder of Jack Layne. Phillips then set a hearing for October 6 at eleven A.M., and Grady was taken back to a cell to wait for justice to unfold.

Later that day, September 28, cops again searched the murder scene for the missing bullet. Finding none, they called the coroner's office to verify that the victim was shot twice. They also discovered that one of the bullets was still in the victim. Since the gun had been fired twice, and the investigating officers had found one spent bullet on the porch the previous night, and the second pellet was still in the victim, the numbers added up and the search was terminated.

At 10:30 that morning, the coroner came in with his preliminary findings.

The first wound was the one everyone had seen, in the chest. The bullet had lodged in the body. The second was located near the back of the neck in the area of the scapula. Jack was shot in the back of the neck as he was fleeing. The bullet had passed through his body, hit the wood above the door, and then fell to the porch beneath.

Later in the day, detectives interviewed Jack Layne's other sister, Eveline Rivera.

"Grady Stiles was opposed to Jack marrying Donna," she told the detectives. "He had threatened Jack before with a gun on a number of occasions."

"How do you know?"

"Jack told me."

"So, you never actually saw Grady threatening him?"

"No. And Jack never really thought that Grady would follow through on the threats. You know, Jack only knew her for three months. Grady was against the marriage but he finally gave the okay. The wedding had been postponed, though, a couple of times because Grady told them that he was sick."

In the days after the murder, Barbara Stiles received a series of threatening phone calls that she reported to the police on September 30.

She claimed that it was Jack's family, that they were threatening to kill her and the girls. And every time she looked out the window, there was this same blue Ford sedan cruising past. She was very worried.

She called again on October 3. This time, somebody broke the left rear window of their car.

The next day, Barbara was relaxing in the house when two bricks came crashing through the front window. The phone rang.

"You're all dead," said the caller, and hung up.

Barbara told the police it was all happening as retaliation for the murder.

* * *

On October 6, a hearing was held before Coroner's Solicitor Stanley Stein. A special van with a hydraulic lift transported Grady to the hearing. It made for a heartrending photograph in the *Pittsburgh Post Gazette* to see the crippled man when he was lowered to the ground.

Donna testified that Grady had not been happy about her impending nuptials to Jack.

"He [Grady] said Jack could come for supper but for him not to smile or snicker at me," Donna testified.

Donna then said that she was with Grady when he purchased the murder weapon. "He told me the gun was for Jack and me," Donna said.

Dressed in a shabby pair of blue trousers, white shirt, and white sweater, Grady could only shake his head in astonishment at Donna's testimony. He still had no conception of the tragedy he'd caused.

She then recounted her shopping trips on the day of the shooting, and what happened when they returned to Foreland Street.

Stottlemyre then took the stand and told Stein how he had taken Grady's statement after he was taken into custody, and the content of it.

It didn't take long for Stein to remand

Grady to the County Jail without bail pending trial.

All alone in his jail cell, Grady had time to think. Despite what the police had told him, he was smart enough to know he was in hot water. They had charged him with first degree murder.

In the State of Pennsylvania, first degree murder is punishable by death in the electric chair. Grady knew that unless he found a good attorney, he would be convicted.

Eight

The taxicab left Grady and Barbara off on Grant Street, in downtown Pittsburgh. They paid for the cab with the little funds they had left. The state had moderated their initial demands and had let Grady out on $10,000 bond.

Barbara helped Grady into his chair, then wheeled him up the sidewalk and into the Grant Building.

When they got off the elevator, they found themselves in a reception area, off which were the offices of five different criminal defense lawyers.

"Can I help you?" the receptionist asked.

"We're here to see Anthony DeCello. We have an appointment," Barbara answered.

They were ushered into DeCello's office. It was very plush and expensive-looking. There was a big, dark mahogany desk, arranged neatly with a phone/intercom, a dictating machine, yellow foolscap pad, pen and pencil set in holders, pictures of DeCello's family, and a statue of St. Anthony. The saint

of lost things, St. Anthony was DeCello's pa-
tron saint.

In front of the desk were chairs made out
of a lighter colored wood than the desk, up-
holstered in a soft, cushiony fabric. To complete the look of elegance, all the walls were
paneled in dark wood.

"The first time Grady came into my office
with Barbara, he was in a wheelchair," De-
Cello recalled. "She did everything for him
as far as pushing it. He wanted me to know
immediately about his physical condition,
which was quite obvious."

During introductions, Grady shook De-
Cello's hand. The attorney would later find
out that this was Grady's favorite thing to do
when meeting someone for the first time. He
always wanted a formal introduction. That's
when he could establish his strength by literally crushing the other person's out-
stretched hand in his iron grip.

Throughout the morning, Grady had been
drinking. DeCello smelled the booze on his
breath. When he tried to tell DeCello what
had happened and why he was there to seek
his help, the words came out in a drunken
slur.

DeCello knew how difficult it was defend-
ing any defendant accused of murder, but
one who was a drunk, whose behavior was
unpredictable, was just too problematic. He
told Grady to go home and the next time

he showed up for an appointment, he better be sober. Otherwise, he would have nothing else to do with his case.

Few people talked to Grady like that and got away with it, but Grady was fresh out of options and staring the electric chair in the face. When he and Barbara showed up for his next appointment a few days later, he was sober.

Barbara, still thin to the point of emaciation, was dressed in ill-kept jeans and a raggedy shirt. "She looked like she fought Sonny Liston and lost. She was bad. She always was bruised. Every time I saw her she had bruises. She was ugly and she was very stupid," DeCello recalls. "And she smelled."

As for Grady, despite the fact that he was in a place of business, he, too, was dressed shabbily. His pants, cut off at the knee, and button-down shirt were wrinkled and faded.

But if Grady was not flashy in appearance, he was still a showman.

He had Barbara position his wheelchair next to one of the overstuffed armchairs in front of DeCello's desk. As DeCello watched openmouthed, Grady used his claws to flip himself from one chair to the other in a single, neat motion. It showed the dexterity he had with his claws, all right, but DeCello wondered why he was trying to impress him so. Coupled with his antagonistic way of shaking hands, DeCello figured he was trying to show off his immense physical strength.

At the time, Tony DeCello was one of Pittsburgh's more prominent defense attorneys. Of medium height and dark good looks, the forty-one-year-old DeCello moved with the grace and fluidity of an athlete.

His hometown was Farrell, a little place eighty miles north of Pittsburgh. If it is known for anything at all, it is the quality of its high-school basketball team.

In 1952, Farrell's basketball team won the state championship. Years later, playwright and actor Jason Miller became fascinated by the little town that could. He interviewed many of the team members, including one of the starting guards, Tony DeCello. Eventually, he wrote a Pulitzer Prize-winning play about the 1952 team. He entitled it, *That Championship Season*.

Opening night on Broadway, Miller flew in the captains of the championship team, including Anthony DeCello. With the actual pictures of the team on stage as backdrop, they watched the action unfold. Afterward, they were ushered to the Tavern on the Green restaurant in Central Park, where they were treated to an elaborate meal.

Now in his office, DeCello asked Grady to tell him the truth in his own words of exactly what had taken place because he didn't want to be surprised in court.

Instead, Grady began to discuss the fact of his physical disability. His tone was sarcastic, and DeCello soon realized that the disability was his armor plate against everything, that because he was physically disabled, everyone should take pity on him.

Finally, after Grady finished trying to garner the lawyer's sympathy, DeCello was able to turn the conversation around to the crime Stiles had been charged with.

"Jack had taunted me and made fun of me and ridiculed me," Grady said in his whiskey-soaked voice. "He told me that he'd had sex with Donna and there was nothin' I could do about it. And then he made fun of me. He said, 'I'm gonna dump you out of the wheelchair anytime I feel like it.' "

To DeCello, though, Grady's fears did not seem real. He could tell from talking to Grady and from the man's physicality that he was not the defenseless cripple he tried to make himself out to be. He was a very strong man who was able to do almost everything a normal man could, including firing a gun.

Despite the fact that Grady was hardly defenseless, he insisted that Jack Layne continued to taunt him with all kinds of names until finally, he just couldn't take the verbal abuse anymore. He thought that in the best interests of Donna, and for his own sake, he had to do something about Jack.

"Donna, she deserved better than this bum," Grady said.

After that second meeting, Anthony De-Cello remembers feeling sorry for Grady Stiles. "Hell, any normal person would have feelings of remorse that someone would have to live a life with those claws. He was poor, he was downtrodden and his own family, he claimed, made fun of him," said DeCello.

Regardless of what Stiles had done, he deserved help. And DeCello was going to give it to him. He would plead "not guilty" by reason of self-defense. Whether he believed Grady or not was not relevant. The man was entitled to the best defense possible. He would do what the law allowed— present his defense as the facts allowed.

In court, DeCello would try to minimize the seemingly cold-blooded nature of the crime with the mitigating factors of Jack's alleged threats, Grady's fear, and, of course, his client's pitiable physical condition.

While Anthony DeCello was trying to figure out a way to rescue Grady from the electric chair, Robert Vincler was doing the exact opposite. As sure as the sun would come up in the morning, Vincler was certain that Grady Stiles had committed first degree murder. As assistant district attorney, and supervisor of general trials for the district attorney's office of Allegheny County, Vincler's job was to make sure that Grady Stiles, Jr., was convicted.

Yet despite the facts of the case, Vincler was struck by the tragedy of the whole thing. Here was the sad case of a young girl who had gone out to buy a wedding dress and returned to her home, only to have her future husband shot by her father and die in her arms. It was also astonishing to Vincler that Grady had so much dexterity with his claw, he was able to pull the trigger on the gun.

Donna was going to be the prosecution's star witness; she was going to testify against Grady. Over the course of the next five months, Vincler spoke frequently with Donna over the phone. She was still pretty broken up about the crime.

After Jack had been killed, his sister and his family blamed Donna for his death. For a time, she hid out at her girlfriend's house. Cathy had been living with Barbara at the Salvation Army. Then, one day, Donna's grandmother, Edna Stiles, called her up on the phone.

"Donna, your mom's been in touch with me. Your mom's sending an airplane ticket to get you and Cathy," Edna continued.

"My . . . mom was only going to take me, because she didn't know if she was allowed to have Cathy. And Grandma says [to Teresa], 'You better take Cathy with you. You take both of these girls and get them out of here.' "

Teresa sent her the plane tickets. Donna and Cathy left Barbara with her children, Little Grady and Tammy.

"We left Pittsburgh and met her and Glenn [Sr.] in Dallas. They were helping a friend with a show. They were sort of taking a vacation and working at the same time."

Glenn was working the bally stage for Ward Hall, a famous carnival entrepreneur. Eventually, they moved back to Ohio.

Donna stayed with her mother and Glenn in the Buckeye State, where Glenn supported the family from a tire business he had established. Because Teresa rarely spoke to Vincler, the task of explaining the family circumstances fell to Glenn, Sr. Vincler found himself liking the man, even though they had never met.

From Glenn and others who were involved in the case, Vincler came away with the impression that Donna was the apple of her father's eye. While Cathy and Little Grady were deformed, Donna was the attractive, normal one. Grady thought she could really make it and was very upset that she had been lured away and was going to marry a guy he thought was a bum.

* * *

For his part, Grady had no knowledge that his family was conspiring with the prosecution to put him in jail. He was certain that once enough time had passed, Donna would forgive him. Eventually she would see that he'd done the right thing, the only thing. She would come back to him.

In his conversations with DeCello, Grady made it clear that he was both proud and envious of Donna.

Over and over, DeCello took Grady through the day of the murder to get his story straight so there'd be no inconsistencies when he testified. DeCello found it strange that when they talked about the murder, Grady showed no feelings.

In his practice, DeCello had found that anybody you talk to involved in a murder has feelings about it, either remorse or hate. But Grady just went over the details like he was describing some routine task. Flat. Never once did he express any emotion over killing Jack.

But when it came to discussing his sex life, his voice took on new vigor.

"Everyone I have sex with wants to have sex with my claws. They love it when I use my claws."

He was proud of that fact. Barbara, who

was sitting across the room, nodded in agreement.

And as if to prove the point, Grady told DeCello this story.

"One of my daughter's [Donna's] teachers came to the house to discuss her attendance at school."

In fact, Donna had failed to attend school on a regular basis during the fall of 1978 when she met and fell for Jack Layne.

"This teacher, she really liked my claws. So we had sex right in the house and she just kept coming back and back and back because of this."

The lawyer came to realize that it was a source of personal pride for Grady that he was able to have a sexual relationship with someone that was normal. "When he talked about having sex with the teacher, it was like he'd just won the Battle of Bataan. It was like a victory. He wanted you to know he had these accomplishments, no matter how totally insignificant they were," DeCello said.

As for what he did to make a living, carnival to him did not mean sideshow freak. It meant Carnegie Hall. Grady Stiles, Jr., was a famous, dominating figure in the carnival world.

Robert Vincler woke up to a cold day, where snow matted the ground. Traveling to work, breath plumed from his mouth in a cold fog.

By 8:30 A.M., on February 20, 1979, he was in the forty-by-fifty-foot space he shared with two other assistant district attorneys. Each had their own office. Because Vincler's was located not twenty feet behind the reception area, he always had a clear view of who was visiting. He looked up from his work when he heard people in the corridor.

"I knew right away who the people were coming through the door. This girl was rather attractive, young, sixteen years old; followed by her mother, who was also rather attractive, thin, well dressed, and manicured; followed by Mr. Newman who was a midget. It sort of floored me that here was this midget," Vincler recalls.

No one had ever given any indication over the phone that Glenn might not be of normal height.

After recovering his composure, Vincler noted that Donna wore a nice conservative outfit. She'd make a good witness. As for Glenn, he was dressed in a pullover jersey and a pair of slacks. His hair was cut rather long.

"Time to go downstairs," Vincler said.

As the women walked quickly down the corridor to the elevator, Glenn settled down in the young district attorney's office.

The trial was about to begin.

Nine

The courtroom of Common Pleas judge Thomas A. Harper was set up in an old-fashioned way, with the defense and prosecution seated at parallel tables on opposite sides of the courtroom.

The trial started with Vincler's opening statement to the jury. Vincler made it crystal clear that he would seek a first degree murder conviction against Grady Stiles, Jr., on the grounds that the shooting was a premeditated act. To bolster his case, Vincler pointed out the following:

"There are a number of key points on which Anthony DeCello, Mr. Stiles's attorney, and I agree on, including the fact that Mr. Stiles did, in reality, shoot Jack Layne once in the chest and once in the back with a thirty-two-caliber revolver he purchased from an East Ohio Street pawnshop sixteen days before Mr. Layne was murdered."

For his part, Tony DeCello emphatically stated that Grady Stiles had no choice but to kill Jack Layne. Layne had taunted and threatened him to the point where he felt he was in grave danger. Layne had lured his daughter away. To save her, and him, Grady had no choice but to take matters into his own hands.

Vincler then called his star witness: Donna Stiles.

Once again, Donna testified that she was with Grady when he bought the gun and that he told her he was going to "use it on Jack."

After explaining how she ran away for nearly six days, she related how she called her father from the home of Jack's sister.

"If you don't get home in five minutes, I'm going to beat the hell out of you. Then I'm going to kill Jack," Donna quoted Grady.

At the defense table, dressed in the same shabby clothes, and despite DeCello's pleas to wear a tie, all Grady could do was mumble and shake his head in disbelief. Throughout the trial, he continued to drink heavily.

On the stand, Donna told about the shopping trip to buy her dress on the day before the wedding, and what her father's condition was.

"And was your father drunk on the day of the murder?" Vincler questioned.

"My father was fairly drunk," Donna testified. "And he tried to talk me out of the marriage by telling me about the unhappy experiences he'd had with his previous wives."

Donna turned and looked at Grady, her face twisted in hatred.

"She's no good, I can't believe she'd turn on me," Grady mumbled.

Donna claimed her father opposed the marriage because she was underage and that she planned to quit school. As for her living conditions, Donna hated living with her father because, among other things, he "made me baby-sit constantly and didn't let me out enough."

"Damn her, damn her," Grady mumbled.

DeCello had been watching Donna very closely. Like Vincler, he, too, had not had a chance to depose her. This was the first opportunity he had to talk to her. It would be difficult to impeach her testimony. It was obvious that the jury believed the story this attractive girl told.

Donna did concede under DeCello's cross-examination that Grady had purchased the weapon before she and Jack had decided to marry. In the jury's mind, DeCello had just planted a seed that maybe the crime wasn't premeditated after all.

Next on the witness stand was Frank De-Salvo, one of Jack's friends.

"I was watching through the front window of the Stileses' home on the day before the shooting. I saw Mr. Stiles pull a gun from the left side of his wheelchair, point it at Jack, and say, 'I will kill you before you marry my daughter.' "

"He admitted shooting Mr. Layne because he said he had 'no alternative,' " homicide detective Joseph Stottlemyre next testified.

Forensic evidence was offered that inextricably linked the murder weapon to Grady's possession. The autopsy results were entered into evidence.

After a brief few hours of damning testimony, Robert Vincler was satisfied that he had proven his case and the defense rested.

Now, it was DeCello's turn to persuade the jury.

DeCello's tactic was to show that there were real reasons why Grady had opposed the marriage.

Barbara Sanaer, Grady's niece, testified that she had been engaged to Jack Layne and had broken up with him before he'd started dating Donna, and that Jack was prone to violence. "He frequently punched me and pushed me against the wall."

Sanaer and her mother, Sarah, Grady's sister, both testified that they had warned Grady that Jack carried a knife.

Perhaps the most interesting defense testimony came from Barbara Stiles.

Barbara said that Grady purchased the

gun at her request after she began receiving
obscene and threatening phone calls. Then,
"Barbara testified as to their home life. She
didn't testify [as to the alleged] threats
[Grady made against Jack] because I think
even though she feared Grady, she didn't
want to get herself in a position where she
would have problems herself.

"I think she was relieved, thinking Grady
would go to jail and get out of her life. She
was in fear of him. You could tell that by
the way he treated her," DeCello recalls.

For her part, Donna hated Barbara. She
was just glad that she was out of her life.

Things were not looking up for Grady, and
he knew it. It was time to bring in the cav-
alry.

Paul Fishbaugh, The Fat Man, entered the
courtroom. Too heavy to fit his six hundred
pounds into the witness chair, he was forced
to sit in a lotus position on the floor of the
courtroom in front of the witness docket.

Fishbaugh, under DeCello's brief questioning, asserted the forthrightness of Grady's
character.

The next character witness for Grady was
The Bearded Lady, whom Teresa would later
identify as Priscilla Bagorno. Bagorno, with
her full, dark beard, related what a wonderful human being and credit to the human

race Grady was. And by the time the third character witness, a carnival midget— not Glenn— had finished his testimony, spectators of the trial were presented with a portrait of Grady Stiles, Jr., as a caring parent and model citizen.

For his part, Vincler was limited by law in the questions he could ask the character witnesses, just as they were limited in what they could testify to. How do you challenge someone's opinion of another human being? The answer is, you don't. You just assume the jury understands that these are Grady's friends, and their testimony, inherently, is going to be tainted. Hopefully, the weight of evidence will prove to them that Grady Stiles, Jr., is not the paragon of virtue his friends made him out to be.

Grady was a showman, first and foremost. He had cut his teeth performing in front of crowds. Now, he would get to perform for a crowd of twelve, with his life hanging in the balance.

"I call Grady Stiles, Jr., to the witness stand," Tony DeCello announced to the court on the morning of February 21, 1978.

The bailiff wheeled Grady up to the witness stand and turned the wheelchair around. He was sworn in and then, under DeCello's patient questioning, began his testimony.

"Tell us first what your daughter's relationship was with Jack Layne," DeCello began.

"Well, Donna started to change shortly after she began dating Layne last July. She would sneak out of the house late at night and come home sometimes with beer on her breath."

"Why did you oppose their marriage?"

"Because Donna was too young. She's only fifteen. And she was going to leave school to marry him."

"Anything else?"

"Donna threatened to live with him without being married."

"A common-law marriage?"

"Right. Rather than see them live together, I'd rather see them get married."

DeCello then asked Grady to describe what had happened the day of the murder.

First Grady contradicted Donna. "I never called Jack into the living room," Grady testified. "He was already in there playing with my daughter [Cathy] when he said, 'Well, I guess I got Donna now.'"

"Then what happened?"

Holding back tears, Grady replied that it would be up to a judge the next day to decide whether or not Donna could marry.

"He [Jack] said it didn't matter what a judge said and that he would live together with her. Then he started coming toward me. I don't know what came over him, but I was scared— I guess of him killing me. He lunged toward me when I fired my gun.

"I didn't even see him when I pulled the trigger," Grady added. "Because of my birth deformity, my shooting is pretty poor."

"Do you recall shooting Mr. Layne a second time as he turned to leave?"

"No. I don't. For four or five days after, I didn't know what was happening."

Grady said he did not recall telling the police that he kept the gun he'd purchased at the East Ohio Street pawnshop by his side for protection when he was alone in the house.

"I bought the gun because my wife Barbara had been receiving threatening phone calls."

Having the gun in the house was just Grady acting in a husband's role, as his wife's protector.

As for Frank DeSalvo's testimony that Grady had pointed the gun with his left hand at Jack the day before the shooting, Grady said DeSalvo was mistaken.

"I cannot support a gun in my left hand," he said, and all attention in the court went to his left claw. It was his weak claw. "It's impossible," he asserted.

As for the testimony of the prosecution witnesses that Grady had previously threatened to kill Layne because he did not want him to marry his daughter, under cross-examination by Vincler, he told the court, "All of them lied on the stand."

Once again, Grady created a public sensation. The *Pittsburgh Post Gazette* reported, "Some of the jurors were visibly affected by Stiles's account of the fatal shooting of his fifteen-year-old daughter's fiancé. . . ."

"He got up there and traded on his condition," DeCello recalls. "He made a helluva witness for himself."

It was a bravura performance, better than anyone realized. "He had no feelings. Had no love for anyone. He had no fears. He was a very sick man," says DeCello.

Vincler had not been able to shake Grady on cross-examination. He attempted to rebut the character witnesses' testimony by recalling Donna to the stand.

"Did you ever see Mr. Stiles beat his wife?" Vincler asked.

"Yes," Donna replied. "I saw him beat my stepmother on several occasions."

During closing arguments, District Attorney Robert Vincler emphasized that the murder of Jack Layne was a cold, premeditated act of a violent man.

"He asks you to believe that all those people," and the dynamic young attorney waved to the prosecution witnesses in the courtroom, "and the police, got together and fabricated their stories.

"Donna Stiles has been out of town since

the incident. How could she have known what anyone else was going to testify to, let alone fabricated her testimony?

"Besides Miss Stiles, several prosecution witnesses indicated that Mr. Stiles frequently promised to kill Mr. Layne rather than allow him to marry his daughter. This was a deliberate act of premeditated murder.

"I would also cite the autopsy report. It clearly contradicts Mr. Stiles's version of the shooting. Mr. Stiles said he was talking to Mr. Layne when the victim came at him and appeared ready to attack him. The defendant also said he could not remember firing a second shot, which struck the victim in the back as he was leaving the living room.

"Well, the autopsy showed that the first bullet, which struck the victim in the chest, traveled in a downward path, after making initial contact with Mr. Layne's body. That shows irrefutably that the victim was seated rather than standing and walking toward him, as Mr. Stiles claimed."

Defense attorney Anthony DeCello countered that "love and compassion" led Grady to defend his daughter and himself, and that the killing of Jack Layne was a pure act of self-defense.

"The greatest hurt and the greatest shame for Mr. Stiles came when his daughter [Donna] told him she'd see him to his grave," DeCello said. "Try and visualize the love and compassion this poor soul has for his children. My client loved his children so much that he obtained a court order in Florida to assume custody of his two children from his previous wife.

"All Grady has is his family," DeCello concluded with obvious emotion. "He has no real friends because people don't want to have someone as him for a friend."

Judge Harper charged the jury and sent them out to deliberate Grady Stiles's fate. While he had been charged with first degree murder, the jury also had the option of convicting him of second degree murder, an intentional killing without premeditation, or third degree murder, commonly known as voluntary manslaughter. With the exception of the last charge, all were punishable by mandatory prison sentences. First degree murder was also punishable by death.

Three hours later, the jury of six women and six men came out of the jury room. Somber-faced, they took their assigned places in the jury box.

"Mr. Foreman, I understand you've reached a verdict."

"Yes, Your Honor, we have. We find the defendant, Grady Stiles, Jr., guilty of third degree murder."

Grady wept crocodile tears. He sat at the defense table in his wheelchair, the same one he had told Barbara and Donna was stolen the day of the murder, the same one he made them search for while he shot Jack Layne.

"I think the jury felt sorry for him. The bottom line is the jury gave him a break. I felt it was first degree murder then and I still feel it's first degree murder now," says Vincler, who's now in private practice.

"One of the things that we tried to bring out on defense was he [Grady] may have had the gun for protection and he saw the kid coming at him and his reflexes were so poor . . . but that's just not true. He was sitting in the house facing the door when they got home. Grady had that gun pointed exactly where he wanted to hit that kid dead-on.

"Another thing. Grady had told me he had no experience with guns, that it was a lucky shot. I didn't believe him. The reason I didn't believe him because there was another time he was telling me when he was in Florida, there was a place down there that show people frequented, and at one time or another, he would fire a gun there with some of his friends. I knew he had some experience with firearms."

"Still," adds DeCello, who no longer practices law, "he convinced the jury that he was defenseless."

Judge Harper postponed sentencing pending a presentencing report by the county's

Adult Probation Office, and Grady was allowed to remain free on the $10,000 bond he had already posted.

The trial had been a draining process for all concerned. Not one person involved in the case, from the police who investigated to the prosecuting attorney, did not feel sorrow at the awful life Grady Stiles had led.

In the presentencing report, the police stated that they had no feelings regarding sentencing. Vincler was even more vague.

"Assistant District Attorney Robert Vincler stated that the present offense was most difficult in terms of sentencing. He stated that the offense was of a very serious nature, however, at the same period of time, he had no statement to make regarding sentencing.

"The present offense is truly a sad case," the report concludes. "It appears that there was some premeditation on the defendant's part and shooting the victim was the only way that the defendant could stop the victim from marrying his daughter. To further complicate the situation, the defendant's physical handicaps would present a problem if the defendant were incarcerated, yet at the same period of time, the present offense is serious enough that a prison sentence might be in order."

Shortly before sentencing, Judge Harper called Vincler.

"Bob, I have gotten a letter from Western Penitentiary [one of the state's penitentiaries] and they've indicated that they did not want him in the system because they'd end up having to put a guard with him all day to take care of him."

"What are we going to do with him, Judge? Realistically, he's wheelchair-bound. And his health's not good."

At Grady's sentencing on April 30, 1979, Grady rose in Judge Harper's courtroom to hear his fate.

Everyone knew Judge Tom Harper, who is now deceased, to be a kind, wise man, and a truly nice guy. He was a man of compassion.

After first noting the difficulties long-term housing of Grady would present to the state prison facilities, Judge Harper got down to the nitty-gritty. He sentenced Grady to fifteen years' probation.

"I'm not so sure that a prison term would not be cruel and unusual punishment in this case. Unquestionably, though, the crime was a serious offense," Harper told the hushed courtroom.

"Society doesn't require vengeance, and I felt a probationary term met the best interests for society and the defendant. In fact, even if the defendant could operate a wheelchair without assistance, prisons in the State of Pennsylvania do not have ramps to facilitate mobility."

Grady would not serve one day behind bars for Jack Layne's cold-blooded murder.

Tony DeCello was happy and thrilled by the verdict and the sentence.

"Judge Harper felt that putting him on probation would accomplish the same effect as putting him in jail," explains DeCello. "By putting him on probation, Grady would dictate his own destiny. If he did something [criminal], he'd go to jail. But he wasn't gonna shoot anyone else. Grady was a [classic bully], to his family especially."

All Grady had to do was report to his probation officer on a regular basis and keep his nose clean, and he would remain free to do as he pleased. He would even be allowed to move to another area of the country as long as he reported to his probation officer in his new habitat.

Immediately after the trial, Grady left Pittsburgh, and never paid DeCello his fourteen-thousand-dollar trial fee. "He never even said thank you. Never," DeCello relates.

The money he saved by not paying DeCello helped him organize his own sideshow. No longer would "Lobster Boy" be working for anyone else. Now, he would be the boss of ten acts, presented as one show, that travel together from carnival to carnival. It was the bizarre world Grady felt most in control of, the one place where he didn't have to put his defenses up, where he could be himself.

"You gotta remember all these people were in the same boat. It's their own little protective world. You or I wouldn't associate with them. You'd have nothing in common with them. And they realized that. They are very defensive people. Very defensive," says DeCello.

Ten

For the remarried Stiles and Newman families, the 1980s were a constant struggle.

Glenn's tire business failed. One day during a welding job, Glenn fell fifteen feet to the ground and hurt his back. Shortly after that, he began to use a wheelchair to get around. Money was tight.

As for home life, Donna remembers it was a time where there was no real fighting, no real arguing. Teresa would have her mood swings; Donna thought that was just natural, especially considering how much she had to wait on Glenn.

In his younger days in the carnival, Glenn was spry as could be. He ran around and jumped nimbly up into the back of trucks. That was in the past.

"Glenn would have her [Teresa] wait on him because he was so small he couldn't reach everything," Donna recalls. And being in the wheelchair, his mobility was cut down even further.

To support his family, Glenn went out on

the road with a show he called The World's
Smallest Man. Donna accompanied him, to
help out in the carnival.

Teresa stayed home to take care of the
kids. On weekends, she'd visit. Unlike Grady,
Glenn liked being near home. He never
toured more than four hundred miles from
their house.

When school finished, she would pack up
her kids and go out on the road with Glenn
and Donna, and help out in the carnival.
She sold tickets, helped to set up and tear
down the tent, and took care of the book-
keeping.

It was a hardscrabble life, like any seasonal
trade. At some point, the family moved back
to Smock, Pennsylvania. Regardless of where
they were, Glenn always managed to pay
their bills.

Everyone who knows Glenn, or has ever
met him, looks upon him as the nicest of
human beings. He treated Teresa's kids as
kindly as his own son, Glenn, Jr.

For Teresa, it was the first time in her life
she lived in a relatively stable environment,
with a man who really loved her.

However, as time passed, Teresa grew rest-
less, tired of having to cater to her husband's
disabilities. "They just couldn't get along at
all," says Donna.

They decided to seek a divorce. Teresa felt she could have a better life. There must be a man out there who could give her more than Glenn was able to give her. A powerful, successful man— like her former husband, Grady Stiles, Jr.

"I was very angry. I was angry at her for even thinking about talking to him. Because I really hated him," Donna says.

"Donna, you know," Teresa continued, "it's been a long time. He's probably changed."

In her bones, Donna knew otherwise, but she held her tongue.

"I still love your dad," Teresa continued quietly.

Donna just could not understand. How could she love someone that had beaten her up so badly?

Teresa phoned Grady and began to rekindle their relationship. Seeing her interest, Grady tried to buy her back. When Teresa was short of cash, he sent her money. She responded to his charm and assurances of sobriety as well.

The phone calls became more frequent.

"I still wouldn't talk to him on the phone. And she wouldn't really talk about him too much with us— with me," Donna recalls. "She would talk a little bit more to Cathy than to me."

During the time that she and Grady were becoming reacquainted, Teresa decided to

move the family once again, this time down
south to Okeechobee, central Florida. Grady,
meanwhile, after his divorce from Barbara,
had relocated back to Gibsonton.

Soon after they were settled in Okeechobee,
Donna was dating a quiet young man named
Joe Miles. They fell in love and got engaged.

Joe's parents owned an eating estab-
lishment called the Angus Restaurant. Teresa decided that for her next date with
Grady, they'd meet there. It'd be nice and
neat. One set of future in-laws meeting another set of future in-laws.

"Donna, can you please— you and Cathy,
please come in [the restaurant] and see your
dad. He's not like he used to be. Please, for
my sake, do it for me," Teresa pleaded.

"We both talked to him, Cathy and me,
and said hello. And he didn't drink. That
bar was sitting right there and he never had
a drink."

Sometimes, Teresa would take the kids
along on their dates. Donna remembers driving over to his house in Gibsonton and going
inside.

The place was a total disaster, always filthy,
always dirty.

"Mom would come in and pick Dad up,
take him out to dinner. The date after the
Angus, when we went up to the house, [he]
gave her a big kiss and a hug. And he was

really nice. He didn't holler; he talked very softly. They went out holding hands."

Grady was even nice to Teresa and Glenn's son, Glennie, the same child who witnessed Grady's assault on his mother years before. Grady showered the entire family with presents. Donna and Cathy got gold necklaces with their initials carved in gold.

Yet, despite all the hatred Donna felt toward her father, watching him with Teresa, the way she enjoyed being in his company, she decided to give him one more chance.

"I love him, Mom," Donna told her mother.

"You're not the same as you used to be," she told Grady with a goodbye hug at the end of a date. "I love you."

"I don't think I ever started loving my father like a dad again. My mom didn't know that, though."

While Donna says she never could love her father again, she recalls thinking that she tried to build a "liking" relationship. As for his abstinence, "It scared me. It scared me remembering what he was, what he was like, and then seeing him, what he was doing. It was like Jekyll and Hyde there. I was scared. I was nervous. I was cautious."

Now that they were a family again, it was time to take to the road. Grady needed everyone's help with his "10 in 1" show. Donna, in particular, had promised to help him at the Dallas Fair.

Grady rented Teresa a spanking new motor home. On the road, she occupied it, along with Donna, Cathy, and Glennie. Grady and Little Grady bunked in an older trailer. In the evening, Grady would come over, and they'd have dinner like a family. On the nights he worked, he'd eat right on the platform where he did his act.

Meanwhile, Teresa disapproved of the way the relationship between Donna and Joe was progressing, and they rarely spoke about it. Grady, though, was different.

Once again, Donna confronted her father with news of her impending nuptials. A sense of fear overwhelmed her.

"There's this guy that asked me to marry him."

Donna showed him Joe's picture. He was still in Okeechobee.

"I really want to go," Donna continued. "I know I promised you I would work Dallas for you, but I got to go back [to Okeechobee]."

"I don't blame you," said Grady. "Do you love him? Are you in love with him? Does he love you?"

"Yes, definitely."

"Okay," Grady said firmly.

He took a wad of bills from his pocket, and peeled off three hundred dollars. It was payment for working the previous date. "And I'm buying you a plane ticket home."

Was this the same Grady, the one who had murdered Jack? Now, he was not only giving her his blessing, he was putting his money where his mouth was.

Donna was finally won over. Teresa was right; Grady had changed.

After that, Donna and Teresa made up, with Grady acting as mediator.

In January of 1989, Joe Miles married Donna Marie Stiles. It was a new life for Donna. This time, it would work out.

Teresa and Grady decided to live together on Inglewood Drive and remarried soon after.

Grady had done it. He had changed. He had turned over a new leaf. He had sought and received redemption from his family.

Donna noticed the first changes a few months after her parents remarried. She and Joe came down from Okeechobee to visit.

"Where's Dad?" she asked her mother when they arrived.

"He's, uh, he's out."

"Out where, Mom?"

"A bar. He's out at a bar."

"Mom, why don't we— "

"I don't want to talk about it!" And that ended the discussion.

Donna and Joe came to visit again two

weeks later. They noticed the half-pint of booze on the countertop, and another one under the sink in the kitchen. Grady had fallen off the wagon completely. He was drinking in the house.

"Mom, if he's starting to drink again, then he's going to be mean," Donna warned. "Why don't you just say forget it, you and Glennie come back with me and Joe. I can put you up in a trailer in the park."

"No, Donna," Teresa replied firmly. "I can't leave your dad now. I can't leave him. He don't got nobody to take care of him."

After that, Teresa clammed up and wouldn't talk about what was going on.

For her part, Donna noticed a difference in her father. His eyes, always an icy blue, turned cold as a winter's day in Chicago. His face took on a hardened look.

Before they remarried, he'd had a ready smile. He never smiled now. Unhappy, he just sat in his armchair, drinking Seagram's and Coke while the TV droned on. Sometimes, he broke the monotony. He went down to get drunk at Showtown USA. It was like Grady was marking time, waiting for something to happen.

With the booze came the abuse . . . again. Suddenly, the good times prior to their remarriage were gone, the years with Glenn obliterated, and she was back in the pain again, reeling from Grady's physical and verbal abuse.

One night during the summer of 1991 while the carnival played New York, Grady was out playing cards. When he returned, he told Teresa, "Fix me a drink."

Teresa took it to him in the bedroom of their trailer. "This is the last drink I'm going to get you," she warned.

Grady grabbed a handful of Teresa's hair, twisted it and pulled her head back, trying all the while to pull the hair out of her scalp. He pulled her head back so hard that she thought he was going to break her neck. He was strong enough to do it.

"Fix me another drink," he shouted.

"We got no more booze," Teresa spit the words out painfully. "There's no more booze," she repeated.

Grady pressed his claw into Teresa's throat, just under her jawbone. It was so painful, it felt like he was going to push it clear through her throat. Finally, he let her go.

"Go out and find a bottle of liquor," Grady ordered. She left the trailer. Outside in the darkness, Teresa remembered feeling she had had enough.

Grady was just too damn mean. What right did he have abusing her and her children? She felt desperate and alone. The trucks they traveled in were parked nearby. They beckoned, with their promise of safety. Yet Teresa chose to stay and endure the abuse.

Eleven

In April 1992, fifty-four-year-old Grady Stiles took to the road to play the carnival circuit one more time. He had begun as a seven-year-old in 1944.

Most of the others, who, like him, exploited their appearance, had either died out or retired. The few who remained were re-labeled "physically challenged" by reformers, who urged the public to stay away from their exploitation, despite the fact that it was the only way these "physically challenged" individuals could make money. But nothing had stopped Grady yet— not time, not age, not cirrhosis, not emphysema, not even the law.

Looking forward to a profitable summer, Grady took along the whole family.

Donna and Joe ran the gorilla illusion, where a girl mysteriously turns into a gorilla right before the customers' eyes.

Daughter Cathy, who had married, and son-in-law Tyrill ran the animal oddities exhibit, which included a two-headed raccoon, and different types of shrunken animal heads. All you had to do was pay the nominal admission price to see nature's mistakes.

Grady himself ran the "10 in 1." Lobster Boy was the star attraction. Stepson Glenn, son Little Grady, and wife Teresa helped out wherever they were needed.

By the end of April, they had gotten as far north as Virginia. They were playing Military Circle, a mall in Norfork. It was there, set up in the mall's parking lot, that Grady realized he needed a new bally man to draw the crowds.

While Joe fronted the gorilla show, someone was needed to do the same for the "10 in 1." It was a desperate situation.

The "10 in 1" was the family's biggest moneymaker. Inside, marks could see everything from "The Human Pincushion" and Glennie as The Human Blockhead to a snake charmer and sword swallower. But without an expert enough bally man to get the marks into the tent, the summer of 1992 could be the worst ever.

Luckily, a young performer known as Merman the Magician needed a job and heard about the opportunity from a friend.

Merman drove down to the carnival and met Grady and Teresa. Grady did all the talking; Teresa stood behind the wheelchair, eyeing the magician closely.

Grady liked what he saw. Here was a well-spoken, good-looking guy with blond hair, blue eyes, and sandy mustache. The girls would love him. And he did magic, which the kids loved. "I also eat fire," Merman added. And he'd had some limited carnival experience.

"Great, we want you," Grady decided. "You'll bally the 'ten in one' and run it. Do some magic, eat some fire."

"What's the wage?"

"Your pay is ten percent of the gate after the rent is paid."

"Done."

They each had personal details to work out before Merman came on board. It was agreed that Merman would join the show that June at the Nassau Coliseum in Uniondale, New York an all event indoor stadium, best known to sports fans as the home of the New York Islanders hockey team.

"We had a helluva good spot on the midway there. I worked my ass off," Merman recalls.

Sporting a tuxedo at night, Merman was the best-dressed guy on the midway.

"I stood there and called people until my voice was gone. I was standing up there with no voice, flagging these people and begging them to come into the tent and, of course, Joe was on the other end. They had the gorilla show going," says Merman.

Almost immediately, trouble started.

"Joe was jealous of me," Merman recalls. "See, he was like the head guy until I got there. He ran everything. When I got there, he kinda got pushed to the side a little bit."

Joe would tell the roustabouts to do one thing while Merman told them something else. That meant nothing got done. Merman told Grady, "If you want me to run this show, get this guy the hell out of it. I can't tell these guys to do one thing and then have him come in and tell them to do something else. It's causing too much confusion."

Grady sided with Merman.

"Joe got bent all out of shape. There was a big fight and he [Joe] was going to take the truck, take the camper, and just drive the hell off and leave Grady there. Grady said, 'You're not going to do any such thing.'

"Grady wheeled his chair in between the camper and the truck so if he [Joe] was going to pull off, he was gonna run Grady's ass over. He pulled the truck right up on him and was pushing the chair. The police came and kinda broke it up," Merman continues.

It quickly became evident to Merman that the season was being compromised.

"He was having so [many] problems with the family, they had to play a couple of bad spots just because he couldn't get along with these guys. I mean, the season was screwed, primarily because of the problems he was having with Joe and Donna, but Teresa was taking sides, primarily against Grady. And Grady was stuck. His wife and these other people; he couldn't do the shit by himself."

That was a fact. The large truck and campers the Stileses traveled with contained all their carnival paraphernalia, including the huge canvas tent that housed the "10 in 1," the accoutrements of the gorilla show, Tyrill's caged-animal oddities, and the exhibition stages that had to be set up at every stop. There was no way that Grady could set everything up. He needed the help of his family.

After the coliseum event, the Stiles caravan made its way to Brockton, Massachusetts.

"Brockton was, like, worse than the South Bronx. Police walking around fairgrounds in gangs of ten or more. Kids walking with sticks and knives, and pulling blades on gangs of policemen. One guy [a carny] was stabbed because he wouldn't put mustard on this guy's hot dog," Merman says.

It was in Brockton that the open dissension between Grady and his family really started.

"What happened was, they set the 'ten in one' and the gorilla show up side by side. And, of course, anytime you run two ballys, the first bally does his pitch and then when that breaks, as soon as that breaks, the second bally starts his pitch."

Normally, two ballys are never supposed to be set up side by side because of competition. Fairs try to break them up by having a kiddie ride or something else in between. For some reason, that just didn't work in Brockton, and Merman and Joe were working side by side.

"I would go out on the front stage and call all these people up to come inside our tent. When I was done, Joe's show was supposed to start their gig and call whoever was left into his tent. That didn't set well with Joe.

" 'No, no,' Joe disagreed. 'I gotta go first.'

"We're gonna make more money because I've got live stuff going on and there'll be more people that we turn away than you'll turn away," Merman pointed out.

Again, Joe disagreed adamantly.

"Fine," Merman replied with a sigh, wishing to avoid further argument. "Have at it."

"So he'd [Joe] go and do his pitch," Merman continues. "I'd start my pitch after he was finished, and before I had even finished my pitch, Joe was back. See, his show only ran five to ten minutes. After his show was over, he'd immediately come right out and start his pitch again. I'd still be finishing up my pitch. It was stupid because most of the money was all going to the same place. It was all Grady's money. They got their percentage but, Jesus Christ, we all worked for the same person.

"Anyway, he kept doing this shit and then he got all pissed off, and run over and started poking his finger in my face. And then he balled his fist up and took a swing at me, so I clocked him.

"By then, he [Joe] had already fought with four or five other people. Mary and Butch, 'The Snake Queen' and sword swallower, he'd already beaten up on their kid a couple of times."

Grady, meanwhile, decided that it was time to act.

"I've had enough of this shit with you, Joe," Grady said. "I don't need you. Take the gorilla show and get the hell out of here. Take Donna with you. You guys do whatever the hell you want. Just go. I just don't need the problems anymore."

Nervous about going out on their own, Donna and Joe hesitated. And then, so did Grady. He remembered that Joe was the only one in their group with a trucker's license.

"Grady, it's nothing for me to go down and get my license. I'll drive the truck," said Merman.

That cinched it. He told Joe and Donna to get lost. Joe and Donna were ready to leave when Teresa went over and tried to talk them into staying. After a few hours, things had seemed to calm down.

"Before we left that spot, everything kind of chilled over and gelled. And he [Joe] was back in good graces."

Grady wanted him to drive the truck again instead of Merman. Later, though, Merman remembers there was another problem when Joe discovered that someone had cut the truck's brake lines, the truck that Merman was going to drive.

Joe wasn't the only one who, according to Merman, was jealous of his position in the carnival hierarchy.

"Glenn got pissed off at me one day because they were late getting there and we'd already set the show up and I had one stage left to put together. It was an awkward stage and just easier for one person to do it."

"I don't need your help. Let me do this," Merman told Glenn.

Glenn got pissed off at Merman, and ran over and told Grady, "You need to fire him. He's an asshole. You need to get rid of him."

"Leave him alone," Grady replied. "You just need to relax and let him do his job."

"Glenn then got so pissed off at Grady that he went over and punched a tree, and broke half the bones in his wrist," Merman remembers.

"Man, I am extremely, extremely sorry.

I've never seen a season like this. I can't afford to go into these big spots and have these people doin' what they're doin' cause they'll never let me back in," Grady told Merman.

"These guys were his family and they would work the ticket box and steal money from him. That was part of my job, to keep an eye on the box. See, these people thought, 'He's just some magician, he's never been in the business.' But I'd sit there and watch them. I'd count the people and count the box when they walked away from it.

"Teresa'd steal money out of the box every chance [she] got. Somebody'd come up with a fifty or a hundred, and she'd double-count the money and shortchange the guy twenty bucks. Then she'd brag about it and then tell us not to do that shit."

Such shenanigans might account for how Teresa was able to save up the $1,500 she later paid to have Grady killed.

"She'd walk out of the trailer, slam the door, and walk down the midway and talk [out loud], 'Oh this sucks. That fuckin' bastard. I could kill him.'

"It would be because he didn't want to go to town or something. Stupid shit. I honestly believe they [the family] were trying their damnedest to make everything fail," Merman says.

But several members of the family were

doing much more than that. They were plotting murder.

While they were on the road in July, Teresa and Cathy had their first conversation about killing Grady.

"I want him dead," said Teresa.

Cathy agreed.

Marco Eno knew Grady well. He had worked for him at numerous carnival sites around the country for the past five years. He knew that Grady had a temper when he drank, that he would get verbally abusive, but he had never seen him get physical with his family. The proposal, therefore, was out of the blue.

"Marco, would you kill Grady for me?" Teresa asked.

He couldn't believe it.

"No, I couldn't do it," he answered.

What a stupid question! What did she think he was, some kind of hired killer? She was watching too many movies.

"Could you get someone else?" Teresa continued.

This had to be a joke, Marco reasoned. That was it. A joke. A stupid joke.

The summer wore on. Every weekend it rained. The crowds stayed away. The wetter it got, the more the money dried up.

"Get rid of the sword swallower, get rid of Satina the Snake Queen," Merman advised Grady. "All the time they're cryin' and whinin'. We'll find somebody else. We'll start anew, make some money and save this season."

"I can't do that," Grady answered.

"Why the hell can't ya? You own the show."

"Look, I took them in and I gave 'em my word that I'd let 'em work the summer. I can't go back on that. When this season is over, fine, we'll get rid of 'em, we'll get whoever you want. Besides, and if I do get rid of them, where the hell they gonna go? Who's gonna take care of them?"

"Grady, that's not your problem. I understand you gave your word, but do something. Tell 'em I'm in charge and the shit's gotta be done this way or it ain't gonna be done."

"Well, you're not in charge, I'm in charge!"

"Yeah, but you know what I mean."

"Look, just deal with them. We'll get out of this thing and make it work. Let's just go with it."

"All right. You're just the boss."

Grady thought for a moment.

"Look, Merman, I know it's been a lousy season. I want to make this up to you. Next season, we're not bringing any of the family."

And then Grady outlined his plans for the future.

"In the wintertime, I want you to come down here, work for me at some of these spots in Tampa and Fort Lauderdale. I'll pay you seven hundred fifty bucks a week. While we're here, that's when we'll pick up our crew for next year. You can interview these people, you can get whoever you want and we'll take 'em with us. We'll get rid of everybody and the hell with them. We'll go out and make some money, I promise you that."

Merman had no reason to doubt the claw-handed man. He had come to admire and respect Grady. "He was an old carny guy who wanted things done his way. No bullshit. He treated me well. There were a lot of little things he did that a lot of people had never done.

"For instance, couple of spots we played were super dead. We couldn't even pay the rent. Like I said, I didn't get paid until the rent was paid and then I got ten percent."

"Look, I need you to take me somewhere. Take a break for a minute," Grady would tell Merman.

Merman wheeled Grady away from the show, away from the prying eyes of his family.

"Look, you know you've been busting your ass out here for me, and I know I got these shitty people working for me. My family, everyone's trying to screw me, you're the only one who's not trying to screw me."

And he'd slide Merman a fifty or a hundred to get through the next week.

At the end of the summer, Grady told Merman to call him the last week in November to set things up for next season.

"They [the family] knew he was gonna get rid of them. When you live and work day in and day out with the same group of people like we did, there are no secrets."

Except one.

Twelve

The strip mall had been erected on the south side of Federal Highway 301 in Riverview, Florida. There was space enough to house three businesses. One of them was Your Place Game Room, a combination billiard parlor/video-game room that catered to the teenagers in the surrounding area.

"Put me behind a counter and I'll rob you," says Chuck Sanders, smiling. The proprietor of Your Place, he was reminiscing about his days in the carny, when he ran the games on the midway.

"You can put me in a game with five people," Chuck continues, "and when I get done, they leave happy and smiling," even though they lost their money at one of the carny games like Screw, Razzle, or Swinger.

"I'm an agent," Chuck says proudly, agent being carny vernacular for "a guy that can rip you off."

Unlike the unlucky residents of Gibtown, Chuck got out of the carny hustle and gives free games for students who run A's and B's in their classes.

Chuck Sanders doesn't remember seeing Harry Glenn Newman, Jr., waiting outside his billiard parlor that day in early November 1992.

Glenn had positioned himself outside Your Place a few yards away from the strip mall's second store, Paws and Claws— Pet Grooming. As instructed, he was there, waiting at the appointed hour.

When his friend didn't show at the appointed time, Glenn called him on his beeper, and left a message.

Soon, the phone rang. It was his friend Chris Wyant, who lived just down the block from him at 11104 Inglewood Drive.

"Meet me at the park. Right down the road from the arcade."

Glenn got back in his car. With the sun setting and dusk fast approaching, he drove quickly, and took a left down a side street. Within a block, he had come to Riverview Community Park.

It was the kind of park you'd find in any residential community with a decent appropriations budget: well kept, approximately two square blocks in size, with an elementary school on the far end, a playing field leading into a children's playground on the other.

He drove over near the equipment shed, parked his car, and waited.

* * *

Dennis Cowell had a birthday coming up. On November 26, he would be nineteen years old. But that was a few weeks off. What was more important to him that night was not his upcoming birthday but helping out his friend Chris Wyant.

Dennis and Chris were good buddies. In fact, Wyant was as close a friend as he had. And when his good buddy asked him for transportation over to the park in Riverview, he was glad to oblige.

Dennis borrowed his girlfriend Lynne Browne's blue-gray Ford Ranger pickup, got Chris, and drove over to Riverview. It took less than ten minutes to get there, but those ten minutes spelled a great difference.

Once in Riverview, the depressing pall of poverty and hopelessness that encompassed Gibsonton was gone.

Riverview has fast-food restaurants; Gibsonton doesn't. Riverview has many gas stations dispensing well-known national brands; Gibsonton doesn't. And Riverview has neat, one-family homes, which are common; Gibsonton, with its itinerant, poor carny population, doesn't.

In short, Riverview is more like your typical American community. It is not a place where murder is common, and its residents do not think about it with any sort of regularity. Yet it is a place where a murder was conceived and, at that, in one of the more innocent places.

Dennis Cowell tooled his girlfriend's truck to Riverview Park. Spying Glenn's car, he pulled over and parked beside it.

As the sun set and another quiet Florida night approached, Chris got out of the truck and nonchalantly walked over. He had blond hair and blue-green eyes. He was five feet nine inches and weighed 135 pounds soaking wet, the type of kid you wouldn't give a second look to on the street.

Already at the ripe old age of seventeen, Chris had a full juvenile record, and while juvenile records are sealed, he bragged to friends and acquaintances that he'd killed people in drive-by shootings. But booking sheets are one-dimensional objects; cold recitations of fact are no substitute for direct observation.

Maybe it was a portent of things to come, or maybe it was just that he was raised to be polite when someone else was doing business; whatever it was, Dennis hung back, barely in earshot.

Glenn got to the point immediately.

"My mom's having a lot of problems with my father, and I need somehow to help her out, make it better for her. So, what can you do about it?" Glenn asked urgently.

They haggled about the price for a couple

of minutes. Then Chris said confidently,
"Give me three hundred dollars and I'll do
it."

Glenn would later recant this part of his
statement, saying that it was actually the
price of $1,500 that they'd agreed on. Re-
gardless, it was precious little for a human
life.

Overhearing snatches of conversation, Dennis Cowell thought the two were talking in
code, that some sort of drug transaction was
going down. That must be it, Dennis thought.
Chris had a history of dealing drugs, so it was
likely this was just another drug transaction
in the making.

Time would prove him wrong, however.
They made a bond drenched in blood.

Chris Wyant was nothing if not a good
and loyal friend. If someone did a service
for him, he had to repay it.

"Come on, Dennis, let's go shopping,"
Chris said gleefully after his meeting was
over. He planned to reward his friend.

Chris bought Dennis a pair of tennis
shoes, a pair of pants, a shirt, and an Oak-
land Raiders baseball cap with some of the
money he'd received from Glenn. Dennis was
very happy with his gifts, so happy that he
accompanied Chris on another trek, this time
to Apollo Beach.

Apollo Beach is five miles south of Gibsonton on Highway 41. It was built on the green

shores of Hillsborough Bay, just another lazy town on Florida's west coast that most tourists pass through without even stopping. Barry Allen, a family friend, lived in Apollo Beach, and Chris and Dennis headed to his house. It was there that Barry's wife, Sally, sold Chris a .32-caliber Colt Automatic for $150.

Chris was nothing if not clever. He convinced his good buddy Dennis Cowell to sign the paperwork necessary to purchase the weapon. Since it had been a cash transaction, unless someone talked, which wasn't likely given Chris's reputation, there was no way anyone could trace the gun back to him.

It would be Dennis who'd take the fall.

The mourning, plaintive sound of the train whistle played through the palm trees of the still Florida night. You could hear that sound every night in Gibsonton, and during the day, too.

The town was bisected by rail lines. Anytime you made a turn and went east across Highway 41, you had to be careful you didn't run into some hundred-car freight. If you did, the lights would flash, the warning gate would come down, and you'd sit there, stalled, unable to move for an interminable period of time, until the train had passed.

Mary Teresa Stiles lived in fear of those trains.

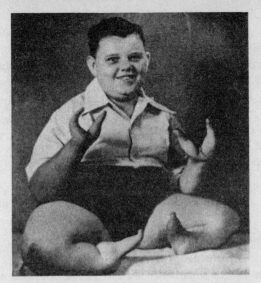

A studio portrait of "Lobster Boy," Grady Stiles, Jr.,
as he appeared on the carnival circuit during the 1940s.
(*Courtesy of Circus World Museum, Baraboo, Wisconsin*)

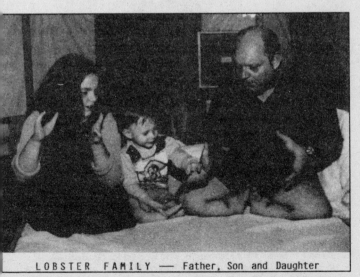

LOBSTER FAMILY — Father, Son and Daughter

Grady Stiles promoted his show by selling postcards like this one,
for anything from 25 cents to one dollar. From left to right: daughter
Cathy, son Grady III, and Grady, Jr.   (*Courtesy of Teresa Stiles*)

STRANGEST MARRIED COUPLE
PERCILLA *Monkey Girl* — EMMITT *Alligator Boy*

Percilla Bejano, "The Bearded Lady," seen here with her husband, Emmitt, "The Alligator Man." Percilla testified as a character witness during Grady's 1978 murder trial in Pittsburgh. (*Courtesy of Circus World Museum, Baraboo, Wisconsin*)

"The Fat Man," Paul Fishbaugh, who worked for Grady Stiles, Jr., in his sideshow and served as a character witness at Grady's 1978 murder trial. (*Courtesy of Teresa Stiles*)

"The World's Only Living Half Girl," Jeanie Tomaini, posing with her husband "The Giant," Al Tomaini. The shot was taken when they were exhibited in "The World's Fair Freak Show" of the 1930s. (*Courtesy of Circus World Museum, Baraboo, Wisconsin*)

BELOW: Jeanie Tomaini, posing in 1993 with her grandchild in Gibsonton, Florida. She and her husband never worked the same shows as Grady, but got to know him as a neighbor. (*Courtesy of Judy Rock*)

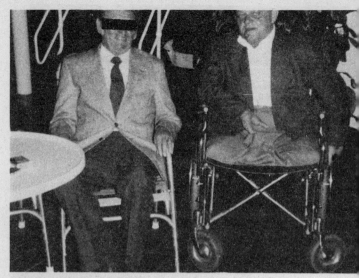

Grady Stiles in happier days, here pictured on a cruise with an unidentified man. *(Courtesy of the Stiles Family)*

The Pittsburgh row house in which Grady Stiles, Jr., murdered Jack Layne, his daughter Donna's fiancé. *(Photo by Fred Rosen)*

Anthony DeCello, Grady's attorney at his 1978 murder trial.
(*Photo by Fred Rosen*)

"Merman the Magician" helped Grady manage his shows
during the summer of 1992. Merman also performed
as a magician and fire-eater in the shows.
(*Courtesy of Merrill McCubbin*)

The Gibsonton trailer where Grady, Mary Teresa, and
Harry Glenn Newman, Jr., lived together.
(*Courtesy of Florida State Attorney's Office, Hillsborough County*)

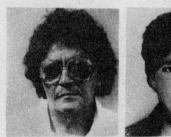

LEFT: Mary Teresa Stiles, 54, on the day of her arrest.
(*Courtesy of Hillsborough County Sheriff's Department*)

CENTER: "The Human Blockhead," Harry Glenn Newman, Jr., 18,
Mary Teresa's son, on the day of his arrest.
(*Courtesy of Hillsborough County Sheriff's Department*)

RIGHT: Gibsonton neighbor, Christopher M. Wyant, 17, on the day
of his arrest. (*Courtesy of Hillsborough County Sheriff's Department*)

Grady Stiles, Jr., shortly after he was shot to death in the living room of his trailer home. (*Courtesy of Florida State Attorney's Office, Hillsborough County*)

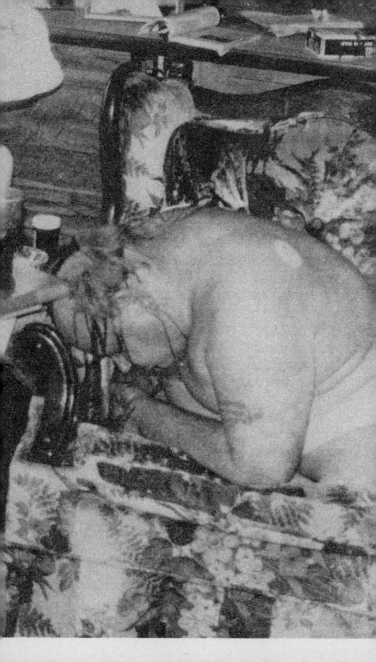

At the murder scene, a police photographer took this grisly still life of a carton of Pall Mall cigarettes splattered with Grady's blood. (*Courtesy of Florida State Attorney's Office, Hillsborough County*)

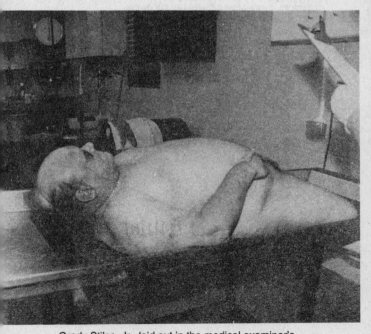

Grady Stiles, Jr., laid out in the medical examiner's room before the autopsy. (*Courtesy of Florida State Attorney's Office, Hillsborough County*)

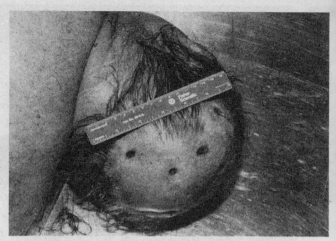

Autopsy photograph showing the bullet wounds to Grady's cranium, three of which caused his death.
(*Courtesy of Florida State Attorney's Office, Hillsborough County*)

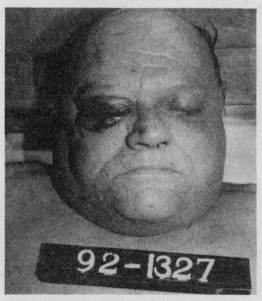

The discoloration of the skin around Grady's right eye was caused by head trauma after the bullets entered his brain.
(*Courtesy of Florida State Attorney's Office, Hillsborough County*)

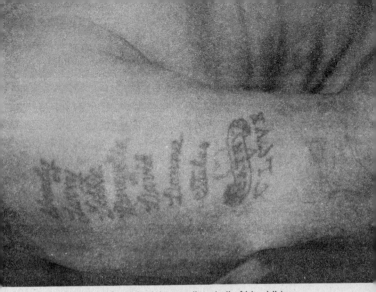

The tattoo on Grady's right arm listed all of his children.
(*Courtesy of the Florida State Attorney's Office, Hillsborough County*)

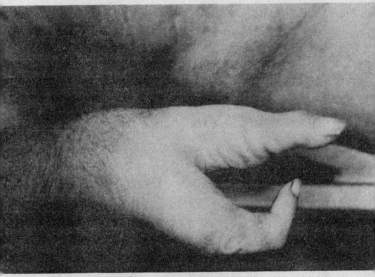

Autopsy shot of one of Grady's hands/claws. The genetic condition known as ectrodactyly caused Grady's fingers and toes to fuse together into claw-like appendages.
(*Courtesy of Florida State Attorney's Office, Hillsborough County*)

LEFT: Dennis Cowell, 18, on the day of his arrest for hiding the gun that killed Grady Stiles, Jr. (*Courtesy of Hillsborough County Sheriff's Office*)

RIGHT: The .32 Caliber Colt Automatic that Chris Wyant used to murder Grady Stiles, Jr. The gun was purchased by Dennis Cowell, who later pleaded guilty as an accessory to the murder. (*Courtesy of Florida State Attorney's Office, Hillsborough County*)

Grady Stiles III, "Little Grady," and his half sister Cathy Stiles Berry. (*Photo by Fred Rosen*)

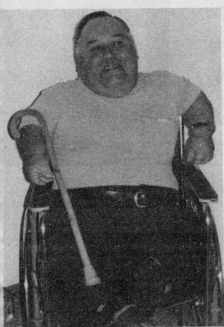

"Midget Man," Harry Glenn Newman, Sr., seen here after his testimony at Mary Teresa's murder trial. He married Mary Teresa after her marriage with Grady fell apart. (*Photo by Fred Rosen*)

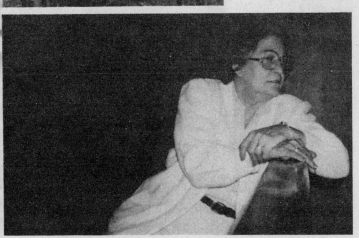

Mary Teresa Stiles during a break at her murder trial. (*Photo by Fred Rosen*)

Assistant State's Attorney, Ron Hanes, first prosecution chair. *(Photo by Fred Rosen)*

Sandra Spoto, Assistant State's Attorney, second prosecution chair. *(Photo by Fred Rosen)*

Mary Teresa and her attorney Arnold Levine. *(Photo by Fred Rosen with technical assistance by Peter Cosgrove)*

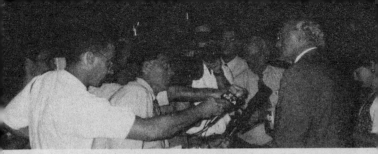

The media coverage surrounding the murder of Grady Stiles, Jr., kept tensions high throughout the trial. Arnold Levine is shown here during one of his impromptu press conferences.
(Photo by Fred Rosen)

Attorney Levine conferring with the Stiles family. From left: Cathy, her husband Tyrill Berry, Mary Teresa, Donna, and "Little Grady" during a brief recess in the trial. *(Photo by Fred Rosen)*

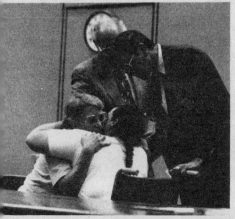

Cathy Stiles Berry comforts her mother after the verdict, moments before the bailiff was instructed to take Mary Teresa into custody.
(Photo by Fred Rosen with technical assistance by Peter Cosgrove)

The entrance gate to The International Independent Showmen
Garden of Memorials in Thonotosassa, Florida, the cemetery
for carny performers in which Grady was buried.
(Photo by Fred Rosen)

The grave of Grady Stiles, Jr.   *(Photo by Fred Rosen)*

The trains were always in the back of her mind when she left Inglewood Drive and drove the few miles into town to go shopping.

At Twin Oaks Plaza, Teresa was momentarily distracted by a display in the window of a store next to the supermarket. There was a momentary pull to go in, to give in to her urge to browse, but then, the fear kicked in like some addictive drug.

No, I can't. I got to call Grady, she thought anxiously.

Then she went into the supermarket and bought a twelve-pack of Pepsi and a pack of Almond Joy candy bars for the boys, and whatever staples they needed.

After loading the packages into the car, Teresa pulled out and went south a few blocks until she got to Showtown USA where she picked him up a pint. Then she made the turn toward the railroad tracks.

She caught a train and was forced to stop. Stalled, waiting for the freight to pass, she kept looking at her watch, willing the second hand to slow down, looking up, willing the slow freight to go faster, and all the while her heart pounding in her chest with fear.

After an eternity of waiting, which was actually mere minutes, the last car finally cleared. She gunned the car across the tracks and raced home to Grady.

Parking the car in the driveway, she raced

across the hearty Florida grass, stiff and green no matter what season it was, through the front gate, and into the brown trailer.

Wordlessly, in a drill born from long repetition, Teresa took the soda pop and the candy bars out of the bag and put them in the pantry. Then she took the rest of the groceries into the house.

Sitting in his armchair, Grady had a stoned look, which wasn't surprising.

Grady Stiles was a creature of habit. Every day, weekday or weekend, he awoke between eleven and twelve. He would crawl out of bed and have a glass of tea in his bedroom. After a while, he'd crawl out of the bedroom on his claws and sit on the chair in the living room in front of the old 1970s-style console TV set. Maybe an hour and a half to two hours later, he started drinking.

He would begin his imbibing with a glass of Seagram's 7 and a glass of tea. Maybe a couple of more glasses, and then he'd leave. He would either get someone to drive him or push himself in his wheelchair down to the local bar, where he would continue drinking, returning in the afternoon to drink more at home, not stopping until he went to sleep in the empty hours after midnight.

"Well, what took you so fucking long? You were longer than what you said you were going to be." His voice sounded harsh.

"I had a train," Teresa answered meekly.

"Don't give me that shit!" Grady shouted. "I know better than that. What were you doing? Where did you go?"

"Just shopping."

"Yeah," he said dubiously, "well, you didn't buy too much, did you?"

Teresa thought of the pop and candy she'd left in the pantry. He always complained that Little Grady and Glenn drank too much soda. She wasn't allowed to buy more than a twelve-pack every three weeks. And just a pack of Almond Joy bars. They ate too much, he said. If she bought more than her assigned quota and Grady found out about it . . .

"No, I didn't buy too much. Grady, your drinking—"

"What about my drinking?" he screamed, making little slurred gestures with his claws. "I'm not in a prison, this is my home, I'll do what I want to do."

In some ways, it was a prison. Grady couldn't see very well and no longer drove. He had to rely on his family and friends to chauffeur him around.

"You won't let me buy a car because you don't want me drinking," Grady continued screaming at Teresa. She just stood there and took it. "I'm allowed to drink, I'm old enough to do what I want to do," he screamed like some petulant schoolboy.

And Grady kept it up, a nonstop verbal stream of abuse. All Teresa could hope for was that he'd run out of steam soon, or the alcohol would anesthetize him and force him to calm down.

As he lay in bed at night, he turned to his wife and said, "I should just kill you. Get it over with." Then he fell off into a drunken stupor.

Weeks went by and Chris failed to deliver on his promise. Then came November 29.

The day of the murder was a lazy sort of day, and Dennis Cowell was visiting his friend Chris Wyant at his trailer on Inglewood Drive. They were just hanging out, not doing much, when Glenn Newman burst through the door at four P.M.

"It's got to be tonight, Chris," Glenn announced breathlessly, "or my mom's going to call the cops saying that you broke into the house and stole the money."

Chris and Glenn talked, planning the impending murder, while Dennis listened. Dennis would later say that the murder had been planned originally for November 30 at an unknown location. Dennis left.

Chris had played chess a few times with Glenn. Ironically, he was the only one of Glenn's friends that Grady let visit the trailer.

"If anything happens, if you turn around and blame me or say that I've done something, I've got a bullet for everyone in the house," Chris warned.

Chris loaded the .32 Colt Automatic with copper-tipped, full metal jacket, .32-caliber bullets. The metal jacket ensured that the lead core would stay intact when a bullet struck the target, in this case, Grady Stiles.

The bullet would penetrate his body in a clean wound channel. Had Chris opted for a hollow-point design, the tip would have expanded on contact, making a larger wound. But in a contract killing, the idea is not to wound, but to kill, and Chris had chosen well both his ammunition and gun.

Later in the evening, Glenn was alone in his bedroom in the rear of the trailer when he heard a knock at his window. The window was broken at the bottom and it flopped open.

"Who is it?"

"Chris," said a voice, whispering from outside.

Glenn stuck his head out, and they began chewing the fat like nothing special was happening.

"Want to play basketball tomorrow?" Chris asked.

"Not sure. Chris, I want the money back. That I gave you."

"Can't do that," Chris responded.

"I want the money back, Chris," Glenn repeated. "I don't want this done 'cause I don't want to get in any trouble my mom and everybody else."

"Can't give you the money back," Chris said. "I already spent it."

He pulled the gun from his jacket and showed it to Glenn. It was wrapped in panty hose. The panty hose would stop the shells from ejecting onto the ground, where the cops could discover them. He was also smart enough to encase his hands in gloves, so there'd be no prints if the gun was recovered, which he didn't plan on happening anyway.

"I'm going to drop the gun in the water," he said. "Throw it in. After."

He said he'd do the job around eleven. Soon after, he left.

About 7:30 or eight P.M., Glenn told Teresa what he had done.

"You said you wanted to get away from this man, that you were tired of him abusing you, and I tried to get it settled. I didn't know how he was going to settle it."

It was curious that Glenn was using the past tense, as if Grady had already been hit.

There was still plenty of time to call the police and stop the murder from happening.

At approximately 9:30 P.M., Dennis went by Chris's house, again to hang out, but Chris was nowhere around. Instead, Dennis went to his girlfriend's, where he spent the night.

Glenn recalled that at eleven P.M., he and Teresa left Grady drunk and alone in the recliner, watching the video *Ruby.*

Apparently, it never occurred to them that Little Grady was also in danger. If he happened to crawl into the proceedings while Chris was doing the dirty work, it would be nothing for Chris to shoot a witness. In fact, he'd have to, so there was no eyewitness to the crime. Apparently, this never occurred to either the son or the mother.

Then again, Little Grady was Barbara's son, not Teresa's.

Shortly after eleven, the back door to the trailer opened. In the light spilling from inside, Chris's outfit could be seen clearly.

He wore a black leather jacket with a Raiders hat turned around backward. On his feet were black Nike Cavericis tennis shoes. His slim torso was encased in a black-and-white

"IOU" T-shirt. Blue jeans completed the uniform of alienation.

Having been to the house many times before to play chess with Glenn, Chris knew the layout. He sneaked along the corridor, passing the kitchen and stepping into the living room. By that time, Grady had seen him.

"What the fuck are you doing here?" Grady raged.

Chris muttered something.

"Get the fuck out of my house. Don't ever come around here again," Grady shouted and turned back to the TV.

Chris retreated to the kitchen hallway. He turned and aimed.

The first shot entered the back of Grady's head. By the time it lodged in his brain, his heart had stopped.

The next two shots appeared in a horizontal row next to the first.

When Glenn heard the shots, he ran out of Cathy's trailer. He saw a young man fleeing from the back door of the brown trailer. Glenn immediately recognized Chris Wyant.

Son of a bitch, he'd done it!

Part Three

The Trial

Thirteen

After Glenn finished giving his statement, the detectives rode back out to Gibsonton, and found Teresa Stiles at home.

"Mrs. Stiles, we've been talking to Glenn and we need you to come downtown with us and straighten out some facts," Willette told her.

"It's not necessary for you to accompany us," Fig said formally, "but it sure would help."

Teresa agreed. On the way downtown to the office, Willette continued:

"Teresa, Glenn talked and gave us a version of what happened out there. He's made statements to us that aren't in your favor or anybody's favor, and we need you to straighten them out. I want you to make sure that you understand your Constitutional rights."

Willette read to her the standard Miranda Warning. After that, they held off interviewing her until they got to headquarters. Teresa, meanwhile, was getting visibly more upset.

When they arrived, Teresa was taken to an interrogation room at Buchman Plaza. The time was 10:30 P.M.

"Glenn told us the whole thing, Mrs. Stiles, about the plot to murder your husband. Do you wish to make a statement?" Willette asked.

Like her son, she, too, signed a "Consent to Interview" form. The time was 10:30 P.M., November 30.

"All right, tell us what happened," said Fig.

"My husband was very abusive. Very abusive, to both me and my kids. He'd beat us. When he drank alcohol, he was just a monster. Uncontrollable. He would beat me and the children with those claws of his. At times, he'd even head butt me, making me bleed.

"Several months ago, I was talking to my daughter Cathy about killing my husband. It didn't matter to me if he was shot or stabbed or whatever, just as long as he was killed. Glenn, he eventually became aware of what I wanted. Glenn said he knew someone who could do the job.

"But I just want to say, right here and now, that I want to accept all blame for the killing. I want my family out of it. See, I gave Glenn fifteen hundred dollars cash as a payment to Chris in order to murder my husband."

"Did you ever meet Chris?"

"Yes, but we never discussed the killing I wanted him to do. See, the arrangement was made between me and Glenn. Then Glenn got with Chris Wyant, paid the money, and made the arrangements for the killing. Then about two weeks ago, I told my daughter Cathy that the contract was off and no killing was going to happen."

Now, Teresa was swearing that the hit had been taken off and Grady was supposed to live.

"Why is it that you left the trailer just a few minutes before Chris came in and did what he'd been hired to do?"

"I did not go outside because I knew Chris was coming. I went outside because I wanted to check on my grandchild who was sick," she stated adamantly.

"Where'd you get the money to hire Chris in the first place?"

"By my own means," she answered defensively. "I'm a showgirl. I have access to my own finances."

"Why didn't you just divorce him?"

"I couldn't get a divorce from Grady because he threatened to kill me if I did."

"Even though you were divorced from him on a previous occasion?"

"Yes, he's much worse now than he's ever been."

"Was," Willette corrected.

* * *

Christopher Wyant was taken into custody at 1:15 A.M. on December 1. Alter being advised of his rights, he refused to give a statement and requested an attorney.

Willette closed the trunk of the LTD. In his hands, he held the dirty rubber boots he always kept in the car's trunk. Quickly, he changed into them, then looked around.

The place was thick with lush, overhanging foliage, wild bushes, weeds, and all kinds of green plants sprouting from the forest floor.

"This way," Cowell said, and led the way down a rutted, dirt road that the fall rains had turned into a sea of dark brown mud.

Seen from the air, the forest was actually large groves of trees, bushes, and plants, broken at jagged intervals by clearings and a meandering body of water that the locals called Bullfrog Creek. Cutting right through the heart of this waterland was a raised two-lane blacktop.

Detectives Michael Willette, Fig Figueredo, and their supervisor, Cpl. Pops Baker, followed Cowell down the road, and into the dense undergrowth. As they went, the sounds of civilization faded, replaced by the incessant croaking of frogs, the occasional birdcall, and the constant hum of insects.

Time after time, Willette had to push back
a branch that whisked toward his face. He
wondered how Cowell had found this place.

No way they could find what they were
looking for without Cowell's help, Willette
thought. But he knew the kid wasn't being
altruistic.

"Look, Dennis, we have a signed confession from Glenn. He says you bought the
gun. He says you gave it to Chris, who did
the job. Now if you don't want to get in any
more trouble than you already are, why don't
you help us?" Willette had advised him.

They'd been walking for a while, Willette
not too sure of the time, when Cowell pointed.

"Over here. Near the palmetto."

Close to a palmetto tree, Cowell pointed
at the ground.

"Over there."

A water-filled footprint in the mud marked
the spot. Taking care not to disturb the footprint, which would later be measured and
photographed for evidence, Willette watched
Cowell bend down and dig down a few inches.
His hand disappeared in the lush earth, coming up with a plastic bag.

Already wearing his rubber gloves, Willette
took the bag and brushed it free of mud
and dirt. Encased in the clear plastic, was an
old, rusty-looking, .32-caliber Colt Automatic. He removed it from the bag, and checked
the clip. The gun was still loaded.

Ballistics should bear out that the automatic was the murder weapon. And they had the confessions. They now had as tight a case as possible against Teresa Stiles, Glenn Newman, and Chris Wyant.

As for his active participation in the case, Willette was finished. He had found the three elements needed to obtain a conviction— motive, means, and opportunity. It was first degree, cold-blooded, premeditated murder. Still, Willette had been around long enough to know there's no such thing as an open and shut case.

On November 30, 1992, Mary Teresa Stiles was charged with first degree murder. A second charge of conspiracy to commit first degree murder was later added.

Her son Harry Glenn Newman, Jr., was indicted on the same charges.

Like his alleged coconspirators, Wyant, too, was indicted for murder one and conspiracy to commit murder one. Because of the cold-blooded nature of the crimes, all were held without bond.

Under Florida law, it is up to the state to decide whether or not to recommend the death penalty in a capital case. Upon conviction, it is then up to the jury to decide whether to go along with the prosecutor's recommendation.

The homicide committee of the state attorney's office in Hillsborough County, composed of upper echelon personnel from that office, met to consider their decision. Showing compassion, they decided not to seek the death penalty against any of the defendants.

The case was then assigned to Judge Barbara Fleischer. Around the courthouse, she had a reputation of being sympathetic to the plight of abused women.

Since the part each defendant played in the alleged conspiracy was unique, and since at any point, one could conceivably testify against the other if a deal was made, each acquired separate counsel, though they would all be tried at the same time.

At first, Teresa Stiles engaged the services of Herbert Sterling, a respected criminal attorney. But they soon had a falling-out and Teresa engaged the services of Peter Catania.

A young attorney in his mid-thirties, Catania is easily the best-dressed lawyer in the Tampa courthouse. He agreed to represent Glenn Newman pro bono. But according to Sterling, "Mr. Catania's contract included representation of the literary rights of the wife and son," which was a direct violation of the Florida canon of ethics for attorneys. According to those rules, an attorney who represents criminal defendants may not take any money regarding literary rights. That part of Catania's contract with Teresa and Glenn was later dissolved.

Realizing the case was bigger and more complicated than he'd thought, Catania brought in Arnold D. Levine to represent Teresa.

Arnie, as he's known to friends, colleagues, and media alike, is a legendary figure in Tampa's legal circles. His multimillion-dollar practice specializes in high-profile criminal and civil cases, which he frequently wins.

Tall, broad-shouldered and silver-haired, the Harvard-educated, sixtyish Levine cuts a dashing figure in the courthouse. Always good for a sound bite, his Bostonian-inflected stentorian tones penetrate to the most remote sections of the courtroom.

By the time Teresa Stiles retained his services, Levine's reputation as a controversial lawyer, who zealously represents his clients, was well established.

As a gesture of his sympathy to Teresa Stiles's plight, and her apparent lack of funds, Arnie agreed to take the case pro bono. Of course, given the bizarre background, and the nature of the crime, the trial was bound to attract extensive media coverage.

That left Christopher Wyant. Since he was the alleged triggerman, there was no public outpouring of sympathy. He had done the deed, pure and simple. No attorney volunteered to take on his case, so Judge Fleischer assigned Brian J. Donerly.

A private practitioner, Donerly is rumpled,

bearded, and bespectacled, an attorney who looks like he'd be more at home in the safe confines of academia rather than the rough and tumble world of courthouse dueling in a criminal trial.

Considering her confession and the facts of the case, it was going to take a pretty unique defense to get Teresa Stiles acquitted, which is exactly what Arnie Levine intended. Arnie figured he had found a way.

Battered wife syndrome.

As a defense in a murder-for-hire, it had never been tried in Florida before. Essentially, Levine would have to prove that Teresa Stiles was so intimidated by her husband and so fearful of her life if she left him that murder-for-hire was her only way out. It was a defense that had been tried unsuccessfully in three previous cases in the United States. Still, Levine, who had a deserved reputation as a brilliant trial lawyer, felt that not only was the defense justified, they would win.

In support of that claim, Levine filed a brief that explained in detail to the court what battered wife syndrome is, and in so doing, the type of living conditions Teresa Stiles was forced to live under. Ultimately, though, it would be up to a jury to answer that question.

* * *

The first trial of all three defendants began and ended quickly in July 1993, when Det. Michael Willette inadvertently blurted out on the stand that Glenn Newman had failed a lie-detector test. Judge Fleischer glared at the homicide detective who sat like a deflated balloon in the witness-box.

It was an accidental response to prosecutor Ron Hanes's questions. As soon as he'd said it, Willette realized his mistake. Since polygraph results cannot be admitted as evidence in a court of law, Judge Fleischer was forced to rule a mistrial.

Judge Fleischer subsequently decided that the defendants would be tried separately. Teresa Stiles would be tried first. Her new trial was scheduled to begin November 1.

In the interim, Ron Hanes decided to file a motion with the state supreme court, asking them to overturn Judge Fleischer's ruling allowing battered wife syndrome in the case of a contract killing as a legitimate defense for homicide. Because the court needed time to review his petition, Teresa's trial was put on hold.

Fourteen

The trial of Christopher Wyant on the charges that he conspired to and then committed the murder in cold blood of Grady Stiles, Jr., began in courtroom number seven of the Hillsborough County Courthouse Annex on January 18, 1994, the type of hot, sunny winter's day that Tampa is famous for.

Maybe it was the weather, though probably it was just a lack of interest. After all, Wyant was just the hit man, not the brains of the plot. And his attorney was the court-appointed, rumpled Brian Donerly, not the charismatic Arnie Levine. Whatever it was, the ten long, plain, brown benches made of worn oak, in the spectator section of the cavernous, green-painted courtroom were practically deserted.

But Chris's mother, Janice Lee Wyant, was there, a worried expression on her pinched face. Her wardrobe for court was tight jeans and a low-cut, tight top that emphasized her youthful figure. Accompanying Janice was her six-year-old daughter Heather, Chris's sister.

Sitting front row left was Carole Brandon, a private investigator who carried her .38-caliber police special in a designer handbag. Brandon, who had done the investigative work on the case for Brian Donerly, looked for all the world like a central casting version of a Floridian female PI— pageboy blond, blue-eyed, with a dynamite figure elegantly encased in a designer suit.

I sat front row right, next to Mike Mahan, the intense beat reporter for the *Tampa-St. Pete Times*. With the exception of a few people who straggled in to kill time, we were the only regulars throughout the trial.

In front of us were two long tables facing each other from opposite sides of the courtroom. At the table on the left sat Christopher Wyant, a pale teenager wearing a "Miami" T-shirt and blue prison pants. His close-cropped hair came down to a widow's peak over his forehead. It was the first time I'd seen him in person, and I was surprised at how young he looked.

Next to him was his attorney, Brian Donerly. Gray-haired and bearded, he wore a rumpled blue suit, white shirt, and a cranberry-and-blue paisley tie. Strewn on the table were various boxes, files, and folders containing legal documents.

Sitting at the opposite table were Ron

Hanes, the intense prosecutor, dressed in a dark suit, shirt, and tie, and his assistant, Sandra Spoto, a lovely woman who favors Ann Taylor designer suits. Spread out on their table appeared to be an identical set of legal papers, plus some official-looking law books in mock leather bindings.

The jury, which had taken a mere few hours to pick, sat in the jury box behind Hanes and Spoto. Predominantly white, it consisted of seven women and five men, with one man and one woman as alternates.

The judge, Barbara Fleischer, sat high up on the bench in her regal black robes. A petite woman, she has short, dark hair in a severe cut that makes her look a lot like Leona Helmsley.

Below Fleischer were the court clerk, who would take down notes of all the proceedings, and another clerk who kept a record of all items entered into evidence. Dressed in official-looking green jackets, the bailiffs were scattered about the courtroom. As for witnesses, they are not allowed into the courtroom until they are called to the stand.

Hanes rose and walked to the lectern that faced the jury. He opened his notes, gazed down at them, looked up, and began his opening argument.

"On November twenty-ninth, 1992, there was a plan to murder Grady Stiles, Jr. On that night, a little bit after eleven P.M. on

Sunday, Christopher Wyant was standing outside the Stiles home. He's an important part of the plan.

"He has a thirty-two-caliber automatic pistol with a loaded clip and he's waiting for his signal. Grady Stiles, Jr.'s, wife leaves, goes outside. Harry Glenn Newman, Mr. Stiles's stepson, also goes outside," Hanes continued in clear, measured tones. The jury gazed at him in rapt attention.

"Chris Wyant takes out the gun, steps into the trailer as Grady Stiles sits there. He has no chance. No chance. But he sees his killer. He shouts at him, yells at Wyant. He's seen Wyant around there; he's a friend of his stepson's.

"At that point, Christopher Wyant takes the gun and *blasts* the first bullet into the brain of Grady Stiles and then fires again and again and again. Two bullets lodge in the man's brain, killing him.

"Christopher Wyant has held up his end of the bargain. It was a plan. The plan had been in the works for several weeks. How to accomplish it and where? Those decisions had to be made. But one thing is consistent throughout. Christopher Wyant chose to take part in it.

"Conspiracy is the case before you. Christopher Wyant shot Grady Stiles, Jr., in the back of the head. He is a born killer.

"You're going to hear about his premeditation," Hanes continued. "About his opportunity to reflect on what he's going to do. [The plot] was weeks in the planning.

"Grady Stiles, Jr., you will hear, was a carnival attraction. He was known as Lobster Boy in the carnival because he had no legs, and hands that never developed. That's the life he led. You will hear that in order to travel, he used a wheelchair. That was his means of transport. He had no chance when Christopher Wyant walked in with a loaded gun."

I couldn't help thinking of Jack Layne's entry into the house in Pittsburgh and the reception Grady had given him.

"Harry Glenn Newman, Jr., had approached Wyant weeks before. He told him that Grady Stiles, Jr., was abusing us. 'No problem, I'll do it,' [says Christopher Wyant].

"The first plan is to murder Grady Stiles outside the Showtown lounge in Gibsonton. The plan was for Teresa Stiles to wheel Grady Stiles out of the bar and Wyant would come up and shoot him and make it look like a robbery. They don't go forward as Grady Stiles only goes there in daylight.

"The second plan is to murder him in the home and make it look like a robbery and burglary. [Christopher Wyant] breaks in, takes his wallet, and the police run around and figure it out. That's the plan [they] go forward with.

"There's an opportunity to reflect on what he's about to do. Christopher Wyant as well as Teresa Stiles and Harry Glenn Newman had some major problems with their plan.

"Number one, within two weeks before the murder, a gentleman you'll hear from, Marco Eno, is living on the property in another trailer in a corner of their lot. He's been living there for a couple of weeks.

"The second problem is it's supposed to look like a robbery so the police don't concern themselves with family members. The key was to take the wallet. He couldn't find it. It was left in Mr. Stiles's pants. That leads them to Christopher Wyant's third problem, which is an attempt to involve others a half a block away.

"Richard Waller and Ann Butterworth lived in a trailer park a few seconds away. Wyant was trying to get Waller involved in the plan. He originally wanted him to pick him up at Showtown after the murder. Now, he wants him to give him an alibi, [to say] that Christopher Wyant was in his trailer all night.

"You'll also hear from Ann Butterworth, who'll tell you that Christopher Wyant tried to get Waller involved. The day of the murder, a few hours before, Harry Glenn Newman and Christopher Wyant come to her house. They're *giggling* about what is about to take place.

"Where does Christopher Wyant run when the murder takes place? Two trailers away from his mother's home to the Butterworth trailer. Waller and Butterworth will say that when he gets there, they see the gun. Chris hides it in Butterworth's trailer and they will tell it's not easy to testify against Christopher Wyant. He was their friend at one time.

"Christopher Wyant tells them at the door, 'I did it, I shot him in the head.' He held up his end of the bargain. Butterworth and Waller are supposed to be the alibi.

"The next day, Christopher Wyant involves Dennis Cowell when the cops are down there. Wyant goes back to the trailer and gets the gun out of the space where he'd hidden it. He gives it to Dennis Cowell. Cowell hides it in the bushes. While this is going on, the Hillsborough County Sheriff's Department focuses on the involvement of the Stiles household. That leads them to Christopher Wyant, Ann Butterworth, and Richard Waller, and to the gun recovered by the Sheriff's Office.

"A firearms expert will testify [that] the bullets found in the Stiles home, and the ones removed from Stiles's brain, all match.

"At the conclusion of the evidence, you will be convinced that Christopher Wyant conspired with [Teresa Stiles and Harry

Glenn Newman, Jr.] to carry out the murder of Grady Stiles, Jr., and you'll see the horrific results.

"At the conclusion, I'll ask you to find him guilty of what he planned. What he has done."

Hanes gathered up his notes and took a seat.

"Brian?"

Donerly looked up at Fleischer, then got up from his chair and started fidgeting around. He shuffled over to the lectern.

"All the evidence will come from that stand," Donerly said in a gravelly voice, pointing at the witness-box. "All Christopher Wyant asks of you is that you give that evidence your careful attention and your best judgment.

"The judge told you during jury selection not to form a fixed opinion [during the presentation of evidence]. Mr. Wyant asks you to keep an open mind.

"Mr. Hanes tells you about a plan while not a great one. You will hear a whole lot about the crime scene, about how Mr. Stiles was shot in the back of the head. There are two witnesses from two different directions who heard arguments. There's nothing in the state's [version] of the [murder] plan about arguments.

"In the state's view, Christopher Wyant is a hired killer. That's the first discordant note. I ask you to listen to the details. Richard Waller told nothing the first time police questioned him. The second time, he [says] he took medication, [but] remembers some things.

"Ann Butterworth has a detailed recollection. Listen to it carefully. See if there aren't the wrong number of shots and other discrepancies.

"You've been told a gun was recovered from a fourth individual, Dennis Cowell. I believe you'll find Mr. Cowell's name appears on the gun receipt that was bought a few days before. These are among the things I ask you to look for.

"When the trial is over, I'll have no hesitation in asking you to find Mr. Wyant not guilty of both charges."

Donerly fidgeted, and walked back, looking at his investigator Carole Brandon with a shy smile.

With the opening statements over, it was time for the state to begin their direct examination.

Hanes stood.

"The state calls Marco Eno."

The door to the courtroom opened and the bailiff led Eno inside. Eno had a black Fu Manchu beard, speckled with gray, grown to a sharp point on his chin. He wore jeans down over his hips, and a T-shirt. Evidently, the style of dress in Tampa's courtrooms leaned toward the casual.

Eno stood before the bench and took the oath. Then he climbed up and took his place in the witness-box, while Hanes positioned himself at the lectern, directly in front of the witness stand, but twenty feet back. Under the rules of evidence, attorneys cannot approach witnesses, unless they have something they want them to examine. Whatever points they want to make must be done with their voice; their physical presence can *not* be used to intimidate the witnesses.

"Whose property did you live on?" Hanes began behind the lectern.

"Grady Stiles's," Eno answered.

"How long did you know him?"

"I knew Grady a few years. I worked for him in the year of 1992."

"Did Mr. Stiles have a stepson?"

"Harry Glenn Newman."

"And what was Mr. Stiles's show business name?"

"The lobster man. Lobster Boy. That was his nickname."

"How many carnival shows did he run?"

"Grady and Teresa ran the human oddities show. Tyrill and Cathy ran the animal oddities show. Donna and Joe ran the gorilla show."

"How long were you on the road together?"

"April to the beginning of November. That's the season."

"You mentioned the gorilla show. What is that?" Hanes asked with curiosity.

"It's where a lady changes into a gorilla."

The jury didn't even crack a smile. They listened intensely, especially juror number two, who leaned forward in her seat.

"And how did Mr. Stiles get around?"

"In a wheelchair."

Hanes then introduced as evidence photographs of Teresa, Grady, and Glennie, and aerial shots of the neighborhood and the trailer where they lived. The idea was to put a face to the names, and give the jury an appreciation of their living conditions.

"Mr. Eno, would you tell us what you remember of the night Mr. Stiles was murdered?"

"A little after eleven, I heard some yelling. Grady kept yelling, 'Son of a bitch, get the fuck out,' a couple of times. Then things went quiet. A little while later I heard four shots. I thought it was someplace else in the neighborhood. I went outside and saw someone leave. I got back in the trailer, got my shoes on, and went to the other trailer where the rest of the family was. I asked them if they heard the shots. They said yes, they heard the shots. We went in the house and found Grady's body."

"How long from the time you heard the shots to the time you came out?"

"I opened the door to see if anyone was in the backyard. It was a couple of minutes before I came out."

"And you saw someone leaving the Stiles trailer?"

"Yes."

"Describe that person to us."

"He was wearing a black jacket, he was about five seven with brown hair."

"What about the family members?"

"They were already outside the trailer. Teresa, Grady, Tyrill, and Cathy had the door open. 'Oh no, it might be Grady,' Teresa said."

"What did you find when you went in the house?"

"Grady was dead. I found the bullet holes in the back of the head."

"Then what did you do?"

"I ran out the front door and ran into the [neighboring] house on the right. I told 'em, 'Call 911, somebody's been shot.' "

"Did any family members go into the home?"

"They came in after me. I was the first one in."

Hanes strode to the prosecution table and reached out his hand. Spoto handed him a photo. It was the murder-scene photograph of Grady slumped in his armchair, the bullet holes a graphic red in the back of his head.

He showed the shot to Eno, who identified it as Grady, and then Hanes went to the jury box. He passed slowly in front of the jurors, giving each of them a long, hard look at Grady Stiles's death. The jurors tried to suppress their emotions but juror number seven, an elderly man in a suit jacket, grimaced.

Hanes gave the shot to the court clerk, who marked it into evidence. The same procedure would be followed for all subsequent photographs and diagrams presented during the trial.

A moment later Hanes was back at the lectern.

"Mr. Eno, when was the next time you saw the man who left the trailer that night?"

"The next time I saw him was on the news. After he was arrested. I recognized him from the way his hair is done in front. I'd seen him before, when he was with Glenn."

"Mr. Eno, do you see that man in the courtroom now?"

Marco Eno looked over at Chris Wyant.

"He's sitting there wearing a 'Miami' T-shirt with his attorney."

Chris Wyant didn't move. He looked bored. His left hand held his mouth in a pensive pose.

"I have nothing further." Hanes sat down.

Donerly stood. Holding his notepad under his right arm, he ambled over to the lectern.

"Didn't Teresa once ask you to kill Grady?" Donerly asked.

"Up in the fair season in Massachusetts."

"What was your response when she asked you to kill Mr. Stiles?"

"Shock. She said they were tired of being hurt themselves."

"No further questions."

What was Donerly up to? Standard defense practice is to try to cast doubt on an eyewitness's identification of the accused.

"Mr. Eno, you're excused," said Judge Fleischer. Eno walked quickly out of the courtroom.

There followed two witnesses whose purpose it was to set the scene: the paramedic who responded to the 911 call; and the deputy who also arrived to answer the call.

Later, Sgt. Charles Phillips of the Hillsborough County Sheriff's Department, one of the supervisors, testified, "After the victim was removed from the scene, the victim's [step]son, Mr. Newman, made jokes. He asked me to order Danishes for the family to eat."

Sharon Sullivan, the crime-scene technician on the scene, testified next. After explaining the nature of her job— sketching the crime scene, taking relevant measurements and photographing it— she identified photographs that Hanes put in evidence that she had taken at the scene. They included an open carton of Pall Mall cigarettes with bloodstains splattered across the logo; a hole in the ceiling of the trailer where she removed one of the bullets; and a picture of a bullet recovered from the trailer's north bedroom. The jury was then shown a detailed floor map of the trailer that showed the location of the rooms, and where the body was lying when the police arrived.

Detective Laurie Eagan, a crime-scene detective, testified that on November 30, the day after the homicide, she went to the medical examiner's office and viewed the postmortem. She took photographs of Grady on the autopsy table and collected two bullets that had penetrated his brain, samples of scalp hair, and his underwear.

Another crime-scene technician testified that no prints had been recovered at the scene, that several hundred dollars were recovered in Grady's wallet, and that Grady was holding a cigarette in his claw.

Throughout the testimony of the crime-scene technicians, Donerly had very few questions on cross. Apparently, he was not going to dispute their findings.

"The state calls Richard Waller," Hanes intoned.

The bailiff led in Richard Waller, a tall, sad-looking young man with slicked-back black hair. He wore black jeans and a blue-patterned sports shirt.

"Mr. Waller, where do you live?" Hanes began.

"I live in a trailer park with Ann Butterworth."

"How far are you from the Stiles trailer?"

"We're two hundred feet away from Grady's home."

"Do you know Christopher Wyant?"

"Yes."

"What's he wearing [now]?"

"I reckon a Miami Hurricanes T-shirt."

"How'd you meet Christopher Wyant?"

"I met Chris through Ann. Chris used to go over and hang out two to three times a week. We considered him a friend."

"Did there come a time when you had discussions about killing someone?"

"We had three or four discussions about a murder."

"When was the first?"

"About four months prior to Grady being killed, maybe a little less."

"What was discussed?"

"He just said a friend of his wanted a job done, someone killed. Me and Ann didn't pay any attention to it. He has a friend who wants something done to his father."

"Did there come a time when he got more specific?"

"He came over and started talking about a bar, the Showtown bar. He wanted to do it up there. His wife would bring him out. He'd act like he was fishing at the bridge. Chris'd run up and shoot the man and I'd drive him away. I'd act as the getaway driver."

"What did you think of all of that?"

"Just a bunch of talk was what I thought. I was really shocked when it happened. When Chris discussed the stuff, it was a big joke."

Then Chris asked him to get involved.

"I said, 'Sure, why not?' I figured it was bullshit. More or less a topic of discussion."

"Did Christopher Wyant give any idea of the family's involvement in the murder plot?"

"Chris indicated it was a plan discussed with family members three weeks before."

"What happened to the plan to kill Mr. Stiles at Showtown?"

"The next thing we heard was that Grady only went there in the daytime. Chris said, 'Everything's off now, he only goes up there during the day, never at night.' He didn't have another plan."

"How was he supposed to be paid for the job?"

"He mentioned something about getting paid from a life-insurance policy."

"Did there come a time where there were further discussions about murdering Grady Stiles?"

"There was another discussion. Chris told me about some plans but said he was talking to the family members about it."

"When did Christopher Wyant talk to you next about these plans?"

"A week before the murder," Waller answered. "The newest plan was to get Little Grady out of the house and all the family members out. Chris goes in and makes it look like a robbery."

"Did you see him the day of the murder?"

"The day of the murder, he came over between four and six. The second time he came over with Glenn. He [Chris] was going to tell his mother he was spending the night at the Stileses'. He'd go in, shoot Mr. Stiles, come back to my place, and I'm supposed to give him an alibi."

"How were Mr. Wyant and Mr. Newman acting?"

"They were laughing. Talking about doing it that night. Chris said he'd do it and Glenn agreed. I agreed to give him an alibi."

Waller agreed because he didn't think Chris was serious.

"No one believed they'd do it the way things were."

"Did you have some sort of physical problem that night?"

"I had fluid on the knee and went to the hospital emergency room. I came back after that."

Waller had taken some medication for the pain in his knee. It made him groggy and he fell asleep. Then, late in the evening, "There was a knock on the living-room window of my trailer. Me and Ann were sleeping. It woke us up. I went out to see who it was."

"Who was it?"

"It was Chris. Chris was there."

"What did he say?"

" 'I dunnit. I shot the man.' "

"What was he wearing?"

"A black jacket and a Raiders cap."

"How was he acting?"

"He was breathing heavy. 'I shot the man,' he said."

"What was your response?"

"I didn't say anything. I was drugged. I was shocked at what went down."

But he did let Wyant in.

"What time was it then?"

Waller wasn't positive, because the kids had unplugged his VCR, but he figured it was between midnight and one A.M.

"After Chris came back from the bedroom, he put the gun in a plastic bag in his jacket.

I told him to put the gun away and Chris hid it. He went into the back bedroom."

After that, Waller, Butterworth, and Wyant went to sleep. The next morning, Wyant took a shower, and borrowed a pair of Waller's pants. Chris then called his mother.

"Chris's mom came over to take him home. He went with his mother."

"Did you have occasion to see Christopher Wyant later in the day?"

Waller was doing some chores out back later in the day when, "I saw Chris and Dennis Cowell coming from Chris's trailer with garbage bags. They went into my trailer. Chris left the pants in the trailer. This was about noon. After they left, Ann came over and talked to me."

"Why didn't you call the police and tell them what had happened?"

"I didn't want to get involved," Waller answered in a frustrated tone. "I was trying to protect my family. I later told the cops what was going on. The first time I gave Chris his alibi, but the second time I told the truth."

At the lectern, Hanes studied his yellow legal notepad. With a ballpoint pen, he checked off questions, then looked up.

"Did Chris say anything about what he did after shooting Mr. Stiles?"

"He said after he shot Grady, he searched for his wallet and couldn't find it. Someone [in the trailer] called him a name. He went up to Grady and fired point-blank."

Now there was a new wrinkle. Wyant claimed someone was in the trailer with him at the time of the murder.

"When you saw Glenn and Chris earlier in the day, how did they act?"

"Glenn and Chris appeared to be stoned and said they were during the second conversation. Chris, he always seemed hyper."

Hanes made one last check mark.

"No further questions."

As Hanes sat, Donerly stood and ambled over to the lectern. In the early part of his questioning of Waller, Donerly tried to discredit his testimony by implying that he was a liar who changed his story every time the cops questioned him.

"Chris used to date Ann at some point in the past?" Donerly asked.

"Yes, sir," Waller responded.

"Did Chris and Glenn do any drugs when they were at your place?"

"They took a few hits [of marijuana]," said Waller.

"How was Chris acting?"

"Chris was really wired, live and active."

"No further questions."

Waller stepped down. Donerly sat. Spoto stood.

"Call Ann Butterworth."

Ann Butterworth wore a pink blouse underneath a cream-colored white suit that billowed out from her stomach that showed her to be very much pregnant. Waller held open the low wooden divider, separating the public section from the trial area, for his wife, who handed him her purse for safekeeping. Without missing a step, she strode to the stand.

Ann Butterworth's face was wan and washed-out. Lifeless black hair fell over pale white skin.

"Ms. Butterworth," began Sandra Spoto, who was doing the direct examination, "could you describe your trailer for us?"

"There are two bedrooms, and one bath," she said.

"Back in November of 1992, were you pregnant?"

"I was three-and-a-half to four months pregnant."

"And how long were you going out with Richard Waller?"

"I been with Dick since October of 1992."

"And Chris?"

"I knew Chris since late June, early July."

"And he visited your trailer?"

"On a regular basis."

"Did there come a time when he spoke about murdering someone?"

"I heard Chris talk about the killing, the plan, three to four times."

"When?"

"I heard him talk about it the first time three weeks before Grady was killed in the trailer. He said he knew someone who wanted someone killed. I thought it was BS, to make conversation.

"Three to four days later, we had the second conversation in the trailer. The gist of the conversation was formulating different plans. He mentioned one way was at the bar, at Showtown. Chris planned on laying the blame on a black person for killing Grady at Showtown."

"Did you talk any further about the murder plans?"

"The third conversation. That one included Richard's assisting, near the railroad tracks off Symmes Road. Richard's part was to sit there with the car [and be the getaway driver]."

"What did Richard think of all that?"

"Richard's reaction was he didn't think nothing would happen."

"Was Chris going to be paid for this murder?"

"Chris said he was going to ask for fifteen hundred to twenty-five hundred before he did it. I got no idea how much after."

"Did Christopher Wyant and Glenn Newman come over to your house together the day of the murder?"

"The first conversation was early in the afternoon. Richard was at work on the fish bar. The second conversation was between six-thirty and seven P.M. He came by with Glenn Newman. I didn't know who he was at the time. He was this short and chubby guy. They called him Glenn. The gist of the conversation was small talk. Then Glenn left. I had come to figure for myself he was the boy who wanted it done. Chris then identified Glenn as 'the client.' "

"How did you react to that?"

"I was in shock. Who'd want to have something done like that?"

"How would you describe Chris?"

"Cool and calm. He knows what he's doing. He's got a head on his shoulders. When he gets excited, he's hyperactive. In between when he was calm and hyperactive was when he was with Glenn."

"So you saw Chris a second time that day, when?"

"Between six to eight. I put the kids to bed. Two of three live with me, and Chris wanted to see Dick privately. They were setting up the alibi. Chris had his beeper with him. The idea was he would meet this girl at our trailer, but tell his mom he was sleeping over at Grady's."

"Did you know what Chris was planning?"

"I didn't realize they were trying to make an alibi. Chris said, 'They just want the pain to stop.' "

"What time did you next see Chris?"

"He came to the trailer late."

She then described the same story as Waller, how they were awakened and they opened the door to find Chris standing there. According to Butterworth the following conversation ensued between her, Richard, and Chris:

"It's done," said Chris, really high-strung.

"What are you talking about?" Ann asked.

"He's dead. I killed him."

"You did what?"

"I killed him," Chris repeated.

"Richard couldn't believe it actually happened," Butterworth continued. "Richard said, 'Chris, go to bed and don't get up till morning.' "

"Did Christopher Wyant describe what he had done?"

"He said he shot him once. His head slumped over and he bent down. They started calling him a 'pussy.' So Chris shot him one more time from behind the ear."

Again, Butterworth had thrown the prosecution a curve. She had mentioned nothing before about someone else being in the room while he shot Grady.

"He said the man he shot had on underwear. He was supposed to have his pants on, a wristwatch, and be in his wheelchair."

Chris spent the rest of the night with Waller and Butterworth. When he came back with Dennis Cowell the next day he asked:

"Could I get it?"

"Get what?" Butterworth asked back.

"The gun."

"Where is it?"

"It's in the furnace."

The trailer had a gas-powered furnace in the rear of the trailer.

"I showed them to where the furnace was," Butterworth continued. "Chris opened it and took the gun out— it was in a plastic bag— and handed it to Dennis. Dennis hid it in his waistband, under a sweater.

"That night the cops searched the trailer and found Chris's black leather jacket."

On cross, Donerly had few questions. What was the point? Butterworth had already done his job for him. She had suddenly introduced the possibility that someone else was in the trailer at the time Grady was killed, egging Chris on. And both Butterworth and Waller mentioned the complicity of Dennis Cowell.

In return for his assistance in solving the case, Cowell had already cut a deal that gave him probation. Still, why wasn't Cowell testifying?

"They know Cowell's a powder keg," Donerly told me when court had recessed for the day. "He'd be a three-hour cross and give me an opportunity to establish a different theory of what happened. That's why they're not putting him on."

Fifteen

Day two of the trial began with testimony from Sally Allen, the person who sold Dennis Cowell the murder weapon. Spoto established that Cowell bought the murder weapon instead of Wyant because Cowell, eighteen, was old enough in the State of Florida to buy a firearm, while Chris was underage at the time.

Detective James Iverson testified that he was the one who went to the Butterworth/Waller trailer and recovered Chris Wyant's jacket.

Dr. Robert Pfalzgraf testified next.

Under Hanes's patient questioning, Pfalzgraf established his credentials as a forensic pathologist, and then testified to his involvement in the case.

"I was called to the scene on November twenty-ninth. I examined the body, which was sitting in a chair in the living room with his head slumped over and gunshot wounds to the back of the head. I had the crime-scene technicians take photographs at the scene. I had Grady Stiles's body removed to my office, where I did the autopsy."

"What did you find?" Hanes asked.

"There were three gunshot wounds to the head. I X-rayed the body. There were two bullets in the head. The autopsy was carried out to recover the bullets. One bullet went through the brain stem and struck the base of the skull. Either shot was fatal. [The third bullet] went in and chipped off the skull and exited."

After Hanes was through with Pfalzgraf, Donerly declined to cross-examine.

Detective Mike Willette was next on the stand.

"What did you do when you got to the scene?" Hanes asked.

"I made sure that the perimeter of the house was secured with crime-scene tape, to preserve the integrity of the crime scene. Then I looked for forced entry to try and develop a motive," Willette testified.

Willette discovered that none of the doors or windows had been forced. Then he found Grady's wallet in his pants and it contained a large amount of currency.

"That seemed unusual. I still didn't have a motive. It was after my second meeting with Glenn that I developed the idea of him as a suspect."

He related Glenn's confession, and how it led him to Chris Wyant.

"At one A.M. on December first, Christopher Wyant was arrested for the murder of Grady Stiles," Willette said. Afterward, "Accompanied by Dennis Cowell, we went down U.S. 3012 to a creek and Dennis Cowell led us back into the woods, about eight to ten miles from the [crime] scene. It was a wooded area. We recovered a plastic bag. Inside was a handgun. It was loaded with a clip, a thirty-two caliber Colt."

"What did you do with it?"

"We photographed the bag and sealed it in a [evidence] box. No prints were found on the gun."

Hanes went over and picked up the diagram of the house, which had been leaning against the clerk's desk.

"From your investigation, where would you say the man who fired the shot was positioned in the trailer?"

Willette pointed on the diagram.

"The shooter was eight to ten feet behind the victim, possibly in the hallway, right behind the table in the kitchen area."

Hanes put the diagram down. "No further questions."

Donerly's turn.

"Detective Willette, what was Dennis Cowell arrested for?"

"Dennis Cowell was arrested for conspiracy to commit first-degree murder and murder one. He was later charged with accessory after the fact."

Through his patient questioning of Willette, Donerly tried to plant the thought in the jury's mind that it was the mysterious Mr. Cowell who might have committed the crime. In light of Cowell's negotiated plea of guilty to the charge of accessory after the fact, and a state recommendation of probation in return for his cooperation of "truthful testimony," it was a practical defense strategy.

Next up was Joseph Michael Hall, a firearms expert.

"I test-fired the Colt thirty-two," he testified in answer to Hanes's question.

"What did you find?"

"That it required seven-and-a-quarter pounds of trigger pull [pressure] to fire it. And the gun was rusty."

"How does the gun fire?"

"You have to depress the trigger every time to fire. The bullet passes through the muzzle and a brass cartridge [casing] is ejected."

Hall also testified that the test-fired bullets matched the ones taken from the victim.

"No further questions."

Again, Donerly had little cross.

"The prosecution rests," Hanes said.

"Mr. Donerly, is the defense ready?" Judge Fleischer asked.

"Yes, Your Honor. The defense calls John Palmer."

Palmer, forty years old, took the stand. Donerly sauntered over to the lectern, notes tucked firmly under his arm.

"Mr. Palmer," Donerly began, "where do you live?"

"I live across the street from Grady."

"Grady Stiles?"

"Yes."

"Did you hear anything unusual that night coming from the Stiles residence?"

"I heard gunshots, and an argument between two people."

"How long did the argument last?"

"Ten to fifteen minutes before Grady Stiles said 'Come back here, you motherfucker.' Three to four seconds later, there was a gunshot."

He stated that he didn't know Grady that well and that he ". . . didn't see anything else."

After some cursory questions from the prosecution, he was excused.

"The defense calls Janice Lee Wyant."

For the second day of testimony, Chris's mother wore black stretch pants and a tight pink-and-white sweater. After being sworn in, she took the stand.

During previous testimony, Chris had occasionally looked at the witnesses. But with his mother, he couldn't meet her gaze and stared straight ahead into space.

"I saw Dennis Cowell bring Chris home

on the day of the murder," Janice Lee testified. "It was three to four P.M. I saw him with Dennis."

"What did Chris do after he got home?" Donerly asked.

"He stayed in the trailer until he asked if he could spend the night with [Little] Grady."

"No further questions."

Once again, Donerly had managed to raise the specter of Dennis Cowell's participation in the crime.

The prosecution had little on cross.

"Mr. Donerly, call your next witness."

"Yes, Your Honor. The defense calls Tyrill Berry."

Tyrill entered the courtroom and pushed through the divider. He wore a blue long-sleeved shirt and jeans.

"Mr. Berry, would you describe what you saw the night Mr. Stiles was murdered?"

"Well, my daughter, Misty, had had a bronchial asthma attack. Anyway, at ten-forty-five, I was [out front] and saw a light blue or silver pickup driving in front of [our] home."

The mysterious pickup made a U-turn and traveled south on Inglewood Drive and drove out of view. He never saw who was inside. Later on, he said, Teresa and then Glenn, came over to check on the well-being of his daughter.

He could add nothing further.

"Your Honor, the defense rests," and

Donerly gathered up his notes and sauntered back to the defense table.

"We'll take a lunch break. Be back at one-forty-five P.M. for closing arguments," said Judge Fleischer.

With the trial testimony over, the witnesses were allowed into the courtroom to hear closing arguments. Butterworth and Waller huddled in the back, trying to look unobtrusive.

Chris Wyant slouched at the defense table, arms folded, exhibiting the same sort of nonchalance he had throughout the trial. Maybe he was a sociopath who had no emotions and could kill a man in cold blood without feeling a thing. Or maybe he was just a scared kid trying to look like an adult.

In the second row on the right side, Janice Lee Wyant looked worried. If her son was convicted of first degree murder, he was going to jail for a minimum of twenty-five years.

At 2:03 P.M. on January 19, 1994, Ron Hanes began his closing argument.

" 'I did it.' "

" 'Did what?' "

" 'I shot him. I shot the man.' "

"A senseless, brutal but premeditated, absolutely premeditated murder."

Hanes looked over at the defense table.

"And he sits there now with his arms folded. Imagine Chris Wyant. That moment.

All talking and planning and bragging taken place. Harry Glenn Newman leaves the house. Put the gun down, walk away, run away. Instead, he fired and fired until he held up his end of the bargain.

"It's awful to imagine how easy that death came to him. Standing outside the door, just as he'd joked with Harry Glenn Newman, just as he coldly set forth to do it.

"There's three things you need for pre-meditation. Grady Stiles is dead. Chris Wyant caused his death. Chris Wyant killed Grady Stiles with premeditation. Oh, the plans changed. What does Wyant tell Butterworth and Waller? 'We're gonna make it look like a robbery.' When he comes back, he says he couldn't find the wallet to make it look like a robbery.

"Surprise! The victim's not wearing trousers."

Then Hanes summed up all the evidence, going back over the testimony of all concerned. Finally, he turned.

"The person holding the life of a man in his hand was that individual," and pointed directly at Chris Wyant who at that moment looked more like Macaulay Culkin than John Dillinger.

"I'm going to ask you to find him guilty, because of the choice he made that night, the conspiracy and murder of Grady Stiles, Jr."

Hanes's closing had taken thirty-five min-

utes. At 2:38 P.M. Brian Donerly ambled over
to the lectern and squarely faced the jury.
In a slow, measured cadence, he went back
over the evidence bit by bit and poked holes
in it.

Eno had not identified Chris for certain
until days after the murder. Both Waller and
Butterworth had testified that Chris told
them there was someone else in the trailer
at the moment he shot Grady.

"You know, in the hit man's handbook, it
says not to mention the crime before you do
it," Donerly said in a dry tone. "And Christopher Wyant certainly doesn't act like a hit
man.

"I want you to acquit Christopher Wyant by
means of reasonable doubt on both counts he
is charged with. I want you to find him not
guilty."

Donerly sat down at 3:02 P.M. Hanes rose
for his rebuttal. Chris listened to him, arms
still folded, but gradually, a different expression came across his face.

Fear.

The summations finished, Judge Barbara
Fleischer charged the jury. She explained
that while the defendant had been charged
with murder in the first degree, the jury had
the option of finding the following:

The defendant is guilty of Murder in the First Degree.

The defendant is guilty of Murder in the Second Degree with a firearm.

The defendant is guilty of Murder in the Second Degree.

The defendant is guilty of Manslaughter with a Firearm.

The defendant is not guilty.

She also explained the differences between first and second degree murder and manslaughter.

On the charge of conspiracy to commit Murder in the First Degree, the jury had only one option— guilty or not guilty.

"Emotions are not relevant, only the facts," Judge Fleischer concluded. Then as one, the jury stood, and filed out to the jury room directly behind the judge's bench. Bull the Bailiff closed the door. It was 3:43 P.M.

Wyant was taken out to a holding cell someplace in the interior of the building. The attorneys stayed seated.

After a while, Donerly said brightly, "Well, they've been out twenty minutes. Looks good for me."

Scattered but nervous laughter. Everyone knew he'd had a stinker of a case. Everyone expected a quick conviction.

By 6:30, the jury was still out.

By seven P.M., sandwiches and drinks were ordered in for the jury with a few extra for

the attorneys. On sighting the food and
drink, the jurors looked positively jovial.

"Hey, it's Bud time," one of the male jurors said, and the rest of them laughed.

Donerly, Hanes, and Spoto were all sitting
together at the prosecution table.

A few hours later, the angry sounds of the
jury's deliberations could be heard through
the closed door. They were screaming at
each other.

The sound of the bell was piercing.

"There's a verdict," the bailiff announced.

The judge left and came back quickly in
her robes. The defense and prosecution attorneys took their places. Christopher Wyant
was brought in and took a seat next to Donerly. Janice Lee Wyant held her daughter's
hand tightly. The judge nodded and the bailiff opened the back door. Wearing an ex-
pressionless face, Bull led the jurors out to
the jury box, where they took their seats.

"I understand you've reached a verdict?"

"Yes, we have, Your Honor." The jury
forewoman rose.

The clock on the wall said 10:38 P.M.

The court clerk read from a slip of paper
she had received from the bailiff: "We find
the defendant guilty of conspiracy to commit
murder in the first degree. We find the de-

fendant guilty of murder in the second degree with a firearm."

Chris Wyant never changed expression. Donerly leaned over to say a few things to him. The bailiffs converged on Wyant, and attached a pair of ankle shackles and handcuffs. His mother watched as he shuffled away like the two-bit con he'd become.

"Attorneys, please approach the bench," Judge Fleischer said with anger in her voice.

They conversed in hushed tones about sentencing dates. When they'd agreed on a date, the judge said, so all the court could hear, "Ron, be ready to give me arguments to go above the guidelines."

"Yes, Your Honor."

According to both Hanes and Donerly, the verdict was a compromise. One or more of the jurors had held out for the reduced charges. The others, tired of sitting in the jury room, acquiesced.

The judge was obviously angered by the verdict. Evidently, she had expected two convictions of first degree. That was why she asked Hanes for sentencing guidelines to go over the maximum. Regardless, Wyant could still be out of jail in ten to fifteen years.

Donerly had done his job and then some.

Everyone agreed that the trial of Teresa Stiles was the main event in the case.

Hanes had already thrown his potential knockout punch when he tried to get the state supreme court to disallow the battered wife defense in Teresa Stiles's case because it was a contract killing. But the court eventually ruled that Hanes, who had had plenty of time to file his motion, had filed it much too late, in fact, on the eve of Teresa's trial back in October. Therefore, they disallowed it. The trial would go forward, and Judge Fleischer's prior ruling allowing the defense would stand.

Score one for Arnie Levine.

The silver-haired lawyer won another when Teresa, who had been in jail over a year awaiting trial, was released on bond, but under house arrest. Fleischer also allowed Glenn to be released under the same conditions.

Score two for Arnie.

In order to prove battered wife syndrome, Arnie Levine needed to introduce expert witnesses to testify to Teresa Stiles's state of mind at the time she ordered the hit. Their job would be to testify that in her frazzled state of mind, she had no other choice.

The state, meanwhile, was struggling to come up with expert witnesses of their own to counter Arnie's. Problem was, the state's own expert, a psychiatrist who'd examined Teresa, sided with the defense.

Score three for Arnie.

By late May 1994, there still wasn't a trial date. The two sides were still dueling over other matters. Arnie knew that the longer things were drawn out, the longer Hanes had to find an expert that would side with the state.

Arnie Levine filed a motion with Judge Fleischer, demanding a speedy trial. Under the law, the court would have to act expeditiously to schedule Teresa's trial within ninety days. It looked like Arnie would win another one. But in his zeal to push the prosecution's hand, Arnie had neglected Judge Fleischer's calendar.

Because Fleischer's calendar was full, they assigned it to Judge M. William Graybill.

Among Tampa's legal community and around the Hillsborough County courthouse, the sixty-year-old Graybill's unusual courtroom manner and seemingly eccentric method of eliciting responses from the attorneys had given him the nickname of "The Riddler." But like his comic-book namesake, behind Graybill's eccentric facade, there was method to the madness.

Graybill made his attorneys work.

More important for the defense, Graybill was not certain that he would allow Levine the option of presenting his expert witnesses. He would rule on that during the trial.

Sixteen

Monday, July 11, 1994.

The Tampa-St. Petersburg metropolitan
area has well over a million inhabitants. Given
that fact, and the media's insatiable desire to
sensationalize, it came as no surprise that
print, TV, and radio reporters converged on
the Hillsborough County Courthouse for the
first day of Teresa Stiles's murder trial.

Parked in front of the courthouse were sat-
ellite trucks that allowed the reporters to edit
their tapes and, using microwave technology,
do live feeds back to the studios.

The state provided a media room in the
corridor next to Judge Graybill's courtroom.
It was filled with broadcast-quality videotape
recorders, one for each of the TV reporters
present. All the recorders were attached to a
central monitor, that in turn was plugged
into the pool camera in the courtroom.

A sign at the back of the media room
made it clear which stations were to operate
the pool camera and on what days.

Each reporter was free to record whatever sound bites they wanted from the pool coverage for the evening news. The two radio reporters present could also plug into the central feed.

With all that technology, there was not much to report on the first day of the trial, which was taken up by jury selection. The reporters spent most of the time doing crossword puzzles.

July 12.

It was a hot, steamy day. The courtroom was packed. The print reporters were in the front row, their electronic brethren back in the media room. All the rows in courtroom number six were filled.

Outside, the witnesses waited, including Cathy, Little Grady, and Glenn Newman, Sr., all in their wheelchairs.

And then there was Donna. She had been impossible to get a hold of because she was always on the road with Joe, who accompanied her that day to court.

From the rebellious teenager who had defied her father and paid a frightening price, she had grown into a mature woman. Her eyes and the dark circles underneath them reflected sadness and fatigue beyond her years. She paced nervously, constantly puffing on a cigarette.

With jury selection completed on the second day, the attorneys gave their opening statements. Judge Graybill watched from the bench, staring alternately at the attorney, and at the computer screen next to him on which were flashed Hanes's words as fast as the court reporter typed them.

Ron Hanes outlined the plot to kill Grady that Teresa had conceived and promised to show that Teresa was not in danger as she claimed, and that she was perfectly capable of walking away from her husband instead of killing him.

Impeccably dressed, Arnie Levine countered that she had no choice and was justified in what she did. He characterized her as a battered wife who had no choice but to pay a neighbor $1,500 to shoot her husband.

In stentorian tones, Arnie told the hushed courtroom, "She honestly believed she had no other alternative but to participate in this terrible act."

Arnie told the jury that even though Grady was deformed and confined to a wheelchair, he was an alcoholic brute who beat his wife and kids with his claws, head butted them and repeatedly threatened to kill them.

At the defense table, Teresa wept quietly.

Ron Hanes presented essentially the same case that he had at the Wyant trial.

There was Eno again, telling what he'd seen and heard, the police officers and lab technicians testifying about the results of their investigation, culminating with Teresa's and Glenn's confessions.

Levine was much more aggressive in his cross-examination of the prosecution witnesses, but it's hard to try a case when your client has confessed to the crime she's charged with. His only hope of winning was to get Judge Graybill to allow his experts to testify that Teresa was so afraid Grady would kill her, she had no choice but to arrange to have him killed.

"The state calls Christopher Wyant."

And there he was, the shooter himself, Chris Wyant. Dressed in blue prison garb, he already looked harder and heavier than the teenager who'd been sentenced six months before to twenty-seven years. Judge Fleischer had indeed gone over the sentencing guidelines.

He did not look boyish anymore, but more confident, more of the Chris Wyant that Ann Butterworth had described on the stand.

During his testimony, Chris related how he had been drawn into the murder plot by Glenn Newman and Teresa Stiles. He claimed to have spent the money for the hit that Glenn had given him, and then Teresa and Glenn wanted the job done. So he went through with it. He had been high when he stole into the house and killed Grady Stiles.

On cross-examination, Arnie poked holes in his credibility by establishing that he'd been a dope dealer and user.

Hanes stood, curtly announced, "The prosecution rests," and sat, leaning over and saying a few words to Sandra Spoto.

With Chris's testimony and the prosecution's case wrapped up, the reporters hustled to put their stories together. But it had been a boring day. Sound bites were scarce. There was a collective hope that the next day would be more interesting.

That night on TV, all the news reports of the trial were supplemented with a short home video supplied by Arnie Levine: Grady and Little Grady wrestling on the floor of the trailer. There was no sound on the tape.

July 14.

The defense was scheduled to open its case at nine A.M. but Judge Graybill was preoccupied with another matter.

Graybill seemed torn, wanting to give Teresa every break he could, but at the same time doubting the veracity of her defense. He didn't agree fully with Fleischer's ruling allowing the battered wife syndrome defense in this case, and granting the experts permission to testify. But this was his court. He wasn't bound by what Fleischer had done. Now, it was up to him to rule.

Arnie had given him legal briefs citing precedents, and throughout this early part of the trial, it was clear from Graybill's acidic tongue and Arnie's mock deferential tone that these two did not get along.

"The court has had time to read Judge Fleischer's order," he said in a pronounced Southern drawl. "I'm going to return to my office and read everything cited by Mr. Levine and whether I will allow or not allow further argument [on battered wife syndrome] to be seen."

He adjourned court until noon so he could have time to read the case law on the matter. Precisely at noon, he came back with his response. As with all rulings from the bench, the jury was not present to hear it, for fear it might prejudice them.

"Battered wife syndrome is not in and of itself a legal defense for murder and conspiracy to commit murder. Mrs. Stiles must first take the stand before evidence of battered spouse syndrome is offered.

"In order for Mrs. Stiles to claim self-defense, she must first take the stand and *admit* she arranged his killing and then if she wishes, to testify that she did so for fear of great bodily harm to herself. I will allow their [the experts'] testimony if Mrs. Stiles admits that she arranged to have her husband killed. Failing that, I will not allow that defense to be used, nor will she be entitled to self-defense instructions [to the jury]."

Arnie Levine didn't flinch, but Teresa looked down at the table, trying to maintain her composure. When she had been examined by Levine's experts, she claimed that she only had a hazy recollection of the plot, and no real specifics. Unless she regained her memory quickly, Arnie's carefully framed defense would wind up on the garbage heap.

"If she has no recollection," Graybill continued, "she will be prevented from testifying as to the relationship [with Grady] as it relates to murder in the first and second degree, manslaughter and conspiracy to commit first degree murder."

He reiterated, "Mr. Levine, I will give you until one-thirty P.M. [today] whether, in light of my ruling, you wish to file for a mistrial, which I will consider, and to confer with your client over this matter. This court is in recess," and Graybill stood, and began leaving.

"Your Honor—" Arnie shouted.

Graybill stopped.

"Mr. Levine, I said this court is in recess!"

"But Your Honor, I just have a question."

Graybill returned to the bench, at which point Arnie asked Graybill to clarify his ruling. He did.

"You can't have it both ways, Mr. Levine. Mrs. Stiles must first take the stand before evidence of battered spouse syndrome is offered. I will allow their [the experts'] testimony if Mrs. Stiles admits that she arranged to have her husband killed."

Her memory of the event would have to miraculously return. And quickly.

"But Your Honor— "

"Mr. Levine, I've made my ruling!"

That afternoon, Arnie requested time to prepare Teresa for her testimony. The judge agreed, and said that court would reconvene at 8:45 A.M. tomorrow.

A few minutes later, at 1:40 P.M., Arnie Levine came to the media room to give a statement to the reporters. The print reporters stayed on the fringes of the crowd, busily taking notes.

He announced that Teresa's memory of planning the crime had returned. "She says 'I did it, I remember doing it and did it to protect my family.' In this type of trauma, this is not unusual," Arnie told the reporters gravely.

Tomorrow, Teresa Stiles would take the

stand. Her memory would return just in time to admit to the world her crime.

Outside the courtroom, her family huddled around the accused murderess. Cathy tried to console her mother. Teresa grasped a tissue in her hands, nervously wringing it out.

"It just keeps getting worse," she muttered.

Seventeen

July 15.

Early the next morning, Graybill reversed himself.

"Battered wife syndrome is not in and of itself a defense for murder in the first degree and conspiracy to commit murder," Graybill began. "The defendant need not take the stand in this case. The defendant has the right to present whatever evidence is proper."

Graybill went on to say that the defense had to prove there was "imminent danger" to Teresa from Grady, that is, she felt in imminent danger of being killed by Lobster Boy, in order for him to allow the expert testimony.

"I will wait and see if there's competent testimony to support a self-defense instruction," he finished.

Levine and Graybill went at it again on the definition of imminent danger while Teresa looked puzzled. But Arnie seemed to get some satisfaction out of the judge's explanation. He was ready to present his case.

"The defense calls Harry Glenn Newman, Sr."

Midget Man was wheeled in and placed in front of the witness-box where he was sworn in. Brandishing his miniature cane, Glenn fidgeted in his seat.

"Mr. Newman, how long did you know Grady Stiles?" Arnie asked.

"I knew Grady for thirty years in the shows," Glenn responded in his gravelly voice.

In the back of the courtroom, Mark Zewalk, the pool cameraman, zoomed in on Glenn while photographer Peter Cosgrove clicked off a couple of frames.

Arnie asked Glenn to relate what occurred the night Grady threw Teresa out.

"Mary called me. She said, 'Come pick me up in the Pittsburgh Airport.' When I picked her up, there was black-and-blue on her face, her arms and legs. She pulled her dress up to show me."

At the defense table, Teresa sobbed into her handkerchief.

Glenn remembered the date as May 22, 1974. "She stayed with me and [eventually] we got married, after Grady divorced her."

"Where'd you live?"

"We moved to Upper Middletown, Pennsylvania."

"What did you do there?"

"I worked as a welder. Mary, she stayed at home."

But Teresa was heartbroken that her kids, Cathy and Donna, were living with Grady.

"Did she try to contact them?" Arnie wondered.

"She sent stuff to them," Glenn responded, "and Grady sent it back."

And then Glenn described their visit to see Grady and the kids in 1976.

"Mary's family lived in Vermont and she wanted to take the family there, so we went to Pittsburgh to pick them up at Grady's."

"During the course of the meeting, did Mr. Stiles pull out a weapon and put it to his wife's head?"

"Objection! Irrelevant!" said Spoto, darting to her feet. The judge asked the bailiff to remove the jury.

Once they were gone, Graybill nodded at Spoto.

"Her relationship with the victim is not relevant," she said.

The judge looked at her incredulously.

"What is the basis of your objection?" Graybill asked.

"We object on the basis of remoteness of time."

Judge Graybill leaned on the arm of his chair with one hand. He looked off into the distance, deep in thought. When he finally turned back around, Glenn looked up at him expectantly.

"Objection overruled," Graybill intoned.

The jury was brought back in and seated. Glenn picked up his testimony.

"Grady pulls out a gun and calls another guy in. Paul Fishbaugh."

"Who was Mr. Fishbaugh?" Arnie asked.

"He was The Fat Man who worked for Grady. He had a sawed-off shotgun in his hand. Grady told him— "

Spoto jumped to her feet.

"Objection. Hearsay."

"Sustained. Mr. Newman, you may testify to what you saw, not what was said," Graybill admonished him.

"Mr. Newman, what did you see?"

"Grady, he poked her in the face and legs and tried to get to her privates with his hand and the gun. I said, 'He'll kill us all.' Then he hit me a couple of times in the face."

"How long did the incident last?"

"Thirty minutes."

"What did you do?"

"I told Mary, 'If he's gonna shoot us, he's gonna shoot us,' so we walked outside and left."

"Did he call you after that?"

"We had an unlisted telephone number where we lived in Pennsylvania. But Grady got it and he called to harass us."

"Mr. Newman, do you drink?"

"When I first got married, I was drinking, but I stopped because she wanted me to."

"When was the next time you saw Grady Stiles?"

"In 1985, Grady came back into our lives. By that time, we were living in Okeechobee. The two girls and my son were with us."

Arnie asked for some clarification of their living arrangements since they had gotten married. Glenn explained that after Grady had divorced Teresa, he had taken her, her two daughters and his son back to Ohio.

"Then I fell from a roof and hurt my back bad. Mary left me in 1985 and divorced me in 1989. She took all the kids and went to Grady and remarried him. Mary didn't tell me she'd remarried."

"Objection." It was Hanes. "Once again, hearsay."

"Sustained." Graybill turned to Glenn and in a weary voice warned, "Mr. Newman, you may only testify to what you saw and what you said, not what someone else said."

"I have no further questions," Arnie said, and took his seat.

"Your Honor— " Glenn began angrily.

"That is all, Mr. Newman."

"I can't believe . . . ," Glenn muttered, brandishing his cane like a weapon.

"You will be assisted out of the courtroom!"

The bailiff pushed the brake on the wheelchair and wheeled Glenn through the wooden divider out of the courtroom.

"The defense calls Mary Teresa Stiles."

"How old are you?" Levine began.

"I'm fifty-six."

A collective rumble and shifting of seats in the courtroom. She looked ten years older. The pretty, svelte showgirl was gone. In her place was a haggard woman dressed in a dowdy yellow pantsuit.

"Would you describe your early life?"

"I lived with my mother and stepfather. My mother divorced [when I was] five or six. I lived with them until I was eighteen."

"What was it like living with them?"

"My stepfather was abusive."

Teresa looked down and sobbed and continued to cry intermittently throughout the direct examination.

"We had a . . . sexual relationship for two or three years."

"Did you do anything about it?"

"I complained to my mother."

"What happened?"

"She slapped me across the face several times. 'He wouldn't do anything like that,' she said."

When she was eighteen, she ran away to join the carnival.

"I was married before Grady for ten months and had a daughter named Debra."

Arnie wanted to know what that first marriage was like.

"I was physically abused by my first husband. He busted all my teeth, poured hot coffee on me. He walked me around with a switchblade in my back and knocked me down the stairs while I was still pregnant."

"And how did that marriage end?"

"He left me."

"When did you meet Grady?"

"In 1958. Working in the sideshow. My first husband was also a carny."

"What was Grady's act like?"

"He would sit on an elevated stage and do a lecture on his condition and family history. He'd started performing at seven, and eventually stopped in 1991. By that time, he owned shows and people worked for him."

"When were you married?"

"The latter part of 1958 to 1959. We lived in the DeSoto Trailer Park [in Gibsonton]."

Then Arnie asked her to describe her childbirth experiences.

"My first baby [with Grady] was born in 1960. It was a girl."

"What happened?"

"She lived twenty-six days and died from virus pneumonia."

"When was your second child born?"

"My second child [with Grady] was born in 1961."

"And that baby?"

"That child lived sixty-three days and died of virus pneumonia, too," Teresa sobbed.

Then Teresa described the rest of her children by Grady.

"Donna's thirty and Cathy is twenty-five. He would beat them," and she sobbed again.

It seemed that Donna, in particular, didn't like to eat.

"He'd make her sit there for hours and hours with the food in front of her and beat her if she didn't eat it."

Arnie asked her about Grady's drinking, which always seemed to trigger the abuse.

"He was drunk on the platform [one night] and couldn't sit up. I asked him to go in the house. He slapped me and told me to get the kids out of his sight.

"A few days later, he jumped off the couch [ran across the floor on his hands] and punched me in the stomach. He beat me up and tore my panty hose," she was sobbing continuously now, "and tried to tear an IUD out. I was all bloody and he told me to get out with twenty dollars."

Despite the sordid details and inconsistencies of fact, there was something up to that point that was strangely unmoving about her testimony. Maybe it was too much preparation or maybe it was just that her life had been so horrendous, it was hard to take it all in.

"[After our divorce], he wouldn't allow me

to have contact with the kids," Teresa continued.

"Was there some sort of incident after the divorce where Grady came to your house and harassed you?"

"In May 1975, we were living in a mobile home in Smock, Pennsylvania. Grady had a friend drive him to the house."

"What happened?"

"He jumped out of the car, ran on his hands up to the door and pounded on it. 'Open the door,' he screamed. He cussed me. He pulled the screen door open and broke his watch. When he left, I put a warrant out on him."

"When did you see Grady again?"

"August of 1976. My mother and stepfather lived in Vermont. I wanted to take the kids up there to visit. Grady says I gotta go in the house to take the kids. Glenn didn't want to go, but we went anyway."

Teresa proceeded to tell the court how Grady had lured her to his Pittsburgh apartment to pick up the kids, instead pulled a gun on her, and while The Fat Man entered and covered Glenn and the baby, Grady proceeded to beat her up while she begged to let them go.

It was a harrowing story. Everyone, including the usually skeptical reporters, was clearly moved. The judge decided it was a good time to take a recess.

* * *

When court reconvened, Teresa described the nomadic life of the carnival, and how Glenn, Jr., lost schooling because of their moving around.

"I divorced Glenn, [Sr.], in 1988. That was the same year I saw Grady." It was the first time she had seen Lobster Boy since 1978. They had been divorced fourteen years, and had not seen each other in ten.

By June or July of that year, Teresa was ill. She entered the hospital in Uniontown, Pennsylvania, and stayed there for two weeks. She sent the kids to live with ". . . his [Grady's] people [parents] in Pittsburgh." And she saw Grady again.

After she got out of the hospital, she took the family back with her to Okeechobee.

"Christmas of 1988, Grady came over and asked me to marry him. I said yes I would."

"Why?" Arnie asked.

"I was still in love with him," Teresa answered. "He appeared to be different. Not drinking. He even treated Glenn like his own. He'd visit in the wintertime, every weekend."

"What happened after you were married?"

"He started drinking again," Teresa said wearily, holding back the sobs. "A half-pint, then a pint went to a fifth. He told Glenn, 'You eat too much food. You're a pig. Get out of my house. You belong to another man.'

"He started calling me all kinds of filthy names."

Then one time, Teresa had a 104 degree fever and had to go to the hospital. Her husband, meanwhile, had gone out drinking. When she got home, a drunk Grady confronted her in their bedroom.

"He asked me where I been. I told him I was sick and went to the hospital. 'You're a liar,' he said, and punched me in the stomach with his fist. I begged him to stop. He slapped me. I went to the motel with the kids. I knew I was in for it that night."

"Did your children try to help you when your husband beat you?" Arnie asked.

"When the kids tried to help me, they were hit. When Cathy was pregnant, Grady knocked her out of her chair. She had an emergency C-section. The placenta had separated from the baby. Knocked her teeth loose."

Teresa recounted another time where "Grady threw Little Grady into a wall."

"Did you ever call the police?" Arnie questioned.

Teresa said they'd called the police sometime during 1990 or 1991. She told them Grady would get drunk and hit her. "They don't do anything. They say, 'This is a domestic problem. I'm sure if you talk it over, everything would be fine.'

"In 1991, we were running the [three shows]. He'd been on a drunk all day." Grady proceeded to hit her and call her a bitch. "Grady," she pleaded, "I can't take any more of this."

Grady slapped her in reply. She asked for a divorce.

"He said, 'I told you once, we're married, it's for life.' "

Arnie asked if there were any other abusive incidents she could recall.

"He grabbed a pillow and held it over my face," Teresa responded. "I couldn't breathe. I tried to push his arms off, but he was too strong. I was scared I was gonna die. He finally let go. I was always afraid of making too much noise. It would wake the boys up."

By that time, only Little Grady and Glenn were living with them.

Teresa testified that she had visible bruises— black-and-blue marks— and wore lots of shirts and pants to hide them. "I lied to the kids about them."

She recalled still another shocking incident of abuse when the two boys and Cathy were present.

"In Uniontown in 1990, Grady cussed me out, then grabbed me by the throat and choked me. Little Grady covered himself with a blanket. Cathy hit him with the phone on the arms and the head," until he stopped.

And still another.

"It was in Nassau County [at the Coliseum]. Grady had been drinking and comes in the trailer. 'Fix me a drink.' I told him, 'Grady, we don't have any more.' He wrapped his fingers in my hair and jerked my head so hard my head popped. 'I told you to fix me another drink. I told you.' He pushed his thumbs between my jawbone and pushed."

The pain was so intense, Teresa almost blacked out.

"Grady said, 'I told you, never, ever run out of whiskey.' I went out and bought some."

In December 1991, she went on, he hit her with a belt buckle. Grady had told her, " 'I'm talking to you, pay attention.' He jumps on the bed and he's telling me I was no good."

"What did you say?" Levine asked.

"Why don't you get it over with?"

Another time, he jumped down, scuttled across the floor, and head butted her in the mouth because she had asked him for a divorce.

"He'd say, 'You know, I killed once before and I'll get away with it again. One of these days [it'll be] you and your family.' "

Teresa rocked back and forth, back and forth, eyes brimming with tears, holding a tissue tightly in her hands.

And then, Arnie asked her about an incident of sexual abuse during the 1992 season. They were playing a date in Hebron, Connecticut.

"I had gone to the show office at night and I carried a large amount of cash to take in. I was gone overly long."

When she got back Grady confronted her. " 'Where you been all this time?'

"I told him, 'At the office.'

" 'You're lying to me. You were laying around with someone,' he said."

Grady hit her and knocked her on the bed of their trailer. " 'I'll fix it so you can't lay with anyone else,' he said."

From his pocket, Grady took out a blackjack. "He tried to shove it up my vagina. It left black-and-blue marks all over my legs. I had a hard time walking and sitting the next day."

If Levine were going to win her acquittal, he needed to prove that she was in imminent fear of her life. He addressed that point now. He asked her about making out her will in 1991.

"At several times, I was fearful for my life. I prepared a handwritten will. I was scared. He wouldn't let me get a divorce. I couldn't walk out and leave. I couldn't hide them," Teresa pleaded, referring to Cathy **and** Little Grady's deformity. "Little Grady said to me,

'What's gonna happen to me, Mom, if you leave me?' "

In December of 1991, Teresa said, she gave Cathy an envelope to hold for her. In it was her will.

Arnie asked what happened after they got off the road in 1992.

"Grady hit me in the back of the legs. It was like watching him do it but I couldn't feel it. He beat the wall and said, 'This is an example of what I can do to you.' "

During that same period of time, "I woke up and Grady was standing by the bed. He was drawing a butcher knife across my throat." Then on November 29, he tried to poke her eyes out with his claws. By that time, the threats and the beatings were more frequent.

"He'd say, 'One of these days when the time is right . . .' "

"Why didn't you leave him?"

"He'd find me," Teresa answered defensively, her voice rising. "I told Glenn something's got to be done. 'I can't take it much more.' I had saved up fifteen hundred dollars. I just told him, 'Something's got to be done.' Glenn knew I had the money. He said, 'I'll find someone to help you, Mom.' "

"Prior to that day, you'd never had a conversation with Christopher Wyant?"

"I never saw Chris Wyant in the trailer. I didn't know my husband would be killed that night. I didn't feel I had any other **alternatives.**"

"Why did you lie to Detective Willette the first time he questioned you?"

"I loved my husband. I still do. I couldn't stand the thought I could do something like this. It's better just to forget it."

"No further questions."

Crying, Teresa gripped the front of the witness-box. She continued to shake back and forth, back and forth.

"We'll recess and reconvene at two-forty-eight," Judge Graybill said.

Teresa Stiles left the stand. Outside, she was comforted by her loving family.

Precisely at 2:48 P.M. Ron Hanes moved in, determined to show that Grady Stiles wasn't dangerous the night he was murdered, that Teresa was not in imminent danger, and that she was not the helpless, destitute victim that Arnie was trying to make her out to be.

Through the early part of his questioning, Teresa admitted that on the day of the murder, they all ate dinner together, and that nothing happened. No threats, no blows.

Grady, she said, ate in the living room on the TV stand, while Little Grady and Glenn ate in the kitchen. Little Grady went to bed around nine, nine-thirty; he had school the next day. Glenn, meanwhile, stayed in his room.

"When I decided to go out back to see how Misty was doing, Glenn said, 'Mom, where you going? Let me get my shoes. You shouldn't be out there alone. I'll go with you.' "

After they had gone out back and been there a short while, Marco Eno had come over to tell them about the gunshots, and then he went into the trailer.

"Marco tried to stop me at the back door. It was the first time I was aware he was murdered. It came as a surprise to me."

Under further questioning, she admitted that she recalled telling Cathy that Chris Wyant stole $1,500 from her, and that Little Grady had known Chris since 1991.

For some reason, Hanes turned back to her early life in the carnival. "I did the blade box and worked the front bally stage. I was paid twenty-five dollars a week."

After her first husband Jerry Plummer beat her, she ". . . went to Connecticut to get away from [him]." After they split up for good, "I got an attorney to get a divorce."

"Did you have any other business duties during your marriage to Grady?"

"I booked shows, had to see to the employees. Grady made up the payroll and gave me the money to give to them."

"In 1992, the family made how much?"

She wasn't sure. "Grady put money aside for all expenses. During the last year on the road, we had three to four shows [to pay for]. We were paid usually on a Tuesday."

Hanes asked her about the family's vehicles, and she listed them— a Ford truck, Cathy's small trailer, her trailer, the trailer Eno had been living in that contained the gorilla show, Cathy's Ford Suburban, and her own van.

"You mentioned earlier that you employed an attorney to get a divorce after your first marriage."

"Yes."

"Did he help you with anything else?"

"I used an attorney to modify the child custody after my first marriage ended."

"You were successful in doing that?"

"Yes," Teresa answered.

"How old are your kids?"

Teresa stated their ages. At seventeen, Little Grady was the youngest.

"Then the only child not of his majority is Grady III?"

"Yes," Teresa admitted.

"Now you stated earlier that you saved fifteen hundred dollars. What for?"

"I saved money because my husband was unsure if he'd have money all the time."

"Now the vehicles you mentioned. Who owned them?"

"I considered all our property to be joint."

"But isn't it a fact that four of the vehicles are registered in your name?"

Reluctantly, Teresa agreed. She was totally dry-eyed, staring straight at Hanes with hate in her eyes. He got her even angrier when he forced her to admit that she hadn't provided for Little Grady in her will.

"Turning to the fifteen hundred dollars. How did Chris Wyant get that money?"

"I made it available. I put the money on the dryer weeks before anything happened."

In some way, she said, it had then disappeared.

"What did you tell your daughter had happened to the money?"

"I told Cathy that Chris Wyant stole the money that was left on the dryer."

Hanes wanted to know what Glenn, Jr., thought of the household situation. She paused to think before answering Hanes's question.

"He knew what would happen to us if we didn't do something. Every day got closer and closer."

"And what did Glenn say he'd do?"

" 'I'll see if I can talk to someone.' "

Under further aggressive questioning by Hanes, Teresa admitted that she ". . . had a conversation before placing the money on the dryer about two weeks before."

"Did you ask Chris Wyant to return the money when nothing happened?"

"I never told Chris Wyant personally to return the money."

"Were you in danger the night Grady was killed?"

"No," Teresa admitted. She was in no imminent danger, ". . . at that precise moment."

Hanes paused, looked down at his yellow pad, checked off a few questions and found a few he hadn't asked.

"Who paid the household bills?"

"I wrote the checks on the household."

"Did you have your own checking account?"

"Yes."

"Were you afraid you'd lose all your properties with a divorce?"

"No, sir."

"Couldn't you reunite with Mr. Newman if you divorced?"

"I wouldn't."

"Isn't it true that Mr. Stiles was free with the gifts he bought the kids?"

"Yes."

"Didn't both boys have TVs, VCRs, and video games?"

"Yes."

"But you don't have any memory of actually planning this man's death?"

"It's too horrifying to think I could do something like this to someone I love, to my husband. It's horrible."

Teresa began to cry. Hanes had no more questions.

Graybill adjourned until Monday morning.

Alone in the courtroom save for Sandra Spoto, Ron Hanes, in a mild voice and methodical manner, was getting his files together. In his own quiet way, he had laid a trap for Teresa and she had fallen into it.

"I didn't know if she had an attorney or not handle her first divorce, when I asked her that question on the stand," Hanes said later.

Hanes had managed to establish during his cross that a woman who was trying to portray herself as a helpless victim had enough emotional wherewithal to hire an attorney on numerous occasions to represent her legal interests; ostensibly, in Hanes's view, a far cry from the battered spouse she was trying to portray.

Eighteen

July 18.

Judge Graybill convened court promptly at nine A.M. He had done a lot of thinking over the weekend.

"The court won't allow battered spouse expert testimony unless more testimony proves she was in imminent danger based upon factual evidence presented toward self-defense. It is for the jury to decide if killing was necessary to prevent great bodily harm."

As the judge ruled, Teresa Stiles looked down at her lap, where she twisted her handkerchief into a tight ball.

"Now this morning, we'll break at about eleven. There's a personal matter I need to attend to. Call your next witness, Mr. Levine."

"Grady Stiles III," said Arnie.

All eyes turned as the bailiff wheeled Little Grady into the room. He took the oath in front of the court clerk and was wheeled over to the witness stand. Grady popped out

of the wheelchair onto the stand in one smooth movement.

After asking the preliminaries, establishing Little Grady's lineage, Arnie asked Little Grady to give a demonstration of hand walking.

As cameras clicked, and the reporters in the media room set their VCRs to record, Little Grady crawled off the stand. Throwing his pelvis in front of him, he hand walked around in front of the jury box and the prosecution table.

The jury watched impassively. No one shuddered. No one even sighed. They did not look impressed one way or the other.

Arnie then showed the silent videotape of the two Gradys wrestling.

The jury watched as Grady had his son in a headlock. With all the faces they were making, it looked like it had been a vicious match.

"What happened during that match?" Arnie asked.

"We started playing around but eventually, I could not breathe," Little Grady answered.

"Did you ask him to stop?"

"Yes."

"Did he?"

"No."

Arnie asked about the hole in the wall Teresa had referred to earlier during her testimony. He introduced into evidence a picture of the hole in the wall in Little Grady's bedroom.

"That's where he pushed me through the wall."

Arnie took Little Grady through a series of questions to reiterate the family history that the other family members had already testified to.

"He [Grady] wasn't using [alcohol] real frequently," when they remarried. "The verbal abuse began first, then the drinking, then the getting physical."

"When did the abuse begin again?"

"The stuff began in the beginning of 1990," Little Grady replied. "Three to four drinks a day, about three days a week. He would drink more. As he drank, he got more aggressive physically and verbally. There were times he would drink fifths in a day or a day and a half. Sometimes, he'd go to clubs."

"He drank every day?"

"Every day he drank."

"Did you do things with your father?"

"We didn't do a lot together. We'd go to movies once in a while and to an amusement park once a year."

Arnie asked what he really thought of his father.

"When he was or wasn't drinking, I didn't really like him. He was always making remarks about his [Glenn's] weight."

"Was Glenn physically abused?"

"I'm not aware of any physical abuse of Glenn."

When the family was reunited, "I got along with Cathy because I hadn't seen her for so long. As for Donna, our relationship was all right."

Grady had answered the last question just as Sandra Spoto was standing to object.

"If you see Ms. Spoto come out of that chair, please don't answer," Judge Graybill admonished.

"Yes, sir."

"Mr. Stiles," Arnie said, "did your father ever abuse you?"

"When he was drunk he would abuse me. And he would say to Glenn— "

Sandra Spoto stood. "Objection."

Judge Graybill did not want to allow Little Grady to testify to what his father said to his half brother. Arnie disagreed. While they argued the point, Teresa nonchalantly bit her nails.

"Mr. Stiles," Arnie continued, back at the lectern, "did you see bruises on your step-mother's body?"

"During the latter part of October, November of 1992, I observed bruises on her legs, arms, and shoulders."

"How often?"

"About every other day."

Arnie then asked him to describe his memory of the night his father was killed.

"I went to my room at nine P.M. I woke up around eleven P.M. I had heard three pops that woke me up. I sat on my back, wondering what had happened. I remembered they'd rented a movie, *Ruby*."

Little Grady thought the shooting came from the movie. Evidently, he did not know his history. Jack Ruby shot Lee Harvey Oswald *only one time* before he was subdued.

"Then I laid back down. [The next thing I remembered] I heard voices. My mother Mary, Glenn, and Cathy. I sat there wondering what was going on."

After they woke him up, "Glenn stopped me from going in the living room."

During cross-examination Sandra Spoto asked, "Think your father kept you on a tight leash?"

"I thought he was overprotective," Little Grady responded.

"We've heard testimony that your father always carried a blackjack. Ever see him use it on anyone?"

"No. The blackjack always stayed in a drawer in the house."

"Ever see him use any gun other than a BB gun?"

"No."

At the lectern, Spoto looked down at her

pad, checking off questions, finding the ones she hadn't asked yet.

"Chris Wyant. You saw him a lot?"

"Me and Glenn always went to Chris when we'd go someplace."

"Where were you the afternoon your father was murdered?"

"All three of us spent the afternoon together."

"In that video we saw, whose hand was that pointing at you when you were wrestling?"

"Uh, that was Donna's hand. It was a family video."

As Arnie began his redirect, Little Grady rocked in his chair.

After Little Grady completed his testimony, he popped back into his wheelchair and the bailiff wheeled him out.

"It's eleven A.M. We'll reconvene in a half hour," said Graybill, and left the bench.

Outside in the corridor, Teresa cradled Little Grady's head to her ample chest and hugged him. Tyrill, Cathy, and Donna crowded around him to find out what was said. Tyrill handed him a paper cup filled with water. The boy's hands shook as he brought it to his lips to drink.

Back inside the courtroom, Arnie told reporters, "It's very difficult to get an acquittal without the experts testifying."

* * *

Levine, Hanes, and Spoto stood at the courtroom's rear door, the one leading to the judge's chambers. It was a long corridor, and at the end of it, Graybill yelled out calmly, "I'm contagious, stay away from me. I've got tuberculosis."

Everyone in the courtroom was on their feet, craning their necks, trying intently to look down the corridor.

"Your Honor, how long might you be out?" Arnie shouted.

"My doctor isn't sure, but probably around two weeks," Graybill replied.

An hour later, Judge Alvarez, the administrative court judge for Hillsborough County, the man who assigned the county judges to their cases, took the bench.

"Your Honor, I'd like the case reassigned to Judge Fleischer," Arnie asked confidently.

"Your Honor, I suggest the case be readjourned in two weeks before Judge Graybill, if he's healthy," Hanes answered.

Judge Alvarez promised to take their positions under advisement. He would rule in the afternoon about the disposition of the trial.

"Bailiff, bring the jury in."

Up to that moment, the jury had been left completely in the dark, cooling their heels in the jury room.

"Ladies and gentlemen, Judge Graybill has gone to the hospital. It's not verified Judge

Graybill has TB, but he might. He does have
pneumonia. His doctor advised him to go to
the hospital for further tests," Judge Alvarez
informed them.

"I will ask you to return tomorrow at nine
A.M. In the meanwhile, the county board of
health informs me that unless you've worked
close to Judge Graybill, you're in no danger.
But anyone who is afraid they might have
contracted tuberculosis can be tested for it.
They're sending a technician down here to
the courthouse to do the testing, and we will
pay for it, of course. I apologize for any inconvenience this may have caused you."

Now the jurors had something else to
worry about: their own health. Six elected to
be tested. Those who had worked close to
Graybill were also going to have blood
drawn, as were two reporters who had recently spoken to the judge.

Outside with her family, Teresa was concerned about her own skin. "I'd rather go
in with another judge than have to postpone
it," she said.

Twenty minutes later, a county health department official carried his testing equipment into the jury room to begin the blood
tests. Meanwhile, the wheels of justice turned
swiftly.

By afternoon, Judge Alvarez decided to go
on with the case. He assigned it to William
"Billy" Fuente, a criminal defense attorney

who had only recently been elected judge. He had just been robed on the previous Friday.

July 19.

Cathy got out of her wheelchair and lifted herself onto a rear bench. She sat next to Donna and Tyrill. Little Grady pulled his wheelchair up to the railing and made eye contact with Mary Teresa. A trace of a smile crept across his features, and then his sparkling blue eyes focused on the man who came through the courtroom's rear door.

"Let me introduce myself," said the handsome, dark-complected, mustachioed man who took the bench.

"My name is Bill Fuente," the judge continued, addressing the jury. "I'll be the presiding judge. The only follow-up question was to ask if you knew me."

None did.

"I'm going to inconvenience you one more time. My intention is to recess until tomorrow at nine or nine-thirty. We'll commence with testimony tomorrow at nine-thirty."

The jury had no problem coming back and working late. They'd even work on Monday, though they'd only committed their time through Friday. They were a dedicated, hardy group.

"I sincerely apologize for this inconvenience," Fuente repeated. And the jury was excused for the day.

"I'll entertain arguments in open court in the afternoon with respect to battered wife syndrome. This is my case and I'm gonna make a decision," Fuente announced to the attorneys. Then he left the bench.

Levine would get the opportunity to once again argue that his experts be allowed to testify. He told reporters how much he was looking forward to the afternoon's proceedings.

It was 2 P.M.

"Mr. Hanes?"

"Thank you, Your Honor," and Hanes rose in his baggy suit to address the court.

"There is no recognizable defense in this case. There is no case in this country which allows it to be brought. The fact there are no cases speaks volumes. There are several cases where you can make the case for battered wife syndrome, [however]."

Hanes himself had told the author during the interview back in November that he would have probably declined to prosecute Teresa if she had shot Grady while he was beating her.

"In conspiracy and contract for hire,"

Hanes continued, "self-defense is not admissible. The facts are incontrovertible."

Hanes continued his arguments, finishing up by quoting a United States Supreme Court ruling to support his position.

Levine rose to his full height. He cut a strong, powerful figure.

"For Mr. Hanes to stand up and say that battered spouse syndrome never comes in [is ridiculous]," he boomed.

Arnie Levine talked and talked, trying, through the interpretation of law and legal precedent, to justify his client's actions. Eventually, he acknowledged that while "My client didn't do it, she should have done it a long time ago," his voice rising and penetrating to every corner of the courtroom.

"When you take imminent, it means at some near time," Arnie explained.

"It shouldn't make any difference who committed the crime if the defendant thought she was in imminent danger, and it shouldn't make any difference that the plot was in place weeks before the murder.

"I just don't make a distinction between hiring somebody and doing it yourself," Arnie continued.

Arnie proceeded to explain that many of his subsequent witnesses, including family members, would testify to the abuse they suffered under Grady's claws.

"I was going to call Tyrill Berry and put

on the video," Arnie added. "That wrestling scene shows things getting out of hand and Grady strangling his son."

He urged Fuente to allow the experts, and to give instructions of what self-defense is when the judge charged the jury.

"I would hope, Your Honor, that you wouldn't be swayed in your decision by the uniqueness of the decision or [the remote possibility of] opening doors to every wife whose husband raised their voice to them and then they shoot them."

They concluded their arguments by walking to the bar. Arnie towered over Hanes.

"We'll reconvene on Thursday at eight-thirty, at which time I'll rule," and Judge Fuente left the bench.

Everyone would have a day off tomorrow while the judge considered his ruling.

July 21.

"I make my ruling solely on the evidence of the case. I have not concluded that self-defense as a matter of law is not applicable in cases of battered spouse syndrome. This is my ruling and my intention is to resume court at nine-fifteen."

Finished, Judge Fuente left the bench.

One, two, three, and it was done. The judge had allowed in the experts. Almost im-

mediately, Cathy turned up in the media
room.

"I'd like to make a statement."

Reporters grabbed for mikes. They thrust
them into her face, then froze for the sound
bite. Cameramen expertly loaded camcorders
on shoulders, turned the image-producing
machines on, focused and waited.

Her face glowing, the pretty, intense-
looking young woman with lobster claws
for hands looked into the cameras. She
paused dramatically.

"I'm very happy, and thank God above for
making the judge make the decision. Now
we definitely have a chance. My mom thanks
the judge very much. This will help a lot of
battered women out there," Cathy said.

Off camera, Cathy admitted that Arnie
had told her to go in and make the statement.

Trial testimony began again with Arnie
questioning Little Grady on direct. Once
again, the bailiff wheeled him in and he
sprang from the chair into the witness-box.

Arnie asked him to tell about a specific
incident of abuse. "One week before the killing, he'd come home from Showtown," Little
Grady remembered. "My father and mother
went to their bedroom. I heard yelling. Both

were arguing. I went to check on her. The door was locked."

"Dad, Dad," he yelled, concerned about his mother's safety. Finally, he hit the door. The lock shattered. He pushed the door open and witnessed a frightening scene.

"My father was choking my mother. On the bed."

"What'd you do?"

"I pulled my father off of her," he answered matter-of-factly.

"What happened on November twenty-ninth?"

"I was with my parents in the morning. We left the house at ten A.M. On the way to the mall [to go shopping], we stopped at Showtown. He had two drinks there. Doubles. After we left, we stopped at the Showman's Club. He had two or three doubles."

"What time was it?"

"About twelve or twelve-thirty."

Then they went to the mall and went shopping.

"When we got home at three, my father drank again. Glenn was present, too. He [Grady] had two or three more doubles."

All through the trial, Arnie had tried to establish in the jury's mind that whenever Grady drank, he turned violent. If he could show that Grady was drunk the day of the killing, then the jury might believe that violence would have occurred again, that Teresa

Stiles felt she was in imminent danger and the use of deadly force was justified.

"Would it be fair to say your father was not a morning person?" Spoto began on cross.

"Yes."

Under Spoto's patient questioning, Little Grady repeated the itinerary of his father's travels from bar to bar on November 29.

"When did you make it to the mall?"

"About one."

"And your dad had more drinks when you got home?"

"At three P.M., he had two or three more drinks. Doubles."

"Did you get out early that morning to get to the mall?"

"Yes."

"You testified today to a violent act."

"Yes."

"Do you remember my asking you [previously] if any violent act stuck out?"

"I remember my answer."

"Was that with Mr. Levine's assistance?"

"No."

At the defense table, Arnie smiled.

"Do you remember your deposition in July 1993?"

"Yes."

"You were put under oath. At that time, I asked you," and now she read from the deposition, " 'Around the time of the murder do you recall any incident of violence involving your mother?'

"Answer: 'No.' "

Little Grady could not explain the discrepancy.

"You never really confronted your father?"

"Not that often. At times, I had to."

"Once again, July sixth, 1993, the same deposition. Line nine, page thirty-six. Were you not asked if you defended your mother from your father, you responded, 'I didn't really confront him.' "

Again, Little Grady could not explain the discrepancy.

On redirect, Arnie stood tall at the lectern.

"Ms. Spoto asked you whether or not I prompted you to testify on redirect. Did you bring to my attention [the information you testified to] during the recess?"

"Yes."

"We met yesterday in my office."

"[Yes and] I just tried to think about what happened and that's how I recalled it."

"Have you testified to the truth?"

"Yes."

"Is anything you said to the jury untrue?"

"No."

Arnie walked away, smiling.

It was Tyrill's turn next.

Tyrill Berry walked in the courtroom.

After establishing that Tyrill was six feet tall and weighed 250 pounds, Arnie showed another videotape where Grady runs across an open field and bowls Tyrill over. Once again, the defense was trying to show Grady's immense physical prowess.

Before Hanes could cross-examine, the judge decided to adjourn court for the day.

During the time I spent researching this account of the murder of Grady Stiles, Jr., I'd become familiar with all the major players both in and out of court. Months before the trial began, I'd been in touch with Arnie Levine's office and received some information about the case, including a copy of the videotape showing Grady brutalizing Little Grady on the floor. When Levine had released it to the media before the start of the trial, it had no sound.

Only my copy wasn't silent. Instead of the desperate cries of a child in pain, it had the sounds of a family's playful banter during the light sparring between a father and his son.

After the session that day, I was walking out of the courtroom and happened to hear Hanes and Spoto talking about the tape and its lack of sound.

"Excuse me," I said, "but my copy does have sound."

The prosecutors stopped and looked at each other.

"That's interesting. Our tape doesn't have any sound."

When I told them how I'd gotten my copy, their interest intensified.

"Where's yours?" Hanes asked.

"Back home in New York."

"That's great. Well, if he calls Grady again, I'll ask him if there was any sound on the tape. Meanwhile, why don't you send for your copy?"

From that moment on, I was no longer simply an observer of this bizarre trial. I became an active participant.

Nineteen

July 22.

The next morning, Hanes began his cross of Tyrill with this casual question.

"Did you wrestle from time to time?"

"Not often. Every once in a while."

"You saw the previous [wrestling] videotape. Did it have sound?"

"The original tape had sound," Tyrill answered truthfully.

"Didn't someone call young Grady a wimp on that tape?"

"I'm not sure," Tyrill answered.

"Do you know if your wife was present, or Mary Stiles?"

"My wife and I were gone at the time."

"Are people talking on the tape?"

"There . . . may be some words exchanged."

"Is the tape shown in court the original?"

"I . . . believe this is the original."

"Were there other matters on the tape?"

"I believe so, sir."

Tyrill was sweating, his voice cracking with the strain.

"And you turned that over to Mr. Levine?"

"Yes."

Arnie came over for his redirect.

"Did the state ever request the sound on it [the tape]?"

"No," Tyrill quickly answered.

Hanes was back again at the lectern.

"You believe there may be sound on it?"

"Some might have sound."

"The camcorder has the ability to record sound?"

"Yes, it does."

"No further questions."

"The defense calls Cathy Berry," Arnie intoned.

The bailiff wheeled Cathy in and like Little Grady, she popped out of the wheelchair and into the witness-box. Waiting for Arnie's first question, she looked like she was on the verge of tears. She put a claw to her face.

"I call your attention to an incident in your home on May fifth, 1990. What happened then?"

"My father was getting ready to strike my mother. I said [to him], 'You preferred the bottle to your family.' "

Then, Cathy said, Grady got angry and struck her.

"I had just gone into my seventh month [of pregnancy]."

Cathy was crying now. Apparently, Grady's blow had brought with it agonizing pain.

"I didn't tell anybody the pain I was in. The morning of the sixth, I started hemorrhaging. I woke up at five A.M. My mother rushed me to the hospital."

When the doctors asked her what had brought on her medical problems, she lied. "I told them [the doctors] I fell out of my chair."

"What had happened as a result of your being hit?" Arnie asked.

"The placenta separated from the cord. My water broke and I needed an emergency C-section."

"He was very nice, when he wasn't drunk. When he was drunk, he was like Satan himself. Sadistic," Cathy added.

At the defense table, Teresa clasped her hands tightly in front of her and cried as Cathy continued her testimony.

"He started drinking more after we'd come off the road in 1992. It was worse. Every day. The abuse was more frequent. He was doing it when he was sober. He constantly threatened to kill us."

"What would happen?"

"He'd jump out of his chair."

Cathy tried to protect her mother by putting herself between them.

"He started beating up on me."

Having tried to establish that Teresa was

in imminent danger prior to Grady's death, Arnie asked Cathy questions that, in her responses, established that she hadn't seen Grady from 1978 to 1988, and that she didn't want to see him because of his brutality.

Later on, when the family got together after the second marriage, Cathy testified that she "stayed with my mother to help my mother."

"Your whole purpose in being on the road was to help your mother?" Arnie questioned.

"Yes," Cathy answered.

Cathy's income was derived, she said, from her social security disability checks.

"Neither yourself or Mr. Berry received any compensation from Mr. Stiles?"

"No. My SSI was enough to buy food with."

"Do you recall having a conversation with your brother Glenn after you came off the road in 1992 about having your father killed?" Hanes asked on cross.

"No."

"Do you know Christopher Wyant?"

"Just to say hi and bye."

She also hadn't heard the gunshots on the night of the murder.

"I never heard the shot. I heard a pop. But you hear that around my house constantly."

"Do you recall any conversation with any person about having your father killed?"

"Objection."

"That's a broad question, Mr. Hanes," interrupted Judge Fuente.

They wrangled it out. Eventually, the judge ruled that on cross of Cathy, Hanes could not talk about the conspiracy to kill Grady.

Back at the lectern, Hanes looked down at his yellow pad. He found the question he wanted and looked up.

"In whose name were the family shows?"

"My father put all the shows in my mother's name."

Hanes paused. He wanted the fact to sink in that whenever Grady died, sooner or later, Teresa would inherit the shows.

Hanes wondered why Cathy would stay at home throughout 1992 with all that abuse going on. Why not just leave so she wasn't a part of it?

"I loved my mother and was trying to protect her in the best way I could," said Cathy.

During a short morning recess, I sought out Levine. Fair journalistic practice is to give a source a chance at rebuttal. In view of my conversation with Hanes the night before, I felt I owed it to him.

Levine was walking around the courtroom and I motioned him over to the railing.

"Is there sound on the videotape?" I asked.

Instead of looking straight at me, his eyes shifted for a moment.

"Am I under oath?" he asked. He smiled broadly.

"I decline to answer." He turned his back to me and walked back to the defense table.

On the other side of the courtroom, Hanes and Spoto were hard at work poring over their notes. I strode over and sat down behind them. Hanes saw me and turned around.

"How'd you know what the audio was on the tape?" I asked.

Hanes explained that that morning they'd come into the courtroom early and Arnie's assistant was playing with the videotape on the VCR.

"I asked," Hanes continued, " 'Can we look at the tape?' They said 'sure.' We turned it up and it's got sound all over it."

But apparently, that was just a copy. They'd asked to see the original. "He [Arnie] said no, you can't see the original tape."

Hanes paused, then said, "At the time, my principal concern was getting the original sound tape entered into evidence. I want that tape."

Spoto turned around. "Did you send for the tape?" Spoto asked.

"Yes," I said. "I'll let you know when I get it."

* * *

"The defense calls Donna Miles."

Without looking at her mother, Donna shuffled into the courtroom and took the stand.

Arnie began with her earliest recollection of life with father.

"I was about seven. We lived on Trenton Street in Gibsonton. I traveled with the show every year I was part of the household."

Arnie wanted to know how often Grady was home when they were off the road.

"He was never home that often. He was out at bars," Donna answered.

"Ever see him drunk?"

"Quite often."

"And the mother/father relationship?"

"A lot of fighting and arguing. My dad yelled a lot at my mom."

"Did he strike her?"

"Yes, he did. He called her dirty names. He choked her in 1972 on Trenton Street."

"What happened?"

"He got on top of her and put his thumb in her throat." Teresa always made the kids go off to the bedroom when they were fighting. As for disciplining the kids, "He would spank us with whatever he had at the time. His belt."

"Buckle too?"

"Both."

"Did your father have a man work for him, Paul Fishbaugh, also known as The Fat Man?"

"Yes."

Arnie asked Donna how Grady would perform his act.

"My dad talked about the history of the condition in his family. Sometimes, he walked across the platform on his hands."

Whether he was drunk or sober, "She [Teresa] would do just about anything he asked her to do."

Then Arnie turned the conversation to Grady's marriage to Barbara and the alcoholism and physical abuse in that household.

Donna testified that Grady would beat Barbara up and ". . . how he'd bite her. . . ."

And then Donna told the court the whole story of how she had fallen for Jack Layne, and how that led to Grady killing her fiancé.

Looking down from the window at Jack's lifeless body cradled in Donna's arms, Donna testified that Grady smiled. "He looked just like he did the day he died."

Years later, when her mother told her she was dating her father again, Donna told her, "He's never gonna change."

After their remarriage, there was an "icy cold look to his face. He looked like he did in Pittsburgh."

On cross, Spoto asked, "Were you present

for any threats on your mother's life by your
father?"

Donna hesitated before answering.

"No," she finally stated.

Then Spoto established that she was married to Joe Miles.

"He's a tall guy, good-looking, with a receding hairline?"

"Very receding," Donna answered with a
trace of a smile.

"What did you do in the carnival for your
father?"

"My husband and I ran the gorilla show."

"A real gorilla?"

"No."

"It's a fake?"

"Yes."

Under further questioning, Spoto was able
to elicit from Donna that Teresa was a jack-
of-all-trades in the carnival, that she did a
little bit of everything to help out, that she
was anything but a helpless woman.

And that was it. Donna stepped down.
With shoulders bowed, she left the courtroom.

After the afternoon break for lunch, the
experts that Arnie Levine had struggled so
long and hard to allow in, would begin their
testimony.

Right from the start, Hanes's strategy with
the experts was to let them have their say.
Regardless of whether Teresa Stiles suffered

from battered spouse syndrome or not, he believed that she was not justified in arranging the death of her husband. Period.

All Hanes could hope was that, in the end, the jury would agree with him.

First up was Dr. Sidney J. Merin.

A clinical psychiatrist in private practice, he frequently testified in Hillsborough County court cases requiring expert psychiatric testimony. He was a hired gun; he'd testify for defense and prosecution alike. This time, he was on the defense side.

"Mrs. Stiles told me of the condition in the home between her and her husband, that he'd punctured at her eye, twisted her nipples, and [tried to] tear them off. He said he'd indeed kill her but didn't say when, and had severely threatened her children."

Merin testified that the threats against her kids were particularly important in terms of her state of mind, because she had previously lost two children.

"She was in a state of constant threat," Merin continued. "She related how he was a very heavy drinker. [After drinking] he became mean, nasty and violent, injurious and battering. She related that this had happened on the day of the shooting.

"She said she returned to Grady because she'd seen him and got the impression he'd stopped drinking and now their relationship could proceed with the love and affection she wanted."

Merin had given her a battery of tests meant to score her intelligence level. Overall, she had an 88 IQ, which was in the low to average range.

Further tests showed her to be a victim of chronic and long-term depression. "She views herself as having a strong conscience, conservative and traditional. She has a tolerant, more passive personality. She doesn't like to act out, is very feminine and views herself as a moral person and wants to view herself as being above human foibles.

"She needs other people to give to her. She is not assertive. She has things happen to her."

It was Merin's conclusion that Teresa Stiles suffered from battered spouse syndrome. "These people [in battered spouse syndrome] learn how to be helpless," Merin explained. "They view themselves as dependent, inferior, lack self-confidence as a consequence of the batterer removing their independence."

He went on to explain that during his examination, she had vague memories of the crime and its planning, which is consistent with those suffering from battered spouse syndrome. "If we understand battered spouse syndrome is an entity in and of itself, it also includes features associated with a dissociative reaction. They lose memories. They detach themselves. The memory is sketchy, easily confused, and will give you different stories. They are helpless."

To Teresa, the threat from Grady was always there.

" 'I'll kill you, but you won't know when.' For herself, she acted reasonably at that time."

On cross-examination, Hanes tried to focus on the concept of learned helplessness, that if Teresa Stiles had learned, through her marriages to be helpless, why was she able to do so many things?

For instance, wasn't she able to get a lawyer to represent her interests when her first husband left her?

Merin could not recall recording information on her first marriage. He also did not recall her telling him about hiring a lawyer to represent her interest after her second marriage was dissolved.

"She's not a blithering idiot," Merin blurted out. "She was seduced" by Grady. "I don't know she wanted to kill him. But she wanted to do something about him."

Hanes wanted to know what he thought of Teresa and Glenn being out of the house just at the moment the murder was committed.

Merin slid through that one. "I think it

was interesting that the family was out of the house at the time of the murder."

On redirect, Arnie asked him what he thought about Teresa's actions.

"I had an opinion that she had no alternative [but to have Grady killed]."

Dr. Marti Loring was a clinical social worker who had flown to Tampa to testify in the trial.

She had examined Teresa on June 24, 1994, in her Atlanta office. She had subsequently come to Tampa and interviewed her for eight hours on July 14.

In a low, tentative voice, as if she was afraid someone was listening, Dr. Loring testified that on November 29, 1992, Teresa Stiles suffered from a very severe case of battered spouse syndrome.

Even if Teresa left Grady, "She believed he'd find and stalk her."

"Is it your opinion that that belief is reasonable?" Arnie inquired.

"Yes, sir," Dr. Loring answered. "She believed if she left, she'd bring on the death of her children."

On cross, prosecutor Hanes tried to get Dr. Loring to admit that Teresa had accepted the responsibility for Grady's murder when she gave her confession to the police.

"No, sir, she gave a semi-denial," Dr. Loring countered.

And then she stepped down and primly left the courtroom for an afternoon flight back to Atlanta. Even with her quiet voice and manner, she had been a most persuasive witness.

"The defense calls Dr. Arturo Gonzalez."

Dressed in a navy blue blazer— red hand-kerchief peeking out of the pocket— gray slacks, red-and-blue patterned tie, and white shirt, Dr. Gonzalez cut a dapper figure on the witness stand. Handsome, tanned face, crowned by a luxuriant growth of white hair, the Cuban-born psychiatrist looked positively regal.

He was also a helluva witness.

"It was a kill or be killed situation," he testified in English, with a Spanish lilt.

"Was she suffering from battered spouse syndrome?" Arnie probed.

"On November twenty-ninth, definitely, absolutely, suffering from battered spouse syndrome."

He explained that with this syndrome, the person being battered does not seem able to break from the abuser, and so continues the cycle of abuse.

Levine also brought up the rather humiliating fact that Dr. Gonzalez had originally been retained by the prosecution as their expert witness, but because he had come to the conclusion that Teresa suffered from battered spouse syndrome, had been forced to be removed as a prosecution witness.

"Did Mrs. Stiles talk of being threatened on the night her husband was murdered?" Hanes asked on cross.

"On the evening Mr. Stiles was killed, she related no threats," Dr. Gonzalez said. But she did talk about being choked by him that day, and Grady trying to poke her eye out during a particularly violent episode.

During the afternoon break, I stepped outside for some air. I stood on the steps of the courthouse, looking at the overcast, gray sky.

After a while, I decided to go back in. That's when I saw Donna Miles sitting alone, smoking a cigarette on the courthouse steps.

It was easy to miss her. A pale, nondescript face and white clothes made her look washed-out.

"How ya doin'?" I asked.

"Okay."

She sucked smoke deep into her lungs.

"I hear you and Joe are truckers now."

She nodded.

"What kind of trucking you do?" I asked.

"Independent stuff. Refrigerated trucks."

"What's it like out on the road?"

"You mean in between the bumps?"

I smiled.

"You get a lot of time to think."

"I was in Pittsburgh and went to the house where you lived."

She looked me in the eye.

"Really?"

"Do you ever think about Jack?"

"That was such a long time ago."

"What do you remember about him?"

She exhaled.

"That he was young. So young. You know, it's funny."

"What is?"

"In 1978, my dad killed a seventeen-year-old and in 1992, he was killed by a seventeen-year-old. It's history reversed."

She stamped the cigarette under the heel of her plain, flat pumps and walked back into the courthouse.

Twenty

July 25.

The tape arrived in a FedEx package. I played it on the VCR in my hotel room. The dialogue was as I remembered, only now, it all fit.

There were Grady and Little Grady wrestling, and Donna and Mary Teresa egging them on in the background. If Levine had introduced the tape with sound in the courtroom, it would make Grady look, at worse, like a father who wrestled too roughly with his son.

Without sound, Grady looked like a brutal, sadistic father. Maybe he really was, but not on that tape. And copies without sound had been sent to all the media.

I went downtown to a video store and dubbed the tape, then drove to the courthouse.

I had missed the morning testimony of the experts. At a little past noon, I rushed through the court corridor and took the elevator up to Hanes's office. I flagged him down as he went by and said, "Let's talk in your office."

Hanes, Spoto, and myself sat down in his office to talk.

The place was a little messier than the last time I was in it. Some of the files were strewn about, just what you'd expect from an attorney who was on trial.

Hanes sat behind his cluttered desk, Spoto and I in armchairs in front of him.

I handed the tape across to Hanes.

"You did the right thing," Hanes said.

"This is now evidence in a murder trial. I'm going to argue that we have the right to see the original tape."

"Yes, we do," Spoto asserted.

"But Arnie did say we never asked to begin with to see the original," Hanes said, legal mind coming into play.

"Well, we'll see what we can do," Spoto countered.

A half hour later, we were all back in the courtroom.

With the jury excused, Spoto argued before Judge Fuente that the prosecution be allowed to enter into evidence a copy of the videotape they had obtained, but with sound.

"Mr. Levine, did you know that the tape had sound?" Fuente asked.

"I knew it," Arnie answered.

Hanes explained that he had previously

asked Arnie to show him the tape with sound but Arnie refused.

"When you disclosed the tape to the state, did you disclose it had sound?" the judge wanted to know.

"Are you posing this question as a discovery violation?" Arnie answered. "This is my client's video. They made no representation [about what was on it] whatsoever."

The state's position was that the tape has an entirely different context when viewed with sound. Arnie, of course, disagreed.

Tap-dancing, but growing more and more flustered by the moment, Arnie told the judge that since the voices on the tape were hearsay, it was evidence he had not introduced.

Sitting in a corner of the courtroom, as he had throughout the trial, Glenn's lawyer Peter Catania looked aggravated. His jaw was tight and he looked warily at Arnie. He, too, intended to introduce the video to show Grady's brutality at Glenn's trial.

"If the tape is introduced by the defense, it suggests a particular inference that the state has an opportunity to rebut," Arnie explained weakly.

Fuente didn't agree. He agreed to view the tape at a sidebar before ruling.

"Is this with or without the sound?" Arnie questioned as the tape was run.

His question was answered a second later. There was laughter on the tape.

"Break the hold," somebody said.

"Push harder," said another.

Fuente watched it until the wrestling match ended.

"There's no question. Viewing the tape [with sound] depicts a scene not of violence but of a family playing around," said the judge from the bench. "They [the state] don't have to object to something before they rebut it. I see it as something other than an act of violence."

It was a cold rebuke of Arnie and his position. But before allowing the tape into evidence, Judge Fuente wanted to know how Hanes received it.

"I got it from Mr. Fred Rosen," Hanes responded. "He's writing a book on the case."

The courtroom went silent. Arnie looked back at me. Teresa Stiles's gaze threw daggers into my skin.

I stood up.

"I see Mr. Rosen standing. Perhaps he has something—"

"Your Honor," Levine cut in, looking back at me with a worried expression. "We are satisfied that Mr. Rosen was not acting as an, uh, agent of the prosecution."

He would not argue any further about the tape being allowed in as evidence. And because of that, he sidetracked my explanation of how I'd gotten the tape.

The judge ordered the videotape recorder set up and the jury brought in to view the tape. And then I saw Arnie Levine.

The grin and the jaunty attitude had vanished. In its place was a skull bearing down on me with flashing, sharp, white teeth. I shifted my tape recorder, which was sitting on the railing, and made sure it was turned on.

When he got to the railing, Arnie leaned down, his face a few inches from mine. I could feel his breath.

"Where'd you get that tape with audio?" he hissed through clenched teeth.

"From *you*," I replied calmly.

"Fucker!" Arnie hissed. "You had the audacity to make that available to the state?"

"How dare you, sir, have the audacity to try to show this court and the media a tape *without* sound?"

"You fucker, you fucker— "

"Keep talking," I urged him on. I pushed my tape recorder closer but Arnie didn't notice. As the jury was being seated, he kept cursing me.

Hanes and the bailiff came over.

Hanes spied my tape recorder.

"Arnie, you're on record. He's taping."

"You fucker. . . ." The bailiff led him away. James Martinez the AP reporter who had witnessed the whole thing was madly writing in his notebook.

In the media room, the reporters were scrambling. I'd thrown them a curve and they had to figure out how to play it.

I took a seat in the corner and watched the reporters talking to each other, pressing the record buttons on their VCRs and taking notes as inside the courtroom, the tape with sound, was finally played for the jury.

"Why'd you turn it over?" one reporter asked, with more than a little hostility in her voice.

"What was I supposed to do?" I responded. "It wasn't given to me from an anonymous source. The jury has the right to hear all the evidence."

Some of the others shouted questions at me.

Suddenly, I was no longer one of their own; I was part of the story.

During the afternoon session, the expert witnesses finished their testimony. Then Levine called Wayne Murray.

Obese and bearded, sporting a big silver belt buckle, Murray took the stand.

"I saw Grady frequently at the club," he replied to one of Arnie's questions.

It seemed that, in addition to Showtown, Grady frequented the bar at the International Showman's Club, also in Gibsontown. Murray, who recorded bally come-ons that carnies played from the platform while on the road, frequented the Showman's Club as well.

"He drank rather heavily," said Murray. "As soon as he finished one drink, he'd put his glass down and Teresa would run up to get him another drink."

Arnie wanted to know if Grady ever got really blitzed.

"They'd cut him off before he got to that point," Murray answered.

On cross, all Hanes wanted to know was if Murray had ever observed Grady hurt Teresa.

"No, I never observed Grady hit Mary or verbally abuse her," he testified, clearly reluctantly.

"The defense rests," said Arnie.

Now the prosecution had one more chance. They could, if they chose, introduce rebuttal witnesses. And Hanes was ready.

"Prosecution calls Betty Tanner."

In earlier testimony, Teresa and Little Grady adamantly claimed that Grady began drinking on the morning of his death at the Showman's Club.

Tanner took the stand, and immediately identified herself as the director of the club in question.

"Did you serve Mr. Stiles a drink on the

morning he was killed, November twenty-ninth?" Spoto asked loudly.

"No," Tanner replied.

"Why not?"

"November twenty-ninth was a Sunday. By state law, we are not allowed to serve alcohol before one P.M."

At the defense table, Teresa sat stunned.

"No further questions."

Arnie could not budge her, and Tanner was excused. Her testimony had taken all of five minutes. It was, perhaps, the trial's most damaging. But Spoto wasn't through yet.

"Call Chuck Osak."

The owner of Showtown USA took the stand. Teresa and Grady had said that Grady had a few on the morning of the murder at the Showtown as well as the Showman's Club.

"Did you serve Grady Stiles alcohol on the morning of November twenty-ninth?"

"No, ma'am, I did not. That was a Sunday. We're not allowed to open until one P.M."

"No further questions."

Arnie sprang to his feet.

After establishing that Grady's regular alcoholic drink was Seagram's, Arnie asked Osak when he served the first Seagram's on November twenty-ninth.

Osak, whose cash register recorded the type of drink dispensed, responded, "Eighteen-oh-eight was the first Seagram's 7."

18:08 was military time. Translated into Eastern Standard Time, it was 6:08 P.M. on Sunday, November 29, when Osak served his first Seagram's. At that time, Grady was home eating dinner.

The state had hit two home runs in a row.

"Call Christopher Boden."

Boden took the stand and immediately identified himself as a forensic toxicologist who worked for the state. He had done a blood alcohol test on Grady's blood.

"Mr. Boden, what was Grady Stiles's blood alcohol content at the time of his death?"

"Zero-point-zero-two grams," Boden replied.

"No further questions."

On cross, Arnie tried to confuse the issue by looking at Grady's blood alcohol level in different ways, which would make it seem like he had imbibed more than Boden indicated. But Boden clung to his testimony.

In Florida, .10 is legally intoxicated. According to the state's expert, at the time of his death, Grady had barely enough alcohol in his blood to indicate that he'd had more than one beer.

If that was true, and it looked like it was, then the entire Stiles family was clearly lying. They claimed Grady was drinking heavily the day he was murdered.

But if they lied about Grady's drinking, what else had they lied about?

"Call Detective Michael Willette."

Hanes questioned Willette about the photos he took of Teresa Stiles the night she was arrested.

"Were there any marks on her face in those photos?" Hanes asked.

"No, sir," Willette answered, and Hanes showed the jury the photos that he then entered into evidence.

"No further questions. Your Honor, the prosecution rests."

"Mr. Levine, any rebuttal witnesses?" Judge Fuente asked.

"No, Your Honor."

"Then we'll begin closing tomorrow morning. I want to see counsel in chambers regarding jury instructions."

July 26.

That morning, the courtroom was packed. The Stiles family crowded along the front row, throwing kisses and thumbs-up to Teresa, who sat wearing a tan suit and a grim expression as her fate got closer and closer.

At 9:35 A.M., Ron Hanes stepped up to the lectern and faced the jury.

"Ladies and gentlemen, I want to thank you for your service, which went above and beyond your duty. On behalf of the state, thank you very much.

"You have heard much about what physically took place on November twenty-ninth. And what took place on November twenty-ninth, was murder."

He paused.

"Mr. Stiles is in his chair. 'Hurry and come back,' he says, and puts the video on pause. And with that, his life is taken. Was there any danger on that day to Teresa Stiles? She didn't even know when the homicide would take place.

"What we have is a contract for murder. The terms of the contract are completely open. The killing can take place when you get to it, Mr. Wyant. That *is not* self-defense.

"They walk a few feet from their trailer. The fifteen hundred dollars on the dryer? How does that come about? [In case of divorce, you must] give up your lifestyle so you don't have to go through a divisional situation.

"Money [for the murder] was made available. Are those signs of helplessness?"

Teresa Stiles looked down at her feet.

"There was no imminence," Hanes continued. "Is there any danger? No. It's an open-ended contract."

Cathy leaned forward on her claws, intently studying the prosecutor.

"I've paid you the fifteen hundred dollars— you haven't held up your end of the bargain. [I'm] considering reporting the money stolen. Teresa Stiles has access to independent funds. It's blood money.

"Blood money," Hanes said loudly. "Imminent death or great bodily harm? No! Not willing to leave the household, yes!

"It was very easy to step out of the trailer and give a seventeen-year-old the opportunity to shoot Grady Stiles in the head. As she said, there was no danger. After all [as Teresa pointed out], Grady couldn't travel anymore. Yet her combination of efforts is to go immediately to what should always be the last resort. For Mary Stiles, killing was the easiest way to continue her lifestyle, not a last resort. There then followed a deliberate cover-up to law enforcement to what has taken place.

"It doesn't fit. Mary Stiles knew that night it was murder and she knows today.

"Doctors [who testified] weren't given all the facts [by her]. Which of those versions were the doctors given? The night after the murder, she had total recall [when she confessed to the police]. From that point forward, recall was denied. Amnesia? Is that amnesia?" Hanes asked incredulously. "She has a specific recall of the day of the murder and everything else. For her to give the details of the murder [to the doctors] would show you a person who acted and was not helpless.

"You judge whether you believe that was

amnesia. She told Dr. Gonzalez, Christopher
Wyant was in the house that night. Are we
dealing with dissociation? No, we just aren't
being given details! A thirty-two caliber Colt
Automatic that he fired into that man's
head. As Wyant told you, he spent the
money and they wanted him to hold up his
end of the deal.

"By entering into an open-ended contract,
Mrs. Stiles knew it was murder. That's not
dissociation— it's deceit. The cover-up itself,
we have no idea who took part in it. But
there is a consciousness of guilt through the
use of a son and a seventeen-year-old.

"That was murder on November twenty-
ninth, that is murder today."

Hanes sat down. The time was 10:15 A.M.
Arnie Levine immediately stood and strode
with all the majesty he could muster to the
lectern and faced the jury.

"I am not here to mislead you. Not every
battered woman kills but Mary Stiles is not
every battered woman."

The courtroom hushed. All that could be
heard was Arnie's ringing voice, the words
and inflection clear as a bell, penetrating to
every corner of the courtroom.

"Mary Stiles is a unique battered woman
who suffered every form of violence, physical, emotional and," voice rising, "sexual,
and the threat she'd be killed, not just orally,
but acting out, too.

"The evidence unquestionably establishes that on November twenty-ninth and prior, Mary Stiles reasonably [believed] that she and her family members were in imminent danger of either death or great bodily harm.

"In this case, there are two killers. Grady Stiles, Jr., who killed without justification and got away with it. Grady Stiles, Jr., and Christopher Wyant.

"It's almost unfathomable that the state prosecuted Mary Stiles for premeditated murder and conspiracy to commit murder. It doesn't make sense. Not at all.

"Back then, in 1988 to 1989, [Grady] drew Mary Stiles into his web and then reverted to what he was and he took his pound of flesh from Mary Stiles and his children. He had killed. Life, soul, and the hope of Mary Stiles and children. Terrorized them, seduced them.

"The state, through Mr. Hanes, brands Mary Stiles a felon. I suggest the evidence says that she paid for what she did. I suggest he [Hanes] never explained the why and he can *not*. She is innocent by virtue of self-defense."

Even as Arnie continued to argue her case, Teresa Stiles could not raise her eyes and look at the jury of her peers that would judge her.

"Everybody said [Mary Stiles suffered from] battered wife syndrome. Where is the evidence to the contrary? They [the state] have the obligation to prove it, not me. Listening to Mr. Hanes, you'd think it had been the O.K. Corral.

"You must judge her by the circumstance by which she was surrounded when the bullet was fired. The judge will say that the danger facing the defendant need not be actual. It has to do with perception, her belief. Is there any evidence to the contrary about violence, dangerousness and alcoholism? They called no witnesses to refute [this] despite the fact they have the burden of proof. Not I.

"[The videotape] shows the father [holding the son] in a headlock he could not break," Arnie continued. "It was family fun? Even sober, he lost control. That's a microcosm of what my client experienced when he was drunk. They're encouraging him to break it. See the look in Grady's eyes. He lets his son up and grabs him again. You could hear Grady III choking on the video.

"How does Mary Stiles face up to that? How could she defend herself against his [strength]? That video is mild and moderate compared to the terror Mary Stiles was living with."

As for the prosecution's contention that Mary Stiles killed Grady to continue her lifestyle, he considered that a joke, considering she lived in Gibsonton.

"There was no big insurance. [Just] a trailer in Gibsonton [to inherit]."

"Kill or be killed. The words of Arturo Gonzalez. There are no other alternatives. It's the circumstances she was in, her frailties, her state of mind. There is only one proper verdict. Not guilty. Not guilty."

Arnie finished at 12:15, two hours of summation. Now, one more time, the prosecution had a chance at rebuttal.

"Ladies and gentlemen, their strategy is to overwhelm you with learned helplessness and dissociation," said Sandra Spoto.

"They tried to put alcohol into his system. Alcohol followed by violence.

"The judge will tell you the defendant must be treated as a principal. If she knew what would happen, and a crime was going to be committed, she was responsible. The State of Florida cares, and you should care."

Arnie objected.

"No, sir," said Judge Fuente, and Arnie sat down.

"Mr. Levine spent time talking about penalty. That's Judge Fuente's job. Test the evidence. Find out how hard it is to put a square peg into a round hole. Strategy. Setting up defense. Learned helplessness."

Spoto reminded the jury to consider Donna Miles's testimony as to what her mother was capable of doing.

"If it's imminent danger, don't you have

a conversation with [the shooter] and say, 'It has to be done. It has to be done.'

"Was she in imminent danger when she went over her Christmas list in November 1992?"

Then she brought up the family's testimony that Grady had been drinking all day the day of the murder.

"Alcohol followed by violence. They forgot that November twenty-ninth is a Sunday and bars weren't open and Grady Stiles couldn't be drinking then."

"Relying on the scientific evidence, Grady Stiles, Jr., had a blood alcohol level of point-zero-two. They weren't being honest with you.

"Let's talk about the video."

"The video without sound. The video with sound. And all of them laughing. Mr. Levine said that video turned violent. Test the evidence.

" 'Don't scream Grady because you're gonna hurt your throat.' That's what you'll hear on the video. And as for that hole in the closet [that Grady threw Little Grady through] it's been there since 1991."

Then she turned to Teresa's story that Grady tried to poke her eye out the night before he was murdered, seemingly contradicted by the photos Willette took of her two days later at the time of her arrest.

"Surely there would be bruises if that

event had taken place. Mr. Levine has inferred that these shadows are bruises. Why wouldn't they show up in a photograph? The answer is the lighting makes her eyes appear she has black circles, like today."

I looked over at Teresa Stiles. Her head had sunk down again.

"She testified that she reported the abuse and the police treated their complaints of domestic violence [as a joke]. She didn't. The State of Florida is not asking you to disregard if Mary Stiles was a battered woman. [But she was involved] in a fifteen-hundred-dollar deal that landed that seventeen-year-old boy twenty-seven years in Florida state prison."

Now, Spoto lowered her voice.

"Grady Stiles was sitting in his home, drinking tea, surrounded by photos of his family. He was sitting in front of the TV, waiting for his family. 'Hurry up and watch the movie.' That scene is real. Imminent danger? Battered wife syndrome is not a license to kill."

Spoto sat down. And just like that, the trial was over.

Judge Fuente charged the jury, explaining the law to them and the charges against the defendant. When he was finished, the jury was escorted into the jury room on the left, behind the judge's bench. The door closed quietly behind them.

We all settled down to await their verdict.

Teresa Stiles left the courtroom. After a while, she and her children left to go to lunch.

It was 2:57 P.M. The jury had sent a note to the judge. They wanted a clarification on two points:

"Does self-defense apply to the second count?"

"We are not clear on the definition of the word principal."

The lawyers battled back and forth over how to answer the questions, Hanes favoring a more narrow answer while Levine somewhat more liberal. In the end, Judge Fuente compromised and sent the jury a note to try and help them as best he could, without influencing their judgment.

By six o'clock, the jury had still not made a decision. The judge decided not to sequester them, and sent them home for the day.

Twenty-one

Wednesday. July 27, 1994.

It was a long, slow day.

Lunchtime came and went. The clock ticked away, minute by minute. By late afternoon, there was still no verdict.

Then the buzzer rang. The time was 5:11 P.M.

The jury had been out nearly eleven hours over a period of two days.

Within a matter of minutes, the courtroom was packed as tight as a sardine can. Inside the media room, TV reporters paused, fingers over record buttons.

Escorted by her children, Mary Teresa Stiles came in and took her seat at the defense table. A few minutes before, Ron Hanes and Arnie Levine had been sitting there conversing like they were the best of friends. Now, with the jury coming back, they had gone back to their respective corners like two fighters waiting for the decision.

The jury was ushered back in. Absolutely no emotion registered on their faces as they sat down in the box.

Judge Fuente entered the courtroom and climbed to the bench.

"Mr. Foreman, I understand you've reached a verdict?"

A man on the far end, closest to the judge, who'd been talking on a cellular phone during breaks, stood up. Earlier, one of the alternates had identified him as an employee of Southwest Bell.

"Yes, Your Honor, we have." He handed the sheet of paper to the bailiff, who gave it to the court clerk, who read the verdict. "On the first count, we find the defendant guilty of manslaughter with a firearm."

Cathy Berry cried out.

"On the second count, conspiracy to commit murder in the first degree, we find the defendant guilty."

Teresa didn't cry, she didn't laugh, she didn't say anything. Donna looked shell-shocked. Tyrill and Little Grady looked down, fighting back tears. Arnie put his arms around Teresa and began speaking to her in soft, soothing tones.

After the court had cleared, Arnie Levine, Teresa Stiles, Ron Hanes, and Sandra Spoto stood before the bar. Arnie was desperately pleading with the judge to allow Teresa

Stiles to remain free under house arrest pending appeal.

"Mr. Levine, I'm certainly sympathetic to Mrs. Stiles, but she has been convicted of felony murder. I order she be taken into custody immediately and bail denied," Fuente said solemnly.

Teresa went back to the defendant's table and Tyrill wheeled Cathy over. The mother took the daughter's grieving face in her hands and pulled her close, trying to comfort her. The daughter wept. Then the bailiff came over, pulled Cathy gently away from Teresa, and led the convicted murderess back through the bowels of the building to begin serving her sentence.

"Son of a bitch," Cathy shouted, screaming and doing a wheelie in her chair. "Killed him," she screamed, the rest unintelligible gibberish mixed in with the screaming. She crashed through the swinging doors of the railing, headed for the courthouse's doors.

In the corridor outside, the camera crews were all ready to shoot the family, but Judge Alvarez, the administrative court judge, would have none of it. He ordered all the camera crews to leave their taping for outside the building.

Outside, Cathy, ever the family's spokesperson, was about to make a tearful speech.

"It's bad to say because I am a Christian.

I hope that Fred Rosen, Mr. Hanes, and Sandra whatever her name is get the beatings and the threats my family has," she shouted.

When asked about the verdict, Arnie said, "Who wants a compromise when you're right? She killed this man because he deserved to be killed."

Epilogue

Before Harry Glenn Newman, Jr., came to trial in late August of 1994, Ron Hanes offered him a deal. Plead to the same charges his mother had been convicted of and he would receive the same sentence.

The deal was carefully explained to Glenn's attorney Peter Catania, to Glenn, and to Teresa. Catania advised Glenn to take it. Teresa disagreed, and Glenn went to trial.

On August 9, after one hour and five minutes of deliberation, Harry Glenn Newman, Jr., was convicted of first degree murder and conspiracy to commit first degree murder. It turned out that it was Peter Catania's first time trying a murder case.

On August 29, 1994, Teresa Stiles was sentenced to twelve years behind bars, followed by five years probation.

On October 14, 1994, Harry Glenn Newman, Jr., was sentenced to life in prison.

When Arnie Levine subsequently filed his appeal, the state cross-appealed with a brief asking that in Teresa's case, the defense of battered wife syndrome be disallowed. They wanted an opportunity to go back into court and convict Teresa on first degree murder.

In the same brief, the state named Cathy Berry Stiles as an unindicted coconspirator.

As for Teresa, Judge Fuente subsequently relented and allowed her to remain free on bond, pending appeal.

"She posted a twenty-thousand dollar bond," Hanes confirmed. "She put the home up for collateral. Basically, she'd signed off on it back in January of 1993, with the proceeds going to her children, who then put it up for collateral.

"In Florida, manslaughter with a firearm is not included in the intestate statutes as specifically prohibiting a person from collecting on an estate."

Afterword

INTERVIEWS IN GIBTOWN

My first stop in Gibsonston was at the Giant's Camp, the nerve center of the community and the home of Jeanie Tomaini, "The World's Only Living Half Girl."

I found Jeanie with her daughter, Judy Rock, in Judy's office at the far end of their trailer court.

Jeanie sat on the floor, two-and-a-half feet tall, on her torso. It did indeed look like only half of her was there. While Grady's death was a shock to the community, it was by no means the first time a major crime had occurred thereabouts.

"There's so much crime here now. Kids are just born different. [Tampa] being a seaport, it's so easy to get drugs and stuff in. There are more street people now. Little jungles of street people [in Gibtown]."

Jeanie recalled that in the old days, "It was just a swamp here. We came here every year and cleared a little more and then, we stayed here.

"I could adapt myself to whatever. Seems to me I was just a country girl who's been traveling and working with shows since I was three." Her mother met up with someone who thought she'd be a great addition to the carnival. And so Jeanie began her life as a sideshow attraction, The World's Only Living Half Girl.

"I enjoyed the show, the traveling. I made friends, I been in every state. The carnivals were family shows. Now it's dog eat dog. People then were more reliable and stable."

A train rumbled by and the office vibrated. Jeanie held her balance on her hips with ease.

"I never actually knew Grady Stiles," she continued. "We were on separate shows, but most people in this area thought mighty well of him. The people at Showtown speak highly of him," said Jeanie in a soft voice.

She looked up at me. There was a tranquility in her eyes that I had rarely seen in a human being.

"Considering what happened, why not walk away?" she questioned with a flash of anger. "Considering his condition and all," she believed it would have been easy for Teresa to just leave.

"It still boils down to that he was a human

being, a live human being, and they took the life away from him."

Judy, who handled the day-to-day management of the Giant's Camp and also has a business making gravestones, also had an opinion. She, too, thought that Teresa should have left Grady instead of killing him.

If the Giant's Camp is the nerve center of Gibtown, then Showtown, USA, with its brightly painted facade of carnival scenes, is the place where jangled nerves are assuaged with booze and conviviality. Chuck Osak runs the place. Fortyish and slim with bifocals, he has a brushy mustache the same color as his sandy blond hair. He was dressed in jeans, a short-sleeved blue shirt, and dark shades.

"Grady was known in this town. He was a good man. He had his own little sideshow, something you could look at. Grady exhibited himself all his life. I'd sit down with him when he came in off the road and ask him, 'How was the season, Grady?' "

And they would chat about what kind of season it had been. "He was never an excessive drinker. Maybe here an hour at most. The only wife I knew was Barbara. She drank a little bit. Whatever Grady wanted to do, she

did. If he said, 'Let's go to New York,' she'd
go. She'd roll with the punches."

As for Teresa, if things were so bad, "She
could have left him," he said forcefully.

Like Tomaini, Osak bemoaned the decline
of the family shows. "You knew the kids; they
helped you set up. I'd see them the following
year and they're a year older. But the family
shows are a thing of the past. How the hell
can you compete against Disney World?"

If I wanted to know more about Grady,
Osak recommended I speak to William
Roberts.

Then he left me with this piece of advice.

"Any carny won't tell you the truth because
they don't want you to know the truth."

William Roberts, a former aerialist, runs
the Pirates Treasure Cove, a Gibtown store
on Kracker Avenue that makes costumes for
circus and carnival people.

"I was on a cruise with him and I knew
the family," Roberts told me. He would pro-
vide me with no further information.

Osak's advice rang in my ears.

The Stiles family live in an out-of-the-way
neighborhood. After a number of lefts and
rights and lefts, past a bunch of apparently
empty fields and a tropical-fish farm, I

found myself on Inglewood Drive. It is a grand name for a narrow, block-long street bordered by a bunch of run-down trailers.

I walked across the parched grass and stopped before a chest-high cyclone fence. The trailer door of number 11117 was open. The wooden sign above it said:

The Stiles
Grady & Teresa

Four dogs smelled me and came out barking.

"Anybody home?" I yelled above the din.

Again, the dogs barked.

"Hello?"

"Yeah, just a second," a young voice answered from inside the trailer.

The door was open. I peered into the dark interior.

On the floor in the shadows was a crawling figure who suddenly turned and popped up into a wheelchair. In one motion, he expertly leaned back, turned it, and wheeled himself out of the gloom, into the sunlight.

"Hey, boys, sit," he said, calling off the four dogs on his side of the wire fence. He introduced himself as Grady Stiles III.

Little Grady wore a dark T-shirt over his barrel chest. Eyes drift down to his claws. They are different from his father's, with two fingers on each hand instead of one.

Politely, he explained, "It's not a good time. Come back at five-thirty when my sister will be here."

I looked at my watch. It was 3:30 P.M.

I rode around awhile, visiting the park in Riverview where Glenn Newman met with Chris Wyant to discuss the murder of his stepfather, and where the money for the hit allegedly changed hands. Then I killed time in the town's only strip mall, the Twin Oaks Plaza.

By 5:30 I was back at the Stiles place but Cathy, the family spokesperson while her mother was in jail, had not shown up yet.

Little Grady and I continued our chat from earlier in the day.

"Hey, I'm a showman," he said proudly, telling me all about how he traveled with and worked the carnival. He particularly loved the gorilla show illusion that Donna and Joe operated.

"I love to watch people's reaction to it," he smiled.

He brushed hair from across his eyes.

"Do you miss your father?"

"Nah, I don't miss him. He was abusive."

"He beat you?"

"Oh yeah. Multiple times. I just miss my mom and Harry. I want 'em back."

His bright blue eyes seem soft rather than hard.

"Harry's father is inside."

Midget Man.

"Mr. Newman?"

"Yeah."

"Okay, well, I'll try again later."

I left to the sounds of the dogs barking. That bothered me.

Why hadn't the dogs barked when Chris Wyant entered the trailer to kill Grady?

A few hours later, the phone rang in my hotel room.

"Mr. Rosen. This is Peter Catania."

It was Glenn's lawyer. He told me that Cathy Berry had called him and said that I had requested an interview. As her brother's attorney, he represented Cathy's interests as well. After I told him that all I wanted was to speak to Cathy to get some background on family matters, he asked me if the family, who was very poor, could, in some way, be financially compensated for their assistance.

"Mr. Catania, I am certainly sympathetic, but I don't pay for information. All I can promise is that I'll get the best obtainable version of the truth. So can I talk to her?"

Catania paused for a long time before answering.

"All right," he said affably. "I'll advise Cathy it's okay to talk with you."

"Thank you."

"You're welcome," and the line went dead.

I called Cathy and we made an appointment for seven P.M. that night.

Everyone acted normal. We just happened to be sitting in your average American living room, in your average American home. Only in this home, the father just happened to have been murdered. His armchair was vacant now and draped with a white cloth.

Harry Glenn Newman, Sr., "Midget Man," lay sprawled in boxer shorts in front of the Japanese television set he gazed at intently. A clear plastic line stretched from his nose to a tank. He was on a respirator because of the lung condition he'd contracted back in Ohio when he was a welder. Near him lay a wooden cane he still used to help him stand and move around because of the fall he had taken.

Cathy Stiles Berry sat in an armchair next to the one in which her father was murdered. A pretty woman, she had the broad shoulders and large arms of a person who has to rely on her upper body to get around. She had no legs and hands/claws like her father's.

Cathy sounded intensely protective of her mother.

"It's too rough for her on the road. I just more or less traveled with her. I didn't work out there. I just traveled mainly to look out for my mother."

"Your brother seems like he likes the life on the road."

"Little Grady? Well, he has no worries. He's seventeen. All he knows how to do is go out there, ride, play the games and have fun. I have a lot more [responsibilities] than that."

"It seems like, for everything that went on, you have it together."

"I had to. Living with him [her father], I had to. There was no way that I was gonna let him mess me up."

"It's real interesting how some kids who grow up with the kind of abuse you did, respond by turning out the way you did."

"I'm levelheaded. He has scarred me emotionally a lot, but right now I just can't let it get to me."

"And your mother?"

"I think my mom is the most wonderful person. There's nothing in the world I wouldn't do for her."

"Why didn't your mother call the cops when your dad got drunk and abused her?"

"If my mother would have called the cops, you better believe things would have gotten ten times worse."

Her husband, Tyrill, who had been in the other room taking care of four-year-old daughter Misty, came in carrying the child. It would be nice to say that Misty looks like a normal, well-adjusted girl, but the truth appears to be anything but.

Her young face, the spitting image of her father's, looked ravaged, old beyond her scant years. She was born without legs. Because the ectrodactyly gene comes out differently from generation to generation, Misty's "legs" stop before the knee; she has a toe or claw up on her hip. She has only one arm with a claw at the end. The other is a stub.

Tyrill went over to the cage where he was raising gerbils.

"You didn't know anything about what your mom was planning?" I asked Cathy.

Cathy wouldn't look at me. She looked away and shook her head no.

"When you finally found out what happened, how'd you feel?"

"I really didn't feel anything," she answered in a loud voice. " 'Cause I knew what she lived with. I'd had it done to me. I feel sorry for her and my brother, not my father.

"He destroyed our love back in 1978 when he shot my sister's fiancé. I didn't see him do it but I heard it because I was right in the backyard. When I came around the house, he was lying on the ground.

"At that time I was what you call 'Daddy's Little Girl.' Daddy couldn't do no wrong. But when the cops came and took him away, and he looked at me and said, 'Yeah, I did it and

I'm glad of it, I'd do it again,' that kind of destroys everything you have for a person. When I get real depressed, I can still see the abuse."

Newman turned around, pulled the respirator off from under his nose, and lit up a Marlboro.

"Pardon me, but considering you're on a respirator, is that a smart thing to do?" I asked.

Glenn smiled. His mustache framed a mouth lifted in an impish grin. It was easy to see why everyone liked him.

"Not too bright, huh?" he answered in a gravelly voice. He turned around and resumed watching TV.

"What about Chris Wyant?"

"I didn't like the kid when I met him," Cathy said firmly. "He looked like the type that takes drugs."

But her father felt differently.

"He was the only boy that my father would let my brother mess with. My father never let anybody have any friends."

"What was it like living with your father?"

"With my father, the more he drank, the worse he got. He couldn't stop at one or two [drinks]. He had to keep going. My dad had the gift to where he could act sober even when he was totally intoxicated. He could turn it right around and make it look like it was a woman's fault. He'd done it with

Little Grady's mother. She called the cops several different times and they came down here to the house and he'd make her look like she was totally crazy [because he acted sober], and not one report was ever filed."

"Your sister Donna said he drank up to a gallon of booze a day."

"Yeah."

"He'd get four drinks out of a half a pint," said Glenn, suddenly turning around.

"Did he drink when he was working?"

"There was many a time he was totally intoxicated while working," said Cathy, a teetotaller. She recalled, "When I was around five my father used to get drunk and put me on the platform 'cause I was identical to him. He would put me out there to work so he wouldn't get in trouble because he was intoxicated."

When she got old enough to say no, she refused to go out there anymore. "It was too boring to sit there."

"Mr. Newman, you worked with him?"

Cathy laughed before he could respond. "He knows who you are," and laughed again.

"Harry Newman Sr.," I said, and added, "What's it like, being on the road with the carnival?"

"It's a very rough life. It separates the men from the boys, I'll tell you that," Glenn continued.

"What makes it so rough?"

"The hours, the work," said Cathy.

"You never have time for yourself. On your day off, you're washing clothes," Glenn added.

"If you have a baby reptile, you have to have heat on them," Tyrill chimed in.

"We lived in trailers, but some of the help, they lived in trucks and tents," Cathy recalled.

"I heard that some people would actually sleep in the joints at night."

"Sometimes you have to for security," Tyrill explained. "Some spots like New York City, you'd get people slash up the tent."

"We got shot at— "

"Shot at?" I interrupted Cathy.

"Oh, yes, in Shea Stadium— "

"Orchard Beach, too," Tyrill added.

"No, we didn't get shot at at Orchard Beach," Cathy corrected.

"Glennie got jumped in Orchard. In City Island," Tyrill corrected himself.

That led to a discussion about the increase in violent crime in Gibsonton. Grady Stiles's death was not mentioned.

I looked up and saw Little Grady walking on his hands into the living room. So swiftly did he walk into the living room and pull himself up onto the couch that I had no chance to react.

"Hi, Grady, how's it going?"

"Cool," he answered brightly. He enjoyed the attention the family was getting.

"What would you like people to know about your father, Cathy, that needs to be clarified?"

"That he wasn't a helpless person. That he wasn't handicapped. He could do just as much as anyone else could do. The state is acting like my father is an indolent person who couldn't abuse anybody."

"How are your mother and brother now?"

"They're hanging in there. Not doing that well."

As I packed up to leave, Tyrill took me aside.

"Do you have a rental car?"

I nodded.

Mindful of the rash of vehicular robberies and murders in Florida, Tyrill advised, "Watch yourself. If someone bumps you, you keep going."

ORDINARY LIVES DESTROYED BY EXTRAORDINARY HORROR.
FACTS MORE DANGEROUS THAN FICTION.
CAPTURE A PINNACLE TRUE CRIME . . . IF YOU DARE.

LITTLE GIRL LOST   (593, $4.99)
By Joan Merriam
When Anna Brackett, an elderly woman living alone, allowed two teenage girls into
her home, she never realized that a brutal death awaited her. Within an hour, Mrs.
Brackett would be savagely stabbed twenty-eight times. Her executioners were Shirley
Katherine Wolf, 14, and Cindy Lee Collier, 15. *Little Girl Lost* examines how two
adolescents were driven through neglect and sexual abuse to commit the ultimate
crime.

HUSH, LITTLE BABY   (541, $4.99)
By Jim Carrier
Darci Kayleen Pierce seemed to be the kind of woman you stand next to in the grocery
store. However, Darci was obsessed with the need to be a mother. She desperately
wanted a baby—any baby. On a summer day, Darci kidnapped a nine-month pregnant
woman, strangled her, and performed a makeshift Cesarean section with a car key. In
this arresting account, readers will learn how Pierce's tortured fantasy of motherhood
spiraled into a bloody reality.

IN A FATHER'S RAGE   (547, $4.99)
By Raymond Van Over
Dr. Kenneth Z. Taylor promised his third wife Teresa that he would mend his drug-
addictive, violent ways. His vow didn't last. He nearly beat his bride to death on their
honeymoon. This nuptial nightmare worsened until Taylor killed Teresa after allegedly catching her sexually abusing their infant son. Claiming to have been driven
beyond a father's rage, Taylor was still found guilty of first degree murder. This grip-
ping page-turner reveals how a marriage made in heaven can become a living hell.

I KNOW MY FIRST NAME IS STEVEN   (563, $4.99)
By Mike Echols
A TV movie was based on this terrifying tale of abduction, child molesting, and
brainwashing. Yet, a ray of hope shines through this evil swamp for Steven Stayner
escaped from his captor and testified against the socially disturbed Kenneth Eugene
Parnell. For seven years, Steven was shuttled across California under the assumed
name of "Dennis Parnell." Despite the humiliations and degradations, Steven never
lost sight of his origins or his courage.

RITES OF BURIAL   (611, $4.99)
By Tom Jackman and Troy Cole
Many pundits believe that the atrocious murders and dismemberments performed by
Robert Berdella may have inspired Jeffrey Dahmer. Berdella stalked and savagely
tortured young men; sadistically photographing their suffering and ritualistically pre-
serving totems from their deaths. Upon his arrest, police uncovered human skulls,
envelopes of teeth, and a partially decomposed human head. This shocking expose is
written by two men who worked daily on this case.

*Available wherever paperbacks are sold, or order direct from the
Publisher. Send cover price plus 50¢ per copy for mailing and
handling to Penguin USA, P.O. Box 999, c/o Dept. 17109,
Bergenfield, NJ 07621. Residents of New York and Tennessee
must include sales tax. DO NOT SEND CASH.*

PINNACLE BOOKS HAS
SOMETHING FOR EVERYONE —

MAGICIANS, EXPLORERS, WITCHES AND CATS

THE HANDYMAN   (377-3, $3.95/$4.95)
He is a magician who likes hands. He likes their comfortable
shape and weight and size. He likes the portability of the hands
once they are severed from the rest of the ponderous body. Detective Lanark must discover who The Handyman is before more
handless bodies appear.

PASSAGE TO EDEN   (538-5, $4.95/$5.95)
Set in a world of prehistoric beauty, here is the epic story of a
courageous seafarer whose wanderings lead him to the ends of
the old world — and to the discovery of a new world in the rugged,
untamed wilderness of northwestern America.

BLACK BODY   (505-9, $5.95/$6.95)
An extraordinary chronicle, this is the diary of a witch, a journal
of the secrets of her race kept in return for not being burned for
her "sin." It is the story of Alba, that rarest of creatures, a white
witch: beautiful and able to walk in the human world undetected.

THE WHITE PUMA   (532-6, $4.95/NCR)
The white puma has recognized the men who deprived him of his
family. Now, like other predators before him, he has become a
man-hater. This story is a fitting tribute to this magnificent animal that stands for all living creatures that have become, through
man's carelessness, close to disappearing forever from the face of
the earth.

*Available wherever paperbacks are sold, or order direct from the
Publisher. Send cover price plus 50¢ per copy for mailing and
handling to Penguin USA, P.O. Box 999, c/o Dept. 17109,
Bergenfield, NJ 07621. Residents of New York and Tennessee
must include sales tax. DO NOT SEND CASH.*